Advance Praise for
RIGHT SIDE OF T

"Anyone who's ever been in relationships will relate to *Right Side of the Wrong Bed*. Frederick Smith is a gifted author who has written a page-turner filled with wit, comedy, and very memorable characters. Don't miss it!"

—Patrick Sanchez, author of *Girlfriends*

"Open *Right Side of the Wrong Bed* to join Fred Smith on a fun, rollicking ride through gay L.A., where the men are fabulous and the wit is as sharp as the latest pair of Diesel jeans. By turns sexy, funny, and heartbreaking, this book is sure to please."

—Fiona Zedde, author of *Every Dark Desire*

And Praise for his sensational debut,
DOWN FOR WHATEVER

"Readers will no doubt recognize themselves or their friends."

—*X Magazine*

"Fun . . . entertaining . . . worth hanging for the ride."

—*Edge* magazine (Boston)

"*Down For Whatever* is mighty fun, with snappier than snappy dialogue and wit. With all the fun, the book does address some more serious issues, including identity, class, HIV, and the down-low community, but never sounds heavy handed."

—*In Los Angeles*

"Frederick Smith's *Down For Whatever* is proudly about life in Los Angeles, about how we all live; trying to find love, trying to make sense of our lives, but few of us write more honestly or so entertainingly about that struggle."

—Jervey Tervalon, author of *Understand This*

"Finally, the boyz come out of the hood. Fresh, funny and real. Queer Latino and African-American male characters living, loving and telling it like it is in present day L.A. Playful with serious insight. Bravo Mr. Smith on your first novel and certainly not your last."

—Monica Palacios, writer/performer, The Original Surfer Chola

"A stupendous debut novel, *Down For Whatever* is a must read! Unapologetically black and unabashedly gay, Smith is a great writer akin to the luminaries of the Harlem Renaissance and James Baldwin. His seductive and wonderfully vivid literary style offers the reader layered complex portraits of four L.A. African-American and Latino gay men searching for love devoid of stereotypes and clichéd sentimentalities."

—Rev. Irene Monroe, religion columnist, *The Religion Thang*

Books by Frederick Smith

DOWN FOR WHATEVER

RIGHT SIDE OF THE WRONG BED

Published by Kensington Publishing Corporation

RIGHT SIDE OF THE WRONG BED

FREDERICK SMITH

KENSINGTON BOOKS.
http://www.kensingtonbooks.com

This is a work of fiction. Although some of the scenes in this novel take place at real places and locations, neither the characters portrayed here nor any of the events that happen in the novel should be construed, understood or implied as real or a reflection of those places and locations. They are all a product and result of my imagination.

KENSINGTON BOOKS are published by

Kensington Publishing Corp.
850 Third Avenue
New York, NY 10022

All Kensington titles, imprints and distributed lines are available at special quantity discounts for bulk purchases for sales promotion, premiums, fund-raising, educational or institutional use.

Special book excerpts or customized printings can also be created to fit specific needs. For details, write or phone the office of the Kensington Special Sales Manager: Kensington Publishing Corp., 850 Third Avenue, New York, NY 10022. Attn. Special Sales Department. Phone: 1-800-221-2647.

Kensington and the K logo Reg. U.S. Pat. & TM Off.

ISBN-13: 978-0-7582-1926-8
ISBN-10: 0-7582-1926-1

First Kensington Trade Paperback Printing: December 2007
10 9 8 7 6 5 4 3 2 1

Printed in the United States of America

Acknowledgments

Last time, I wrote a novel-length acknowledgments statement. This time, it could be a set of encyclopedias. So first, if I acknowledged you in my first book, know that my feelings are still the same.

These past two years have brought a number of phenomenal new people into my life, and have also strengthened my relationships with my established family and friends.

Silly me will try to thank everyone anyway: Mom, Monica, Dad (who's always here), and the families Davis, Lytle, Thomas, Burks, Franklin, Neal, Vernon, Watkins, and Herrera.

Supporters A—L: Jenoyne Adams, A Different Light Bookstore, Alexander Book Co., At The Beach L.A., Joseph Aguirre, Bryant Alexander, Noel Alumit, Julio Alvizo, Dayne Avery, Oskar Ayon, Patrick Bailey, Corliss P. Bennett, Bluestockings, Derrick L. Briggs and Books Are Sexy Book Club, Booked L.A. Book Club, Books Inc., Keith Boykin, Brother Well Read Book Club Atlanta, Eric Burton, Clay Cane, Jasmyne Cannick, Brent Dorian Carpenter, Kevin Chambers, Alana J. Chulick, Eric Claiborne, Zandra Conway, Cross Cultural Centers at CSULA, David Curry, Ivan Daniels, Rashid Darden, Michael Datcher, Herndon Davis, Daniel Dejene, Mel Donalson, Bitta Farahmand, First Fridayz L.A., Reyna Grande, Deondray Gossett, Erasmo Guerra, Denise Hamilton, Bernard Henderson, David Herrera, Darrious Hilmon, Javaki Hilmon, Sam Ingram, In the Life Atlanta, In The Meantime Men's Group L.A., Crystal Irby, Christopher Jackson, Monica Jackson, Trent Jackson, Maurice Jamal, Jewel's Catch One, Tayari Jones, Michael Kearns, Jeff King, Marcela Landres, Quincy LaNear, Lotus Brothers Book Club San Diego.

Supporters, M—Z: Kerry Madden, Matais Books, Rod McCullom, Colleen McLaughlin, Minneapolis AIDS Project, Rhonda Mitchell, Alphonso Morgan, Jarrell Moseley, Sam Myers, Douglas Nowling, Outwrite Books Atlanta, Liza Palmer, Cynthia and Ibarionex Perello, Pride in the City (Brooklyn), Sofia Quintero, Cydney Rax, Corey Roskin, Isaac Salazar, Eduardo Santiago, Joe Sedlacek, Roland Johnson Smith, John Taylor, Jervey Tervalon, Joel Torrez, Jr., Toyce, UC Santa Barbara MultiCultural Center, University-Student Union at CSULA, Alisa Valdez, Belinda and Javier Vazquez and family, Cordero Vigil, Vincent E. Vigil, Chaz Walker, West Hollywood Book Fair, Andre "Antar" Wright, Daria Yudacufski, Fiona Zedde, and if I've missed you, write your name in here, and know that it totally was not personal☺.

And of course agent Nicholas Roman Lewis, editor John Scognamiglio, and the entire staff at Kensington Publishing. I appreciate all you do. And you make the job a whole lot of fun!

Now, I want to introduce you to a friend of mine: Crystal Tennille Irby. After graduating from Florida State University, Crystal moved to Los Angeles to pursue a master's degree in Theater Arts and Dance, which she finished. An accomplished actress, writer, and activist, Crystal just completed her first book, *Milk: Poems, Short Stories, & Lessons From God*, and she graciously agreed to let me share one of her poems with you. I think it sets the tone for *Right Side of the Wrong Bed*. If you like it, visit her online at MySpace or e-mail her at crystalirby@hotmail.com.

All the best,
Fred

Broken hearts are like
Once green grass
Now sunshine dry brown
Hoping . . . Praying
For rain
To help it grow again
Restore its beauty
Reveal what once was
Never to be again
Return it back
To what could have been
If the sun had not burned so long

—Crystal T. Irby, 2006

Chapter 1

Jeremy Lopez slipped into my life as smoothly as the rum going into my second mojito.

"You from Cuba or something?"

He smiled. Grill gleaming like he never missed a cleaning, straight like he never missed a tightening. All six feet of him, dressed in his Daddy Yankee look-alike attire. Slim-fitted, yet baggy, low-rise jeans. White-on-white K-Swiss. Pink-and-white-striped polo shirt, flipped collar. Oversized belt buckle. White blazer. Dog tag and silver cross pendants, on one long and one longer silver-link chain. Plain, white baseball hat, planted vicariously on his head and tilted to the side. Bling shining on his earlobes. I was glad to see the preppy look was trendy again, after years of suffering through gangsta or grungy gear on the scene. And Jeremy wore it well.

"*¿Eres Cubano o que*?" he asked again, this time adding a head nod. I guess to see if I understood Spanish or English, or if I could hear him over George Clinton's "Atomic Dog" which entertained the club patrons.

I looked down at the Heineken he had just ordered. And though I could tell from his light brown skin and dark eyes and hair he might have descended from some country south or some island southeast of the United States, I decided to play along with his geography game.

"You Dutch or something?"

Blank, confused look. "Huh?"

"The beer you're drinking. It's kind of an import from Holland. Just like my mojito originates from Cuba."

"Oh. Okay," he said, but looked over across the crowded room, smiled at someone, and then turned back to me. "Nah. I'm straight-up Latino, half Mexican, half Dominican."

"Serious? That's an interesting pair."

"For real, huh?" he said and smiled again, first at me, then at the same someone across the room. "My dad was military and came out here from New York. But I'm East L.A. born and bred."

"Cool."

"Sometimes people think I'm full black, mixed with black, or something else 'cause of my skin."

"I get that, too, sometimes, but both my parents are black—African-American," I said. "But you're part Dominican. There's some African roots there, so people would make some assumptions."

"True," he said. I guess all the ethnicity talk and explaining who he was bored him. He continued looking across the room, and I wanted to ignore who my new bar friend was checking out, but managed a peek. I guess a long peek.

His clique was a group of similarly urban-prep-dressed men. College age definitely. Running in that mixed-race nontourage young L.A. residents tend to travel in, trying to look like A-List music stars but never quite making the guest list. In this case two Latinos, one black, one Filipino, a white guy, and another who looked to be a mixture of all the above. But who could really tell these days in L.A., especially in club lighting, and especially with the high number of mixed-race kids coming of age in California?

"I don't want to keep you from anything or anybody," I said and grabbed a twenty from my wallet. "My friends are around here somewhere."

"Oh. A'ight." He dug a wad of crumpled singles from his pants pocket.

"I got the drinks. Keep your money."

"Thanks, bro," he said and smiled. Clinked his Heineken against my mojito. Slid his dollar bills back in his pocket. "I'll holla at you lata."

"No prob."

"Next time the Cuba Libre is on me," he said and winked. "Lata, playa."

And he glided across the room, said hello and high-fived a few in the crowd, before settling back with his boys on their side of the room. Seemed so popular and a charmer—I bet he'd never paid for a drink in his burgeoning club life.

Though I was ten years past having my master's degree, working around college students at the university kept me young-at-heart and in tune with the language and ways of youth. Still, I didn't expect the crowd tonight to be so full of younger people. Was looking forward to a low-key, but fun, evening with my thirtysomething friends and acquaintances.

My colleague and best friend, Carlos, was throwing an eighties party to celebrate his partner Ricky's thirty-fifth birthday. He'd rented out a hip West Hollywood club and bar, which usually housed Ivan Daniels's Wednesday night hip-hop set, Metro, that brought out the younger, urban prep crowd. And since word never seems to travel about these private party rentals, the old and the young mingled, suspiciously and tentatively, over the songs that the old grew up on while the young were being born.

Carlos and Ricky were a popular and successful couple—in fact, role models, in a way, for those of us on the not-so-successful relationship track. Carlos, my colleague, was the director of campus multicultural affairs, an office that worked closely with my department, which I directed, campus organizations and leadership. Ricky was a firefighter for the city. A little on the conservative, ¡*VIVA* Bush!, red-state side at times. But loved his eighties music. And loved his Carlos. For the past seven years. Loyal, faithful, and oh-so-generous with his love, time, and money. The way a relationship should be.

Unlike the one I'd ended right before Labor Day last year, just five months plus earlier, with Ricky's best friend and fellow firefighter, DaVon Holloway.

Part of me knew DaVon might stop by to give his best friend a birthday greeting, though their friendship had slipped in the past months due to DaVon's dishonesty and lack of integrity regarding our relationship. And honestly, it was the only reason I'd ventured out of my house on a cold February work night. I wanted to see how DaVon was surviving since I gave him the ultimatum, "Paper or plastic?" when I gathered his things and put him out of my house. Not that I was a particularly vindictive person. Resentment, I've found, is kind of like taking poison, but hoping another person dies. I wished only the best for DaVon, though I wondered how he could give up a stable, upstanding, and cosmopolitan person like me.

Came crashing down just like that.

Months, though most likely years, of unprotected sex brought something to my household and life I never expected to deal with. Women. Paternity tests. Sexual relationships outside of ours. Children. He denied them all. Said they were gold-digging widows looking for a quick and steady dollar from a successful brotha. And at first I believed him. Six years living with someone, being with someone whom you loved and respected, makes you give the benefit of the doubt. Makes you borrow off your retirement, or refinance your mortgage and pull money out the house one more time, or cash out the few stock accounts you hold in order to pay attorney and court costs to defend your man, despite the fact he made a healthier income as a firefighter than I did. Until you learned there are countless examples of firefighters, trauma workers, police officers who give comfort to the families and widows of victims. Until you learned there were hundreds of pending lawsuits from other women claiming their children came from relationships with those hired to serve and protect. Until the DNA tests came back and conclusively identified DaVon Holloway as the father of not one, but two, toddlers—a boy and a girl. Possibly more out there, who knows. Really didn't want to know. All I know is after I put DaVon out, he married one of the women. A marriage formed more out of his desire to avoid further courtroom drama over visitation and child support than one based on love.

I'd given DaVon six, almost seven, years of my life. Started out real fast and furious. Boyfriends after three dates, living together after three months. We just felt each other and found each other at the right time. Six, almost seven years. In my mind, I'd transitioned from fine, to cute, to handsome as I left the mid-twenties and entered my early thirties. I imagined DaVon and I being together forever as we transitioned further to wrinkles and old age. That life out in "the scene" was over and that we would settle down into my white-picket-fence Mr. Black America suburban fantasy. That I wouldn't have to worry about going out there again and trying to market myself to today's single scene. A CeCe Penniston-bred boy in an Beyoncé-led world.

Part of me blamed myself for DaVon's ability to not be faithful. That I knew the deal. That he had been with women long before me, and that I was his first real date with a dude, then boyfriend, then partner, and that it was all new for DaVon. An experiment, or new experience, who knows? Carlos tried to caution me. Ricky reassured me DaVon's interest in me was sincere, and that DaVon was sure of the new direction of his love life and attractions. So I let DaVon Holloway, one of a few black recruits in that year's class of new firefighters in Los Angeles, pursue me. It was good. And I let him move in with me. First, to my one-bedroom apartment in Pasadena. Then, to the town house I bought in the Leimert Park area. Then to the home I purchased in the hills of Monterey Park, a suburban enclave jokingly called "The Chinese Beverly Hills," which was about ten minutes east of downtown L.A., and the entering point of the San Gabriel Valley. We were living the dream that I thought would last forever.

I held no resentment. And was far from bitter. Some might have disagreed.

As I sat at the bar and nodded my head along to "Planet Rock" or one of those other eighties electronic songs, Carlos joined me and sat down. His white T-shirt clung to his skin, a result of sweating to the eighties oldies, no doubt. He ran his hands over his hair and grabbed a handkerchief out his pocket to dry his face off.

"Thanks for coming tonight," he said and smiled. "I hope you're having a good time."

"I am," I said and sipped on the mojito I'd just ordered. It was terrible. Too much rum, not enough sugar. I slid it toward the bartender and pointed to it. "The drink sucks. Can you make another one? Thanks." Then back to Carlos, "Yeah, Carlos, I'm cool. And no, I'm not thinking about DaVon. I know that's your next question."

"Good. As long as you're not here requesting Toni Braxton sad love songs. There will be no slow or sad songs tonight."

"Not at all."

"Or Sade sad love songs."

"Not even."

"Or Nina Simone."

"Fine, Carlos, I get your point," I said. "So, is DaVon coming or what?"

"We invited him, but who knows what's in his head these days."

"Who knows?" I said. "Who cares?"

"Anyways," Carlos said and smiled again like he was about to instigate trouble. "Where's the young child you were talking to?"

"You saw that?" I asked.

"Yeah. He was cute. Young, but cute."

"I don't know. Probably off flirting, looking for his newest piece. We just ran into each other at the bar while ordering."

"Mmm hmm."

"It's true," I said. "I'm not *even* ready to start dating someone new."

Which was true. Though I wasn't singing Toni Braxton songs anymore after five months, and could definitely breathe again, I had too much on my plate to consider letting my heart open to someone else. It was barely healing from DaVon. But I had more going on in my life than the need to jump into anything new with anyone.

My job at the university was in jeopardy as usual, with the California state budget always in limbo. You just never knew which positions would be deemed essential and those deemed not. And Carlos's and my new boss, Allison Perez, some woman out of Texas who became Vice President of Student Affairs, swooped in after the new year with her agenda of compassionate conservatism, questioning everything that came out of Carlos's and my departments. *Only* Carlos's and my departments. Said she wanted to see more work from our departments that was more broad and campus-wide. Broad, meaning white. Campus-wide, meaning whiter. This, at California University, East Los Angeles, affectionately known as CUELA, which was home to a majority minority student body, but was attempting to increase its pool of white, and male, numbers. An initiative from our campus president, though it was never put on paper or e-mail. You just knew and saw, based on who walked through the campus entrance each new semester. Regardless of Allison's agenda for me or my job, I had a successful business on the side as a private college coach, charging the rich and paranoid healthy fees to prep their teens for college entrance exams, while doing the same job for free with the economically challenged students I mentored at Big Brothers/Big Sisters.

I also had just moved my mother from the winter wonderland of Ohio to the back house behind my home in Monterey Park. Third separation from my stepfather in recent years. Most of us looked forward to the day of moving out and away from our parents, but I brought her near for a few reasons. One, because she was retired and bored and alone in Ohio in the middle of winter, and my sisters, Tonya and Cecily, were too busy and crowded raising households of kids to take her in. Tonya's in Phoenix. Cecily's in Oakland. Two, to keep my mother out of the casinos in Detroit and Canada that she and her other retired girlfriends would road trip to twice a week. Spending all their little retirement checks on deflated dreams. Causing the tension between her and my stepfather. At least here, I'd be able to keep an eye on her, and prayed she wouldn't find a *Thomas Guide* and figure out a way to drive herself to the Indian reservations in the Inland Empire, San Diego, or, God forbid, the big casinos in Vegas. Getting her adjusted to life in Southern California was enough of a chore to help distract me from DaVon and his infidelities. Third, I just didn't want to be alone and figured my mom and I could be alone together while sorting out our lives and loves. Not that I needed to have DaVon, or any man, or any other person living with me. I wasn't codependent like that. I just had room and a void in my heart and my house.

I was definitely too busy to let someone new into my life. Yet, knew it was time to let someone new into my life and my bed. Five months was definitely enough time, though I wasn't sure if I wanted to pursue or be pursued.

"Whatever you say," Carlos said to me. "I'm taking that one home with me tonight."

"Which one?"

"This one," Carlos said as Ricky slid behind him and kissed the back of his neck. Ricky was a man's man, to use a tired cliché. The mythical kind everyone wanted, but rarely got: athletic, outgoing, yet considerate, kind, faithful, and able to blend in with gay or straight crowds with no problems, yet was not ashamed of his sexual orientation. At. All. "I just cruised him in the bathroom and told him I had a special, private birthday gift for him at my place."

"You guys are so lucky," I said. "Happy birthday again, Ricky. How does it feel to be thirty-five?"

"Better than twenty-one, that's for sure."

It was great seeing my colleague, and I guess best friend (the best one I've got in L.A.), so in love with his Ricky. They were my relationship role models, even though at times I had to put thoughts of questioning Ricky's judgment of character aside and stop blaming him for bringing DaVon into my life. It wasn't Ricky's fault DaVon turned out the way he was. Ricky was just a convenient scapegoat. You just never really know a person. You can only really know yourself.

The bartender slid a new mojito across the bar to me. I sipped it. Much smoother. I tipped him a couple bucks for the trouble. I offered up my glass to Carlos's Cape Cod and Ricky's Heineken. Tapped cheers.

"Well, don't just sit here at the bar all night," Ricky said to me. "Come on back and dance with us to some real music from *our* generation."

"I'll be there in a minute. I'll finish this off and dance the buzz away with you guys in a bit."

"You better," Carlos said and placed his empty glass on the bar counter. "The wicked witch, Allison, is off all this week, so we can go in late tomorrow."

I slapped him a high-five and watched Carlos and Ricky head back toward the dance floor area. Sounded and looked like a fun time for all, even the younger set. It was an eighties party, but not the typical Devo, Go-Go's, Depeche Mode eighties. Ricky, in all his ¡*VIVA* Bush! enthusiasm, liked black people eighties music. Songs like "Egyptian Lover," "Funkin' For Jamaica," "Meeting in the Ladies' Room," "Oh Shelia," "777-9311," and "Juicy Fruit." Songs I learned while visiting cousins up in Detroit in the eighties and watching their local dance show, *The Scene* with Nat Morris on Channel 62. It amazed me how similar musical tastes could be among people from different cultures and backgrounds. Me. Blue collar, black, first generation college grad, Midwestern. Ricky. Rich, Hispanic (his word, not mine), eighth generation American, West Coast.

I looked forward to joining my friends out on the dance floor and continuing the celebration. Until I turned around and saw him walk through the front entrance.

DaVon.

Damn. Not the way I wanted to be spotted the first time since our breakup. Drinking alone. At a bar. No hottie on my arm or by my side to make him jealous, or at least to make him reconsider what he gave up (even though I'm the one who gave him the boot).

DaVon Holloway. In the flesh.

Minus his wife. With his real wedding ring on his third finger. Showing off his shoulders and bicep muscles in a tight wife-beater T-shirt. Baggy jeans and L.A. Dodgers hat tilted to the side. Trying to fool himself from thirty-five to twenty-five, I guess. Still looked good. Always been attracted to tall, dark men like DaVon. Our eyes met immediately, and though I tried quickly to look down and sip on my mojito to ignore him, and maybe hope/pretend like I was turning invisible like Casper the Friendly Ghost, he walked my way and stood next to me at the bar. Still wore Obsession, even though I had bought other fragrances, newer ones from the 2000s, for him to try. Still smelled good on him.

"Whassup?"

He looked nervous, kept his hands in his pockets, but managed a head nod. His full lips parted, a little nervously, to show off his perfect smile. He'd grown a goatee in the past five months and looked a little older than he did during his clean-shaven years with me. Probably the stress of living with a toddler and getting woken in the middle of the night for feedings or diaper changes.

"Hey," I said and took a large swallow like a binge drinker. The sooner I finished the mojito, the sooner I could get away from DaVon and dance with my friends.

"You alone?"

"Uh," I said and pondered. Really quickly. Saying yes would indicate I was a loser: single, alone, not over him, no prospects, the one who should break out in Mariah's "We Belong Together." Saying no would answer the question, and no explanation would really be needed. What to say to DaVon? "They're dancing."

"Cool." He looked at me and smiled. "How's the party?"

"It's all right, I guess," I said nonchalantly. "I haven't been in West Hollywood in a while. Club scene is different from when we were out and about."

"Yeah."

"But Ricky is back on the dance floor if you want to find him."

"I'll find him," DaVon said and looked at the bartender. "One seven and seven, and whatever my man is drinking."

"No thanks, DaVon," I said. "I'm leaving soon anyway. And I'm driving."

"Slow down, babe," he said and put his hand on my shoulder. Gave it a squeeze. "It's a party. Drink up."

DaVon tossed his AMEX on the bar counter and sat down while the bartender finished mixing our drinks. The last thing I wanted. Didn't want to be seen alone by DaVon my first time running into him since the breakup. Didn't want him feeling sorry, sad, or nostalgic. Or looking at me like he'd won, I'd lost, and I was wallowing in my sorrows at the bar. The bartender rang up the transaction, slid our drinks toward us, and took DaVon's credit card.

"How you been?" DaVon said, half looking at me, half looking over my shoulder at the crowd around us. Needed to keep that wandering eye still, with his wife and kid at home, and countless others popping up every other month it seemed. "I drove past your house the other day and saw your mother planting flowers out front. She's in town?"

"What were you doing in Monterey Park?"

"Is there a law?"

"You live and work near USC, right? You have nothing to stop by my house for."

"Just driving. Just thinking. That's all." DaVon looked at me, and for that moment I looked back into his eyes. Would have been so easy and quick to lean over and kiss him. Make up. Or at least attempt to. DaVon probably thought the same thing, and leaned toward my face.

"Don't."

"What?" He smiled. "Six years with someone. You think about things."

Five months wasn't enough time. Memories started flooding back. How perfect it was in the beginning. Vacations. Family reunions. Arguments. Make ups. DaVon's spot below his navel that made him lose it, and how he, in turn, would ravage me like I was all he needed and wanted to be satisfied in life.

Stop. Kenny.

I'm supposed to be celebrating Ricky's birthday, not going down memory lane. Besides, there's a reason we're no longer together. And I needed to remind him.

"How are your babies? Your wife?"

"Smooth like gravy."

"That's it?"

"It's cool. Don't worry about it. Unless you still care."

I did. As a human being. I couldn't exactly turn off seven years of feelings overnight, though I was slowly getting there. Make that six. The last year, when the paternity suits started popping up and I supported and believed him, made me question if what I'd had was real. When the first DNA came back conclusive, that DaVon had indeed become the father of a little girl with Miss Mexico wannabe, Vanessa Flores, and had conceived the child sometime during the fifth year of our relationship, I realized that not everything that seemed perfect was. Not that I'd been one of those people with their heads in the clouds, thinking that relationships were all sunshine and happiness, eternal blue skies, white picket fences, and matching Volvo wagons. Still, I'd had some expectations that people were who they said they were, that some sense of honesty and integrity existed, that without believing in the potential and good side of people, what good was it to give your heart to someone. Vanessa Flores Holloway would now have DaVon's demons and issues to deal with. He'd chosen which side of the fence he wanted to live on, and apparently Vanessa's grass was greener than mine. Her bed, apparently, was more comfortable than mine.

The bartender tapped DaVon's credit card on the counter and nodded. Declined. I reached for my wallet. Grabbed another twenty. Always to the rescue for DaVon. Always to the rescue for everyone, it seemed. In relationships. With students at the university. For my "mentees" and their families at Big Brothers/Big Sisters. My family. Everyone always needed something, it seemed. At times, I wished I could just let it flow and not care about the consequences or outcomes of situations—even for myself.

"Thanks for the drink, DaVon," I said, hoping he would catch the sarcasm in my voice. The nerve offering to buy drinks with a bad credit card.

"I'll spot you next time."

"Won't be a next time."

"We'll see."

"Paper or plastic?" I sang and smiled my famous last words to DaVon from five months earlier.

DaVon snickered, got up and walked through the crowd, all eyes on him. Found his friends. Our friends. A bunch of gay firefighters and gay law enforcement agents, their partners, and the teenybopper boys who didn't know their hip-hop night was cancelled for eighties night. I watched DaVon all the way to the dance floor. Why he was out, past midnight, when he had a wife and baby at home was a mystery to me. But not mine to solve. I finished the newest mojito in two swallows, left a few dollars for the bartender, and got up to leave. I wasn't ready to see DaVon. And dancing with him and Carlos and Ricky would have reminded me of our good old days hanging out as a foursome. Would have reminded me of our trips together. Our dinner parties and dancing with the other couple on the backyard patio. The comfortable and friendly way we used to connect. Definitely not ready for friendship with DaVon.

Outside the club, the winds were picking up, and a light drizzle was coating the winter air. I handed my valet slip to the attendant and waited for my SUV. I noticed my Heineken friend, with two of his boys, standing next to the bar entrance smoking cigarettes. He made some hand signal, looked like gang signs. Couldn't have been signaling to me. I don't do gang boys. I turned away and looked down the street for my SUV to arrive. Felt a tap on my shoulder.

"What's crackin', playa?" Heineken man asked. Cute boy-man voice, with a tinge of East L.A. I guess he was straight-up East L.A. as he told me earlier. "Why didn't you come here when I called you?"

"I didn't know you were talking to me," I said and smiled. "Sorry."

"Where you going so soon?"

"Home. I work in the morning, and I've had enough celebration to last me 'til Memorial Day."

"Too bad you're leaving," he said. "I was gonna get your Cuba Libre. To thank you for the drink earlier that you got me. That was real nice of you. Half these mofos cheap and won't offer you anything."

"No problem," I said. "It's cool. Thanks."

He pulled out his cell, a Treo.

"Can I holla at you sometime, then?"

"Me? Please."

"Why not?"

"Uh, it was just a drink. No need for future conversation."

"Dude, don't leave me hanging out here in front of my boys," he said and winked. "Come on, playa. Don't leave me hanging."

I laughed. Well, smiled a little. Okay. A lot. This Usher-slash-Daddy Yankee–dressed Latino kid was hitting on me. Was flattering. Maybe I passed for a teenybopper. NOT. Well, it wasn't my intention. I had on my favorite True Religion jeans, a chocolate brown and light blue T-shirt, and brown-and-blue sneakers. And now, he pulled up his pink polo just a bit. Knew he wasn't itching. Just showing off that young, tight torso and that sexy thin trail of hair going down . . . Stop. Kenny. Now.

"Here's my card." I handed him my card from the university. The way professionals and grown-ups did it. Wanted to see his reaction. See if he would run away once he realized I was way out of his target demographics. He read my card out loud.

"Kenneth Kane. Director of Campus Activities and Student Leadership, California University, East Los Angeles," he said. "Damn. You got a good job. A real job."

"Yeah, a real job," I said and laughed. "But I go by Kenny, not Kenneth."

"Cool. Kenny," he said and put out his hand. Did the three-part Chicano-style handshake. "Jeremy Lopez."

"The Mexican-Dominican from East L.A., right?"

"Yeah, how'd you know?"

"Duh, you told me at the bar, remember? You're straight-up Latino . . . East L.A. born and bred. The military dad from New York. And the handshake confirmed it."

"Yeah, right," Jeremy said and put out his cigarette on the sidewalk. "Where you stay?"

"MPK."

"Shut up."

"Excuse me?"

"We're like . . . neighbors. That's cool."

"Yeah, I guess so."

"So I can holla and step to a brotha on a regular basis, then?"

"Uh, I didn't say that."

"Well, I'm ready to jet from here, too," Jeremy said. "Can you give me a ride back to East Los?"

"What about your boys? Won't they be looking for you?" I hadn't known this boy, except for a brief, shallow conversation at the bar. I wasn't the type to pick up random people and give them rides. "If your friends . . ."

"Nacho, tell them I'm gone," Jeremy shouted to his friend standing solo by the bar entrance. "I got a ride home."

"You go, boy," Nacho shouted back.

"Oh, God, Jeremy," I said and looked around to see if any of my friends were within earshot. "Tell him it's not like that."

"Nacho, tell them I found him again." Jeremy laughed. "He taking me home."

"Nacho, tell them not like that," I said. "Just dropping him off."

"Claro qué sí," Nacho said and laughed.

The attendant pulled up to the sidewalk with my SUV. My baby. BMW X5. Silver with silver-gray leather interior, wood trim, panorama moonroof, and heated seats. A very-needed luxury on a cold February night in L.A.

"Damn, this your ride?" Jeremy asked, grill gleaming in the midnight air, cigarette steam still billowing from his mouth. "Take our picture, Nacho. Me and my Kenny."

Nacho put out his cigarette and grabbed Jeremy's phone. Snapped two pictures of us next to my SUV. Felt real car show at a swap meet or something.

"Thanks, man," Jeremy said and took his phone back. "And tell them what I'm riding in when you go back in, Nacho."

I tipped the valet attendant a five and got in my side of the SUV. Jeremy got in the passenger side and buckled up. Slipped into the warm leather seats like he belonged there. And I guess, in a way, he did belong.

Chapter 2

As we drove east on Santa Monica Boulevard, toward the Hollywood Freeway, Jeremy switched satellite radio channels in my SUV at least fifteen times. Station was earning its money that night. Changed my smooth R&B to the all hip-hop station, to Eminem's station, to G-Unit's station, back to hip-hop, and then to smooth R&B again. All this while he sent multiple text messages from his Treo to who knows who. His boys. Other boys he'd met that night, who knows? Didn't really matter anyway. He was some bar kid who happened to live near me and whom I was kind enough to offer a ride home. Still, it fascinated me that I'd made a new acquaintance, friend, whatever, at my friend Ricky's birthday party. It had been a long time since I'd done the whole pickup bar thing.

Before we reached the freeway entrance, Jeremy put his phone away and reached into his jacket pocket for his handheld Game Boy Advance.

"You hungry, Kenny?"

"I'm cool. You?"

"There's a taco stand up on Santa Monica and Vermont," Jeremy said. "I thought we could eat and talk."

"The one by the Metro Line?"

"Yeah, let's go. I'm hungry."

I looked over at Jeremy. He was engrossed in his video

game. Barely paying attention to me or the music anymore, but knew he wanted food. Obviously metabolism wasn't a concern with that tight torso and all. To be young again.

"What are you playing?"

"Pokémon," Jeremy said as he pressed buttons frantically. "You got one? We could hook up and double our killing powers."

"Uh, nope. No video games for me."

"Dude, you don't know what you're missing," Jeremy said. "I got a friend who works at Circuit City. I'll see if he can hook you up with a freebie, if you know what I mean."

"Uh, that's cool," I said and turned down the stereo volume on my steering wheel. "I'm over my video game phase. Used to play Atari when I was a kid, but . . ."

"Atari? What's that?"

"Uh, nothing. Forget it. We're here," I said and pulled into the parking lot of El Gran Burrito or "Gay Taco" as some patrons called it. Despite the drizzle and wind, club goers braved the elements for some after-club grub. I parked the SUV in the rear of the lot, away from the other cars. No scratches for me. "You coming?"

"Oh, I just want four tacos *de cabeza*. Everything on them," Jeremy said and continued his murderous rampage in the Pokémon village. "And *una horchata, por favor.*"

I knew he had to be joking. I stared at him, seeing him engrossed in his game in the passenger seat of my SUV. I started it up. My name is not Mamie, thank you. Not even when I was with DaVon did I do the serving-my-man thing. Well, at least not the subservient food thing.

"You're obviously not hungry, Jeremy. So let's just go on home."

He slammed the game closed and put it in his pocket.

"Dude, I'm sorry," Jeremy said. "I thought I was with Lalo."

"Lalo?"

"Oh, my ex," Jeremy said and opened his door. Slammed

it a little too hard when he got out. "Dumped him last week. Bitch was too possessive."

"Funny," I said while hitting the alarm sensor. "So you're single now?"

"You could say." He smiled. "Or you couldn't say. Depends."

"You can stand under my umbrella, Jeremy," I said and opened up the super-sized contraption. He joined me. "It's cold."

"I eat fast," Jeremy said and giggled. "Well, that depends on what I'm eating."

"You like head in your tacos, right. *Cabeza?*" I asked.

"Yeah, head. You want some?"

"I want a torta de carne asada."

"Why not just go for the big enchilada tonight?" Jeremy squinted his eyes at me. Nodded his head.

"Because I don't want a big enchilada tonight," I said, knowing full well how flirtatious and dirty people can get with food names. I wasn't looking for anything. Not a one-night stand, nor a new relationship.

We ordered our food—I paid—and sat in a corner at a table made for two. Lucked out that there was a heater just above our heads, creating a mini tropical oasis in the chilly February air. It was a little after one in the morning. Way past my usual bedtime. I knew my mom might be wondering, but not worried, when I'd be back at the house. After all, I was grown, and she was a temporary visitor and resident in the small house on the back of my property. I laughed in my head, thinking about the adolescence of it all. Jeremy snapped me back to reality.

"So, Kenny Kane. Tell me more about yourself."

"What do you want to know, Jeremy Lopez?"

"First, how old are you?"

I had expected the question, but not so early in our getting-to-know-you-late-night-dining experience. Too bad I hadn't rehearsed my answer. It had been a good seven years since I'd been out on the dating scene, and though this was no date, I wasn't prepared for the direct line of questions. Should I tell him? Thirty-three. Should I lie and tell him what my college students guess as my age, twenty-six or twenty-seven? Should I tell him my younger sister Tonya's age, twenty-eight, since I can recite with ease all the significant years of her life . . . year she started kindergarten, middle and high school, high school and college graduation class, and more importantly, which songs and TV shows corresponded with those years. It was pretty simple to remember. My college and her high school years corresponded. I could do the math in my head from there.

But then I thought, why lie? Why be embarrassed? I'd already lived a full life, had my degrees, started on a good career path in university Student Affairs, had one significant relationship behind me, and traveled around the country and world on my own and with DaVon. That was a lot to be impressed with. Nothing to be ashamed of. Still, I could gather from Jeremy's ways he was twenty-two, maybe twenty-three tops, and if I remembered correctly from my early twenties, the quickest way to turn a promising relationship sour was to mention the number thirty. And forty? Forget it. Deal breaker. Might as well be six feet under, or at minimum ready for the nursing home. So what would this Jeremy kid think when I told him how old I was? And why was I worrying so much? He was just some kid I'd met at Ricky's birthday party and was taking back to his house, which happened to be pretty close to mine.

"Hellllloooo, Kenny. I asked you a question."

"Oh, I know. I just spaced out a minute."

"Because my friends think you're probably twenty-three or twenty-four. But with your SUV, and the kinda job you have, I'd say twenty-five at most. Which is cool with me. I like older guys."

"I'm thirty-three."

"Shut up," he said, eyes and mouth wide open. Does the wider the mouth mean the bigger the shock? And is that a good thing? "You serious? Get the fuck out!"

"What? You got a problem with my age?"

"Hell no. You look fucking good. I thought twenty-five was a stretch, but damn . . ."

"I work out and take care of myself. I don't do any drugs, unless you count alcohol, and try to get enough sleep."

"Obviously. You look younger than some of the guys my age. Damn."

"Really? And how old would that be?"

"Twenty-one."

I choked on my torta. Twenty-one would make him . . . born two years before I started high school. I stopped and redid the math again, just to make sure I wasn't imagining things, hallucinating.

"You're barely legal. Drinkingwise, that is."

"What? I'm too young for you, Kenny?"

"Well, first, let's get something straight. You're not for me. I'm just giving you a ride home."

"Aww, come on, playa," Jeremy said. "I told you I wanted to holla at you back at the club."

I was starting to get sick of Jeremy using the word "holla" so much. Like it was his newest and only vocabulary word of the week. And "playa"? Maybe it was just me. I was, after all, older and not used to hearing such words in everyday conversation with my circle of friends. And especially not within the academic circles at the university, though at times some of them were often a sentence away from me going "urban" on them. Whatever that means.

"You want to holla at me?"

"Yeah. But you probably got a man or something."

"Actually, I just got out of something long-term. Well, five months ago."

"Cool. So ya single now."

"Aren't there boys, I mean men your age you could . . . holla at?"

"Yeah, but they ain't rollin' in a SUV like yours."

"So the age thing? The different ethnicity thing?"

"If I didn't wanna kick it with you, I wouldn't be sitting here," he said. "The age is a little bit to get used to, I'll admit. But the different races, I've kicked it mostly with black dudes anyway. Another Latino feels like being with a cousin or something, though I've dated a few Mexicans and other Dominicans here and there. Dick is dick. Except I don't date white boys."

"Interesting," I said. "I messed around with a white boy in college at Northwestern, but that was a one-time experience."

"But the question is, do those things bother you, Kenny? The age and race?"

"Well, hypothetically, if we were to hang out," I said, "I don't think you'd have been what I had in mind. I mean, you look good."

"Of course I do," he said and laughed.

"But I just never pictured me being with someone that much younger than me . . . or not black. But you're part Dominican, so what am I saying? It's more the age thing."

"I see," he said. Looked a little disappointed. "It's all good, playa. We'll holla and play it by ear. At least you think I look good. You look damn good, that's for sure."

I smiled. "So, what do you do, Jeremy?" I asked, wanting to change the subject. Too much holla and playa and rollin' for my ears. "How do you spend your days?"

"I'm in community college. East L.A. Junior. Almost done with my Associates in psych. Gonna transfer to university in the fall. And I work at the admissions office on campus, giving tours and calling prospective students."

"What do you want to do with your life?"

"Damn, twenty-one questions. You sound like my dad, dude," Jeremy said and finished off his third taco in one bite. He wiped salsa off the corner of his mouth.

"Sorry, didn't mean to come across like your dad," I said. "I guess that makes me officially old if I'm like your dad."

"It's cool, Kenny," he said. "I wanna be a college counselor. Do student activities or leadership stuff. Stuff like you do."

"Really?" I asked. "I bet you say that to all the guys whose business cards you collect."

"You're the first . . . business card I've gotten at a club. Kinda classy, Mr. Kane."

"Please don't call me mister. I'm not that old."

"A'ight, Kenny."

"You ready?" I asked and gathered up my napkins, foil wrapper and salsa containers on my plastic tray. "I've got to work at eight in the morning. What time are your classes starting?"

"I'm up at six every morning to get ready. Gotta beat the family before all the hot water is gone from the shower."

"Really?"

"Yeah, it's just some wetback relatives staying with us for a while."

"No you didn't."

"What?"

"Use that word."

"Yeah, I did," Jeremy said. "Just a joke, Kenny. I'm an equal opportunity offender, by the way. It's my mom's peeps from Mexico. I can use the word."

"Great to know," I said. "But for the record, I don't use it."

"Good for you," he said. "Anyway, let's jet. Don't want you getting fired. Someone's gotta pay the notes on my ride."

"*My* ride," I said and smiled. It felt nice being flirted with, even if just for a few minutes after a club by a man-boy twelve years younger. "Don't you forget it."

"My boys are not gonna believe I'm talking to you,"

Jeremy said. "Half of 'em wanted to step to you, but I'm the only one with the balls. So I got the prize tonight."

"You're gonna make me blush," I said. "And black people don't turn red."

We'd made it to my SUV. Still safe in its lonely spot in the lot. No scratches. I pressed the button to deactivate the alarm. When out of the blue, Jeremy grabbed me and pushed me against the driver's side door.

"Come here," Jeremy said and kissed me. Tongue, tongue piercing, slobber everywhere. It was flattering, but not nice. I stopped and pulled away. "What's up, Kenny?"

"If you're going to kiss me, then you gotta take it nice and slow. There's no race."

"Like this?" Jeremy leaned in and closed-mouthed kissed me, gently tracing the opening of my lips with his tongue, until I slowly opened my mouth to tease his tongue with mine. I heard the parking lot security guards whistle and pulled away. Gently. "Damn."

"Like that, Jeremy."

"That was nice."

"It is what it is," I said. "That's how you kiss someone."

"Damn, I can't wait to see what else you got to teach me, Kenny."

"Let's go." I was a little embarrassed and taken off guard that I was kissing a stranger in public . . . in a parking lot. Something felt real high school, real illegal. But it was over and that was that. Wasn't going to happen again.

I hopped in my side and started up the SUV. Jeremy got in the passenger side, buckled up, and started to reach for his Treo, Game Boy Advance, or some other gadget in his pocket. Then stopped. Instead, he grabbed my hand, which was resting on the center console, and held it all the way to his house in East L.A. Again, real high school crush. But definitely flattering.

"Here's my ghetto shack," Jeremy said and squeezed my hand as we pulled in the driveway. It was a small, pastel green-colored stucco house, lit by a dim porch light. *"Mi casa es tu casa."*

He leaned over and kissed me.

"I'll holla at you probably tomorrow night, when I'm home from school."

"All you have is my work information," I reminded him. Not that I was desperate and wanted to leave every single number and way he could contact me. Not that I was expecting anything further beyond the night.

"Then look for an e-mail from me. Brown Child 1986. I'll e-mail you the pictures from outside the club."

"All right. Cool. Thanks."

"Thanks for the ride, Kenny," he said and handed me a folded-up club napkin. "Here's my number."

Jeremy hopped out of the truck and up the dark driveway. He opened a gate at the side of the house that creaked with age and rust and disappeared once he passed through. Once I knew he was safely in the house—I saw the living room light turn on, the front porch light turn off—I backed out and drove away. Five minutes north on Atlantic Boulevard and I'd be home in MPK.

Chapter 3

I knew I'd have a hard time waking in the morning. But twenty minutes after finding the right spot in my bed, I decided to answer the "Unidentified Caller" on my cell phone. Figured it must have been Jeremy wanting to have one last conversation before going to bed. So sleepy and so giddy at the same time.

"What you doing, babe?"

It was DaVon calling at fifteen minutes to three. Surely he was home by now.

"I'm sleeping, DaVon," I said with a groggy voice. I'd just fallen asleep. "Why?"

"I'm outside. Can I come in?"

"What? Are you serious?" I made myself wake up.

"Take a look."

Although it would be a little chilly in just my underwear and T-shirt, I jumped out of bed and scrambled to the front window of my house. Sure enough, DaVon's truck was parked in front. He blinked the headlights on and off to make sure I knew it was him.

"What do you want?" I said into the phone.

"You."

"Not tonight," I said. "We've been through this already, DaVon."

"Let me just come in for a minute," he said. I watched him

get out of his truck and start walking toward the front door, which against my better judgment I opened. We both hung up our phones, and he put his in the front pocket of his black hoodie pullover. "We don't have to do anything. Just talk or cuddle."

He and I both knew what "just talk or cuddle" meant when it came to us. All those years ago, just after our third date—a steakhouse in Marina del Rey—DaVon and I took a midnight walk along the water, talked about our dreams and desires, and made it official that we wanted to be together beyond the third date. After the hour drive back to my Pasadena apartment, we shared a short cocktail in the living room. DaVon said it was a little late for him to drive back to his place with the alcohol, and wanted to stay—just talk and cuddle. Needless to say, it was our first time talking, cuddling, and taking it to the next level. It was special, really nice. And during our years together, his lovemaking continued to amaze me and connect us.

But it wasn't where I wanted to go that night, though it would have been easy and comfortable to do. I was on a five-month post-DaVon drought, and any attention would have been nice.

"DaVon." I probably sounded like I was whining, but oh well. I was. This late-night visit wasn't what I expected or wanted.

"I have to take a piss anyway, babe," he said. "I'll be just a minute, and then I'm out."

"How classy."

"And so are you, standing here in the front door in your underwear. Muah."

DaVon mouthed a kiss toward me and walked through the door, down the hallway to the guest bathroom. At least he knew he wasn't getting anywhere near the bedroom suite and the bathroom we'd shared. I found a blanket in the front closet, wrapped myself in it, and sat on the arm of the living room sofa, waiting for DaVon to return and leave.

"I like the new decorations," DaVon said. He went to the front door and opened it. "I'm out."

"Like that?"

"Well, if you make it worth my while I could stay," he said and nodded his head. "If you want. It's up to you."

"I have to work in the morning."

"I see," he said. "Well, I have to get home anyway. They'll be wondering where I am."

"You mean your wife and kid."

He walked toward me and cupped my face in his hands. So warm and reassuring as I remembered.

"It was good seeing you again, Kenny. I realize how much I missed . . . miss you. I didn't know all this would rush back the first time seeing you again."

"Too bad you didn't realize this before you messed it all up."

"Muah." He mouthed a kiss toward me again. "You and your smart mouth. I hope the kid is patient enough to put up with it."

"What kid?"

"Trading in a Cadillac for a low-rider, babe? Good luck."

"What an ass," I said and backed away.

"I never knew you liked Latinos," he said. "I can't believe you're replacing me with a dude like that."

"I'm not even close to wanting anything new with anyone, even though you've had no difficulty setting up house so soon after us," I said. "That's kind of insulting if you ask me. And with a Mexican woman, no less."

"But I didn't ask."

"Okay. You should go now," I said and motioned toward the door. "We'd still be a strong black couple if you hadn't played on the other side of the yard. And then you've got nerve to try and confront me over some stranger who happened to talk to me at a bar? Please."

"I'm sorry."

"Yeah. Sorry, DaVon."

"I don't get you. I'm trying to make peace with you." He put the hood up over his head and walked out the door, down the walkway, and got into his truck.

I watched the taillights grow dimmer as DaVon drove away from my house and down the hill. I knew if there was a chance of us talking about getting back together, that would have been the right night and the right time. But for every good thing I saw in DaVon, there were two or three bad things I remembered. And those were memories I didn't want to relive with him again.

Chapter 4

"So how was your night, Kenny?"

Carlos sat down at my desk five minutes after I'd arrived, like clockwork, pretty much every morning with his coffee and nonfat blueberry muffin. Been the same routine for almost seven years, when we joined the Student Affairs staff at California University East L.A. Became colleagues and then best friends pretty quickly, once we noticed we were the only like-minded and like-lifestyled people on staff. We'd shared a lot of significant moments, primarily Carlos's relationship with Ricky, and then my subsequent relationship with Ricky's best friend, DaVon. We'd endured at least a dozen bosses over the years, a result of CUELA's revolving door of bait-'em-reel-'em-in-burn-'em-out staff dysfunction. And we shared similar family backgrounds—oldest sons, only sons, same sexuality issues. Except our families both had been cool and open with it all, to our surprises. Helped us to turn out halfway empowered and a little more confident in a world that tears down black and brown boys like us.

Most mornings it would be just a quick ten-minute catch-up session. But I knew that since Allison, our boss, was out this week, we'd be able to talk for much longer. I opened up the egg and tomato sandwich my mother packed for my breakfast and added a few dashes of pepper and RedHot hot sauce. Carlos stirred his coffee and cut up his muffin while I figured the best way to respond to his question. It was a mixed night, but I didn't want to disappoint Carlos and let down what was a fun birthday celebration he'd planned for Ricky.

"Why? What have you heard?" I asked back as I put the sandwich together again. I shook and opened up a small orange juice.

"A little birdie told me you robbed the cradle," Carlos said and laughed. "That you're ready for your membership in the man-boy love club. That you pulled a Chris Hansen *Dateline NBC*."

"Oh, really?" I asked. "Not even funny."

I knew what Carlos was talking about, but wasn't going to be the first to break the news. In case he was bluffing. Not that it was big news that I'd given someone a ride home. I assumed most of Carlos's friends within eyeshot could see Jeremy getting into my SUV. But that was as far as the story could go, unless they'd followed us to the taco stand or to Jeremy's house in East L.A. And unless they were that paparazzi-ish, that definitely didn't happen.

"Unless my sources are wrong," Carlos said. He stared at me and raised one eyebrow. "But my sources are never wrong. So spill it, mista."

"And did that source tell you he stopped by my house at almost three in the morning, trying to get some?"

"Hmmm. Maybe."

"I bet," I said. "Anyway, I just gave him, I mean Jeremy, a ride back to his place in East L.A."

"Hmmm. How convenient and close to your place."

"It was just a ride, Carlos," I said. "And it was all innocent."

I wasn't ready to admit to the couple kisses we'd shared in the parking lot or in Jeremy's driveway. I could hardly admit to myself that the first person I'd been remotely physical with since DaVon, besides myself, was a twenty-one-year-old. And it was not even expected, at least not on my part.

Carlos looked skeptical, but stopped his inquisition.

"Well, I'm just glad that you're finally at a point where you can see life beyond DaVon."

"Nothing's going on," I said. "And I am *way* over DaVon. Trust. Though he tried to flirt a little last night. I couldn't believe he showed up."

"I could. He knew you'd be there."

"But he's married now."

"It takes more than a few months to really get over a six-year relationship, as the late-night visit should tell you," Carlos said. "But anyway, tell me about Jeremy."

"I don't know much," I said. "Hmmm . . . he's twenty-one. His name is Jeremy Lopez. Latino, mixed Mexican and Dominican. A student over at ELAJ. He loves all his little gadgets and video games. He eats fast. He's cute. Loves hip-hop. Drinks Heineken. Lives in East L.A. with his family. That's all I can think of."

It was for precisely this reason that I couldn't even think of dating. In my years off the market, I hadn't continued developing my list of questions to get the information needed to distinguish a potential date, from a sex buddy, from a friend or acquaintance. And the fact that I knew nothing about Jeremy Lopez, except for a few superficial facts that didn't really add up to a full picture of the man. Who was he really? Was he a man with values and integrity? Family issues and drama to deal with? Drug, alcohol, or mental instability in the past or present of his life? Happy with his life? A man with goals? Which reminded me of one more fact to share with Carlos.

"Oh, he wants to go into Student Affairs . . . like us," I said.

"No way."

"Way. He wants to do student activities or leadership."

"Well, at least he's got a plan," Carlos said. "Maybe you can be his career mentor, mmm hmm."

"True," I said and giggled. "One more thing, though. Don't laugh, even though I am."

"What?"

"The boy could not kiss. I had to slow him down and give lessons."

"Kenny, you so nasty," Carlos said and high-fived me. "I'm gonna tell yo' momma."

"Stupid."

"So you two kinda dug each other, huh? I knew it."

"Maybe. I don't know," I said and shrugged. Looked down at my egg sandwich, which had gotten colder during our conversation. Didn't really want it anymore. Didn't want to go hungry either. "We didn't really exchange numbers or anything. I gave him my card, and he's supposed to e-mail me some pictures from the party. Didn't really talk about much else. Lies . . . he wants to holla at me sometime. Got so sick of him saying that."

"Holla? Is that his way of saying he wants to talk to you?"

"Yeah."

"Hmmm. I guess we'll see if he hollas back. And take it from there."

"I ain't no hollaback boy," I said. Laughed at my own dorky joke. Lame, I know. "I doubt he contacts me. What would he want with an old guy like me anyway?"

"Please, we're far from old. I'm not old," Carlos said and threw away the empty paper wrapper from his muffin. Took a sip from his still steaming coffee. "When did thirty-one or thirty-two become old?"

"It was old when we were twenty-one, duh," I said and laughed. "But anyway, he seems cool with the age thing. He thought I was twenty-four or twenty-five."

"Interesting," Carlos said. "Well, I read an article that said fifty is the new thirty. So that means thirty is the new . . . I don't know. Twenty-one. Eighteen."

We laughed.

My computer chimed, signaling new e-mail had arrived. Carlos jumped up and ran around my desk to look at the screen. Just as promised. E-mail from Jeremy. I felt giddy and clicked to open it. Carlos chided me on.

To: *Kenneth.Kane@cuelamail.edu*
From: *BrOwNcHiLd1986@e-mail.com*
Subject: 2 FiNe bOiS n WeHo

What up foo? Your nikka Brown Child, aKa, Jeremy here giving you a holla before I hit da classroom. Open the pics n put one on your screensaver. Remember how fine a nikka is. Holla back. Class til 5. My digits: 323.555.1986. Hit me back sometime. Lata playa! Jeremy.
P.S. Where is your MySpace page? I tried looking you up and couldn't find you???☹

"Wow, he's sure mastered the English language," Carlos said. "He's Mexican American and Dominican, you said? How many generations here?"

Carlos had this thing about how close or distant other Latinos were to their country of origin. He prided himself on being fifth-generation Californian, and tended to look down on those whose journey had brought them to the state and country more recently. It's what made him and Ricky such a perfect match. Snobby Latinos who didn't associate with *gente corriente*, the running people—as in running across the fictitious border.

"I don't know how long his family's been here," I said almost defensively of Jeremy. "His dad's from New York, I assume the Dominican. His mom is Mexican. But anyway, he doesn't talk like that e-mail sounded. A few slang words here and there, but otherwise . . ."

"Well, open the pics. I wanna see this boy."

A few more clicks and we were staring at Jeremy and me, arms around each other, next to my X5. Looked like lovers. Or at least like we had some strong chemistry. I was glowing in the pictures.

"So what do you think?"

"Looks like one of our students, cradle robber," Carlos said. "But he's cute. Real cute. I'd do him . . . if I was single."

"Whatever," I said. "It's not like we're anything anyway. Probably be the last time I hear from him . . . not that I'm looking for any more contact."

"Whatever . . . back at you."

"I'm gonna delete the message," I said and hit the delete button. "Got work to do."

I looked at the time on my computer and hated that my back-to-back meetings would soon start. The only salvation was that Thursdays at CUELA were like everyone else's Fridays, due to no Friday classes, so my weekend would be starting in just eight and a half hours.

"So glad Allison's not in today," I said and tossed the remainder of the breakfast sandwich in the trash. "She coming back Monday?"

"Or whenever her Botox-detox session ends."

"She's at a conference, I thought."

"Convenient excuse for a quick little skin rejuvenation in Santa Barbara, which I'm sure she'll stick into her conference agenda."

"You're wrong for that, Carlos. Don't kick a woman when she's down."

"She'd do the same thing if she could," Carlos said and headed toward the door. "Call me if you wanna do lunch. I got more dirt to share from Ricky's party."

"Will do."

After Carlos left, I turned to the computer screen and clicked on the deleted files icon. Reopened Jeremy's e-mail.

Saved both pictures and the e-mail. And hit reply. Gave him my home and cell numbers, and included my signature with all my work information. Even left my personal, nonwork e-mail address. Just in case Jeremy wanted to get in touch. Not that I was interested or anything.

Chapter 5

I arrived home to a full, home-cooked dinner. Southern style. Smothered pork chops. Mashed potatoes. Fried corn. Baked apples. All kept piping hot in foil containers and ready for my arrival. Though I would be eating alone, as my nine-thirty arrival home was way past my mom's bedtime.

One of the benefits of having my mom staying in the back house was little perks like this. Real food. A clean house. Laundry. All the things I loved and appreciated as a kid growing up in Ohio. Mom respected my privacy for the most part, and often would lock up after her visits up to the main house. Would leave a list of things touched, moved, cleaned, or tended to if she hung out in my house. Things had always been that way in the Kane household. Respectful. Kind. Honest. God-fearing. For the most part. Mom and Dad, then Stepdad, always said they vowed to raise their kids in the kind of home they didn't have as kids. And though we were no *Cosby Show* Huxtables in terms of money—neither Mom nor Dad nor Stepdad had finished college, and worked overtime in the auto plants and other UAW jobs in southeast Michigan to support us—we grew up with high expectations and beliefs for ourselves and those around us. Being black, blue collar, and working class was no excuse for limited living or thinking, though we could get a little boisterous at times when we all got together.

Ice crackling in room temperature glasses of whiskey, icken sizzling in hot oil, and adults raising their voices over game of spades are some of the sounds I associate with my owing up years in Toledo.

Whether it was just before sunset or a little after sunrise, irs was the home where everyone seemed to end up spending a little time. Our living room never seemed to be without neighbor, a relative, or one of my parents' work friends, nd as a child I got used to having social parents, having very little privacy, and sharing my space with adults and their children who, due to their parents being friends with mine, became friends by default.

Growing up in the kind of house I did, in our very working class way, I learned a lot about the importance of community, family, watching out for others, and helping when you could. My mother's back porch sessions with her sister-friends, destringing and snapping fresh-picked green beans or collards, saved many a marriage, or at the very least, put a weary wife on the path to competing confidently with the other woman lingering on the sidelines. My dad's basement gatherings with his buddies, sitting around and listening to a game on the radio or playing Johnnie Taylor albums while sipping on Johnnie Walker whiskey, encouraged his brother-friends to stay hopeful that the recession and auto industry layoffs were just temporary setbacks. Sometimes they'd loan money to neighbors short on cash during those times. Never borrowed, though at times, we could have used a little extra. Too much pride. Sometimes they'd talk about missing home—for some, Arkansas, Tennessee, or South Carolina; for my dad, Mississippi—and how once retirement time came, they'd trade life up north for simpler times in the places where they grew up. Somehow, I was able to slip in and out of "adults only" spaces unnoticed and hear some of what I was destined to experience in adult life.

Even though we were familiar with playing card games, fixing drinks for adults, or singing along to blues music, we also did our share of going to church on Sundays. We weren't regulars, but we weren't there only on Easter, Mother's Day, and Christmas either. The same people who graced our halls during the week, we'd see at Sunday morning services, proving what my parents always insisted. That Jesus wasn't just for the saved.

As far as I knew, my mom and dad never strayed outside of their marriage for the comfort of another. Of course, if they ever did stray and ever had problems, as any good parents would, they kept those issues to themselves and didn't make my sisters or me aware. Good as I was slipping in and out of adult spaces in the daylight, I never knew what went on in the privacy of my parents' room after dark and when all company was finally gone for the day.

My realistic side says they, like any other couple, had their share of problems, and the wisdom they shared with their friends had to come from experiencing some of the things they counseled others on. My idealistic side says they never had such problems in their years together, and if they did, I wouldn't want to know. All I knew to be true was my dad went to Mississippi to help his brothers and sisters tend to family business after their father died. I was fifteen. He was to be gone for a month. He never moved back to Toledo. My mom, sisters, and I never moved to Mississippi.

Still, I am grateful for those early years of togetherness.

As the oldest, I was expected to set an example and to help my sisters on their paths. And I did, mostly in the area of education. Finished college and then went back for a master's straight through. Finished by twenty-three. Tonya and Cecily did the same. Followed my footsteps. Guess I was a good mentor. Something you learn to do when you're the oldest and, at fifteen, the only man in the house.

Tonya's five years under me, twenty-eight years old. She married a news anchorman, quit her job as a nurse, and was raising two girls in Phoenix. We're opposites. She sees life very black and white, right and wrong. "I'm not prejudiced,

Kenny, but this man thing . . . I just don't see it for you," Tonya said when I came home for holiday break freshman year and brought my first boyfriend, Will, a junior, and vice president of the campus Black Student Union. She was the first to get on the phone to Dad and our cousins in Mississippi to tell them about "Kenny's friend." To this day, she leans toward being tolerant rather than appreciating and valuing my sexual orientation.

Cecily, the youngest at twenty-four, and I are the closest, not just because of her being cool with the gay thing, but because she's whimsical, follows her instincts, and has no regrets. She married her college boyfriend, an artist, her senior year in college, and never got a job in her major, chemistry, so she could help run an African art store they bought in Oakland. Together, she and her husband were raising one-year-old twins—a boy and a girl. Every year for San Francisco Gay Pride and Oakland Black Gay Pride, they throw huge bashes for their artist friends and let me and DaVon stay with them, when we were together. She's quite the fagnet, my upgrade on the term "fag hag."

Since I was without kids, by default, I was the one to take Mom in for the winter during her most recent separation from my stepdad. We all got along, even with our occasional tiffs, tried to have Kane family reunions with our dad included at least once a year on the West Coast or back in Ohio or Mississippi, and tried to keep each other's space sacred. Except this past Christmas, when I needed lots of love, hugs, and support, trying to get me through the DaVon breakup. Each day of Christmas week, over huge breakfasts reminiscent of our childhood in Ohio, each of my blended family members offered their opinions or reassurances.

Mom: "Rejection means direction."

Tonya: "He should have kicked rocks the moment he couldn't, or didn't, contribute to your household bills."

Cecily: "I have an artist friend who looks just like John

Legend who'll be perfect for you. When you wanna come up to the Bay Area again and we'll hook it up?"

Dad: "It's not about you and thinking you're rejected. It's about DaVon and his process."

Stepdad, the strange: "But he's probably happier getting back to the natural way of things . . . man, woman, children." And he wondered why Tonya, Cecily, and I never gelled with him when he came along five years after Dad moved away.

I chuckled as I reminisced about that holiday family time just a few weeks earlier. Let my pork chops, potatoes, and apples cool down, and went to grab the phone off the kitchen wall. Checked the caller ID. A couple 800 numbers. Probably telemarketers. No private numbers. No Jeremy. Grabbed a printout of Jeremy's e-mail and the pictures from the night before. We looked cute. Almost like a couple, though it was foolish to think of us as anything but passing strangers. New friends. Acquaintances. Felt silly being so giddy over a stranger. I hadn't learned anything significant about Jeremy, but knew that's what phone numbers were made for. I decided to call.

"*Hola,*" greeted the husky female voice on the other end of the line. Sounded like a lifelong smoker.

I panicked a little. A Spanish-speaking household. I quickly put my high school Spanish lessons to use and hoped they wouldn't think I was slow or anything.

"*Hola. ¿Puedo hablar con* Jeremy, *por favor?*"

"*¿Con quien hablo?*"

"*Soy* Kenny, *un amigo de* Jeremy."

"*Un minuto,*" she said and slammed the phone down on a hard surface. Had to have landed on its side, because I could hear what sounded like two televisions, a stereo, a half-dozen children, and a few adult voices talking loudly in the background.

I walked back over to the table and stuck a fork into the apples. Nice and cinnamony. Finished them in three forkfuls. Cut up my smothered pork chop into bite-sized pieces.

Dipped them, one by one, in the pool of gravy sitting on top of my mashed potatoes. Finished them. Stirred the fried corn in the remaining potatoes. Finished them. Drank a glass of red Kool–Aid. Realized I'd finished my dinner in the fifteen minutes I'd been on hold. Wondered if I should continue waiting? Hang up and try again? Just hang up? So stupidly giddy over this little man-boy. I wasn't doing anything else. Why not wait?

Then a thought occurred. Why hadn't he given me his cell number, the phone he'd been sending text messages from when we met the other night, instead of the home number? Just when I decided to hang up, I heard Jeremy's voice.

"What happened?"

"What?" I asked.

"Who this?"

"Kenny."

"Who?"

"Kenny. The X5. Last night. The eighties party."

"Oh, yeah," he said like it finally registered. "Whassup?"

"You tell me. You're the one who took almost twenty minutes to answer the phone."

"Serious? They just told me. Hold on."

I heard Jeremy holler at the kids to shut up, and then yell at someone else about the phone. So much activity for almost ten at night. On a weeknight.

"Sorry about that, Kenny. My crazy family."

"It happens."

"You got my e-mail?"

"Yeah. Thanks for the pictures."

"No problem, buddy."

"So what's going on?"

"Uh, not much," Jeremy said. "Just getting ready to go out. No school tomorrow."

"Hmm, that's cool."

"Me and my boys going down to Long Beach. That club Executive Suite."

"Fun. Sounds like a good time."

I felt a little awkward. Didn't want to interrupt his plans. And I obviously hadn't been part of his agenda, or else I would have heard from Jeremy earlier in the day.

"So you wanna do something this weekend?" Jeremy asked. "My folks will be gone, so we could chill here, eat, go catch a movie. You free?"

"Yeah," I said. "I've got stuff to do Saturday and Sunday morning, but I'm free in the late afternoon and evenings."

"I got a little homework, but I can get that shit turned out and be free for lata," he said. I heard another phone ring in the background. "Hold on, Kenny. It's my cell."

"Cool."

He hadn't put the phone we were talking on too far away, and I could overhear his other conversation.

"Whassup, nigga? . . . Hells yeah, I got a bag from my neighbor. We gettin' crunk tonight, foo . . . Nah, nigga, you betta pay me first before you smoke up all my shit. You never paid for the last time . . . I'll believe when I see . . . Yeah, I'm talking to him now . . . Nah, he got work and shit, foo. I got a professional nigga, who makin' big dollas . . . He not that old, whatever. Better than what you picked up, but I'm not playing dozens on you . . . Fifteen minutes. Cool. Holla."

He picked up our phone. "What happened?"

I hated this ill-mannered, rushed way of answering the phone Jeremy had. Annoying.

"What?" I asked.

"Still there, Kenny?"

"Yeah."

"Sorry about that. My best friend, Ignacio . . . Nacho, from last night. Remember?"

"The photographer. Yeah."

"So he being real stupid already. I can tell it's going to be a crazy night."

"Well, have a good time," I said. Had I said that before? Was I sounding like his father? "Get crunk for me."

"Stooge," Jeremy said and laughed. "Don't be using my words. It freaks me out. Anyway, you wanna go? We leaving in fifteen minutes, though."

"No thanks," I said, though I'd run a mental inventory of the first outfit I could possibly put together that didn't need ironing. What was I thinking? I had work tomorrow, even though it was Friday and no students would be around. Perfect day for catching up on projects and no meetings. But not a fan of last-minute sympathy invites. "I'll see you this weekend. Just me and you."

"It's a date, Mister Kenny."

"Don't call me mister. It freaks me out."

"Whatever," he said. "I might call you after the club. Is that cool?"

It wasn't. Didn't want drunken booty calls substituting for glorified conversation, but I made an exception. Didn't know why.

"Yeah."

"Cool. I'll holla at you later, Mister Kenny."

He hung up. I rinsed off my dinner dishes and put them in the dishwasher, not that I needed to ever use it with my mom helping me around the house lately. Looked at the clock. It was a little after ten. If I hurried, I could shower, change, and surprise Jeremy over at the club. Couldn't imagine me running around like a teenager, even though I was grown, with a professional job, and recently single. But that's exactly what I did.

Chapter 6

I picked up Carlos at his house near the Quiet Cannon Golf Course and the 60 Freeway in Montebello. He'd been restless, looking for something to do, and with Ricky working an overnight shift at the firehouse, going out with me was welcome relief for his boredom.

"You know you sprung," Carlos said when he got in and buckled up. "Running the streets looking for your little boy toy."

"He invited me."

"If you say so," he said. "This was *his* boys night out. Not ours."

"It's cool. Chill."

Carlos flipped through my CD case and put in Alicia Keys's musical diary. "If you wasn't my boy, Kenny Lucy Ricardo, I don't think I'd be part of this little adventure."

"We won't stay long," I said. "An hour or so, have one drink, talk to Jeremy, and then we'll leave."

"Jerr-a-meeee. Ooooh. I do have to admit, when you jump you go all the way. Bye bye DaVon."

"That's right," I said. "Bye bye DaVon."

We drove south on the Long Beach Freeway, through all the little blue-collar and working-class cities where most of our students came from. Bell. South Gate. Huntington Park. Compton. In just under twenty minutes, we were on Pacific

Highway and looking for parking in the neighborhood around Executive Suite. I hated neighborhood parking, especially with my new baby, but had no choice. No valet service. We parked about two blocks away, on a tree-lined street, with dozens of other club goers getting out of their cars. It would be safe.

The line wrapped about two-dozen deep around the outside of the club. Everyone was a Jeremy look-alike. Young. Latino. Some tall, some short, most average height. Spiky gelled hair. All wearing their best urban prep gear. Or their casual G-Unit, Ecko, or L.A. Dodgers gear. A few multicultural non-tourages rolled up behind us. A few Chris Brown and Usher look-alikes. Either way you wrote it, it was a young crowd. Definitely twentysomething. I looked at Carlos. He looked at me. We laughed. Knew we had at least a decade on most of the guys in line, but at least Carlos was being a good sport about me wanting to see Jeremy.

One thing. We looked like we fit in. Carlos had on a long-sleeve UCLA T-shirt, baggy jeans, Pumas, and UCLA baseball cap turned sideways. I went more Jeremy/Usher. Blue-and-white-striped, open-collared shirt, white T-shirt underneath, long chain with "K" pendant, loose straight jeans, and new white Adidas. Working at the university, and very closely with college students, kept us in the know on trends in clothes, music, and the latest lingo of our younger brothers on the scene for the most part. Even if we didn't totally buy into all the eighties babies' culture. Not that we were necessarily trying to buy in or fit in with them. With one serious relationship behind me, a house and mortgage, degrees, and a professional job, I couldn't. Neither could Carlos. But that night we were thirty-three going on twentysomething.

Carlos and I made our way into the club, ordered two Coronas, and walked up the steep staircase to where the main crowd and dance floor were. For a club advertising the night as a Latino Night, it was a pretty ethnically mixed crowd of Latinos, blacks, and Asians. And for a scene that catered mainly to the new, young, and hip, for some reason the DJ began spinning what she proclaimed an oldies set—JJ Fad's "Supersonic" blended into Salt-n-Pepa's "Push It," which transitioned into Rob Base & DJ E-Z Rock's "It Takes Two." Just the kind of music that lured Carlos and me directly to dance for the fifteen-minute set, before finding an empty booth near the stairs when the Spanish-language pop music started.

"You seen Jeremy yet?" Carlos shouted over the Paulina Rubio song now playing. Or was it Thalia? Hard for me to keep track. With computers, everyone sounded alike in Spanish or English.

"No, not yet," I said and glanced around the room. "But I saw a couple of his friends out there dancing. He's here somewhere."

"Cool," he said and held his Corona bottle up. "Refill? I'm buying."

"Sure."

"Back in a minute."

Carlos left. I pulled out my cell phone and checked for missed calls or messages from Jeremy. None. Not that I expected any. But still. Why was I getting so stupid over some man/boy I'd just met a night earlier? Especially when I was just starting to get over DaVon and his paternity-suit madness that ruined our relationship. Was five months enough time to move on after a six-year relationship? Even though the last year was basically written off on depositions, blood tests, and hearing DaVon's confession that at least two of the paternity allegations were true. That he'd indeed had multiple affairs with women during our years together. I was justified in starting a new relationship, or at least getting to know someone new. And it looked for the moment, young Jeremy Lopez would be the one. At least be the one who got me through the meantime.

I swallowed the last of my Corona and saw two of my students, members of the campus Gay Student Union and other campus clubs, walking up the stairs, martinis in hand, and laughing up a storm like the fun-loving gossipers they were. Blake and Jabari were two of my favorite students. Seniors. Active. Leaders. With the sharp-tongued wit of a Joan and Melissa Rivers duo, Blake and Jabari kept everyone at CUELA on their toes in the fashion department, and kept me in-the-know with all the student and staff gossip I knew to be true but had no way of confirming. They noticed me and sat down at my booth.

"Funny seeing you here, Kenny," Blake said. "Trolling for the young ones?"

"It'll get better, baby," Jabari chimed in his motherly voice impression he often used with the younger, newer gay students on campus. "All alone, with your beer, at the top of the stairs where everybody can see you. Posing for your blues album cover. All that's missing is B.B. King and Lucille."

We laughed and raised our drinks together in a toast.

"I'm here with Carlos. He's at the downstairs bar."

Jabari shook his head and put his arms around himself like he got the chills. Chimed in, "I'm staying away from downstairs. Saw my ex and two of his pot-head friends."

"Which one?" I asked. "Your boyfriends are like the movie-of-the-week. New one every weekend."

"Good one, Kenny," Jabari said. "This one's the abuser, and not just of alcohol."

"And he's tore up from the floor up already," Blake said and sipped on his drink.

"Fucked up," Jabari said. Frowned. "Oh, well. Guess I'm not good enough."

"Not your problem," Blake said. "Ignore JJ."

"Yes, ignore him," I said. "Ignore him. Move on. That's what I'm doing."

"Amen to that," Blake said.

Not that I made it a habit to confide in or hang out with

my students. I'd known Blake and Jabari since their freshman year at CUELA, when they were younger, more innocent, and barely coming out the post-high school closet. I'd seen them grow into fine young men who were about to graduate. They'd looked up to me. Presumed I had a perfect life. Assumed I had all they were aspiring to get and become.

"I'm meeting some guy I met last night," I said.

"Cool," Jabari said. "I hope to meet someone new tonight."

"Though it's all the same tired queens and JJ's friends out there," Blake said.

"JJ the ex?" I asked.

"Yeah. So over it," Jabari said. "But whatever. I'm gonna get my head swung tonight, that's for damn sure. Oh, here's Carlos."

Blake and Jabari stood up and made room for Carlos to sit. Greeted him, made small talk, moved on to the dance floor. Mariah beckoned them to have a party.

"It's crazy down there," Carlos said. "Passed out boys, boys causing scenes, married boys."

"Married?"

"I swore I saw Allison's man. Husband."

"Our boss Allison? No way."

"Way."

"I always thought."

"I always knew."

"He acted weird when Allison introduced us at the campus Mardi Gras program last month. Like he wanted to avoid us."

"Squeaky door wants to get greased up the most."

"Amen to that," I said, and we clinked Corona bottles. "Poor Allison. If this is true."

"Poor Allison, my ass," Carlos said. "Bitch walks the halls inspecting everything like she's the Queen of Sheba or something."

"When the real Queen of Sheba is her husband," I said. "So sad. She's out of town and he's creeping with the boys."

"Not your problem," Carlos said and looked around. "Where's Jeremy?"

"I don't know." I looked at my watch. Half past midnight. "I guess he changed his mind. He'd be here by now."

"You wanna stay?"

"You wanna leave?"

"Up to you, Kenny," Carlos said. "You're the one looking. And you're the driver."

"We can go," I said. "I don't want Blake and Jabari seeing me get stood up."

"Shouldn't have told them you were meeting someone."

"I know."

We downed our beers, stood up, and walked down the steep staircase.

Walked right into Jeremy, being escorted/carried out the club by security.

"Kennyyyyyyyyyyyyyyy, I'mmmmm fuuuuuuucked up," Jeremy slurred, head nodding like it was coming unattached from his body. He attempted a smile, but exhaled, instead, an alcohol-and-weed-reeking burp. The front of his jeans was wet like he'd peed on himself, the "Ecko" from his sweatshirt smeared with yellowish green slob or something, his silver chain torn and held tightly in his right hand.

"You know this cat?" the fatter of the two security guards asked.

"Yeah."

"Take care of your buddies better," the less fat security man said. "Here. He's yours."

They carried Jeremy just outside the club door and handed him to Carlos and me. My adult rag doll.

"Hellllllp, Kennyyyyyyyyyyy," Jeremy sighed. "Hoooooooooome."

"I'll take you home," I said and braced myself against the brick wall of the club while supporting Jeremy. "Carlos, get my truck, please."

I handed Carlos my keys and held on to Jeremy. So out of

it. Sweating. Ears bright red and hot. Barely breathing, but alive. I patted his forehead with a napkin left from my drink. He leaned more on me, head on my shoulder. Heavier than I thought. Solid build.

"Fuuuuuuuuck," Jeremy said and bent over into a series of dry heaves and finally . . .

In my student life career, I'd seen my share of fucked-up, out-of-it students, especially in my first job as a residence hall director, i.e., dorm director. I'd been there myself. That was all part of my twentysomething life. Some called it a rite of passage for college life, a getting-messed-up night here and there. Not something I thought I'd have an up-close-and-personal experience with that night.

"Sorrrrrrrry," Jeremy said. Held tighter to me. Like I was his lifeline. Like he needed me.

"Don't worry," I said. "You'll be okay."

Fat security guard brought over a roll of hard, dry bathroom napkins. I cleaned off Jeremy's face. He held on to me tighter. Kept apologizing. The small crowd of queens standing outside and smoking offered support in the best way they knew. Stared. Snickered. Pointed. Thanks, but no thanks.

"Fuuuuuuuck thooooosh bissssshes," Jeremy slurred and slobbered. "Fuuuuuuck them uuuuuuup."

"Chill, Jeremy. Carlos is coming with my car. We'll be home soon."

"Sooooo sorrrrrrrrry. Adiooooosh muuuthafuuuuuuck-aaaaaash."

The security guards helped me lift Jeremy into the backseat. The nosy queens continued gawking and gossiping. Great. The man Carlos thought to be Allison's husband was indeed Allison's husband, and he walked by thinking he'd made a discreet exit from the club. Made a mental note of his presence, but tended to the business at hand.

Carlos drove. I sat in the backseat with Jeremy, held his hand, his head on my shoulder. He apologized most of the way to East L.A. Didn't get sick again, thank God. And by the time we pulled into his driveway, Jeremy was still messed up, but could get through the side gate and into his house without assistance. We saw the living room light turn on. The porch light turn off. He was home safely.

Carlos and I didn't say a word as we drove to his house. What else could be said?

Chapter 7

"You hear that?" Mom asked in her husky voice, made deeper over the years by her smoking habit. She was rubbing her thumb and forefinger together, wearing an oversized T-shirt that said, I GAVE HIM THE SKINNIEST YEARS OF MY LIFE. In her other hand was a skillet of popping bacon and grease. In her mouth a cigarette. I didn't allow smoking in my house, but overlooked it during Mom's breakfast-cooking ritual. She was a guest and doing me a favor making my breakfasts and lunches every morning after my gym workouts and before I left for work.

"Yeah, Ma, I know."

"That's the sound of the world's smallest violin," she said and pulled her cigarette out her mouth. Blew a cloud of steam out and continued, "And that's what I'll be playing when you get fucked over by this one. Don't say I didn't tell you so, 'cause I'm telling you now."

I'd just told my mom about Jeremy. Everything. His age. The rides home. How I'd wanted to surprise him by meeting him out, only to be surprised by his drunken stupor and almost passing out in the club. But how cute he was and how intrigued I was for no reason at the moment, other than he was cute and funny and liked to have a good time.

"You want these eggs scrambled or sunny-side up?" Mom

asked. She put her cigarette out and cracked the eggs into the bacon grease.

"Sunny-side up."

"Damn yolk broke," she said. "You getting scrambled."

"That's cool," I said and clicked on my electronic planner. I knew I didn't have anything major planned, with it being a Friday, but I didn't exactly want to hear the truth from my mother. Moms always know. And mine was no different. She wasn't the kind of mother who always disapproved of the choices her kids made in lovers and partners. In fact, there had been many choices she gave her blessing to. Made it easy to talk to her, because you knew you weren't facing an automatic rejection of your thoughts and feelings. You'd just get honesty. Just like that moment in the kitchen.

Just like when I had "the talk" with her, freshman year of college, when I met Will, my then love-of-my-life, in a Black Student Union meeting at Northwestern. I didn't have to tell her I was gay. I just told her about Will, and she listened as I talked about him. He was vice president of the student organization at the time and a junior. He also had a girlfriend, Kim, president of her historically black sorority, and runner-up in the Miss Illinois pageant two years in a row. On the surface, Will and Kim had everything going for them that should have led to a future wedding spread in *Ebony* magazine—forthcoming degrees from an elite university, card-carrying members of the Talented Tenth, Northwestern's version of Dwayne and Whitley from that TV show *A Different World.* Instead, they had me, a third wheel. I needed her advice.

"He might come play in your backyard for a little bit," Mom had said, while I sat in the dorm stairwell with my cordless phone. I prayed my voice didn't echo too loud, or that some dorm busybody wasn't eavesdropping on my affair with Will. "But when the streetlights come on, he's going back home."

"What do you mean, Ma?"

"All that stuff you told me about their saddity credentials,

Kenny, that means too much to people like that. He ain't giving up that dream for too long."

"How do you know?"

"This storyline is old as Jesus," she said. "The other woman always gets the short end of the stick at the end of the day. They never leave their wives for long."

"Like Dad," I said.

"He didn't leave me, Kenny," she said. "He went back home—there's a difference. He always said he was going back to Mississippi to live one day. I wasn't going to stand in the way of his dream."

"I see," I said. "So you don't think this will last? The thing with Will?"

"I don't know much about this man-on-man thing, but I'm trying because of you," she said. "I can only tell you what I know based on my experiences."

"He said he's coming home with me for part of Christmas break. His family is in Detroit."

"That's fine. I want to see this young man who's going to break my baby's heart."

Even then, she knew. Much like she was telling me in the kitchen about Jeremy.

"No, it ain't cool, Kenny," she said while stirring the eggs around in the skillet. "You done already got your heart broken by Mr. Reverse Down Low DaVon. How that ever happened, Lord only knows. He told you exactly what you were dealing with in the beginning. And look what happened. Crept out with how many women? And let's not mention Will, from your college. This Jeremy doing the exact same thing, except he telling you who he is without words. You'll end up paying for his AA meetings or worse yet, on *Oprah* crying out your heart about how you got fucked over by a younger guy. You ain't that writer Terry McMillan. And the white lady law don't apply to gay black men, sorry."

Mom, and Dad, too, had schooled us in their version of race relations survival. In their interpretation, white women stood at the top of the racial pyramid, and could do, be, or say no wrong, no matter how ridiculous or naïve it was, while the same rules didn't apply to any other group of people. Dad always said to remember that white women were often the root of lynchings of black men in the U.S. Mom often said white women could cry, yell, pull a tantrum, commit a crime or other moral offense, declare herself superior or an innocent victim (and really believe it to be true), and still garner instant sympathy, service, and support. Everyone else just had to suffer and shut up. But the ironic part was that Mom could pull a "white lady" when it came to taking care of bill collectors, getting a manager's name in a store, or making sure we got a fair shake with our schooling and teachers.

"I know you're right, Ma," I said. "But DaVon never lied about his attraction to women and men. I just gave him the benefit of the doubt. And at least he's being a responsible black man and taking care of his kids."

"You listening to yourself, Kenny? You're making excuses. Not acceptable for someone you consider a partner."

"I know you're right."

"And that's without a fancy college degree, thank you very much," she said and spooned eggs and grits on my plate. She made her plate, grabbed toast from the oven, and brought everything over to the table. "Sometimes I wonder if sending you and Tonya and Cecily off to college did you any good. You got book smarts, but sometimes I have to wonder about your life smarts."

"You mean Cecily," I said and laughed.

"I mean you and Tonya, too," she said and laughed. "But especially those two girls. Quitting their jobs to stay at home with the kids. Lose your job, lose your vote and control in the house."

"Well, that's their choice, and they support their husbands being the breadwinners," I said. "Though I agree with you."

"Tell that to your father or your stepdad."

"Don't tell them about this Jeremy situation," I said. "I don't want them thinking I'm a weak son. It's really nothing."

My father was a nebulous supporter at best when it came to my sexuality, mainly because of the moving away to Mississippi thing. There wasn't much he could hold against my sisters or me, having moved away . . . or gone back home, as my mom liked to put it. Hard to parent with over a thousand miles separating you from your kids. It hurt, his being away, but eventually we got used to it. Stepdad, the strange, was old school and held on to old school opinions about men, women, and their roles. Luckily, he and Mom married while I was out the house at Northwestern, and I only saw him on breaks. Otherwise, there would have been problems in the Kane household.

"Ain't nothing to tell, Kenny," she said and laughed. "You only known this boy—and that's exactly what he is, a boy, being only three years younger than Cecily—for two days. Don't let a case of the lonelys exaggerate this thing with Jeremy. What's there to tell?"

"I guess nothing. You're right, Ma."

She stared at me. I could see the skeptical look on her face. The Kanes could read each other and know exactly what was on our minds.

"Unless you plan on saying one thing and doing another, which if that's the case, let's just flip you over the pool table right now and tell the hospital to get the rape kit out already."

"Ma," I said, my voice going up an octave or two. "Don't talk like that. That's awful."

"Shoulda talked *more* like that, and maybe you'd have better luck with men," she said. "And Cecily wouldn't be up there with her little crayon drawings, slapping five-figure price tags on them, and maybe selling one or two a year."

"You on a roll this morning," I said. "What's gotten into you?"

"Nothing," she said and pulled a folded piece of paper out her pocket. "This."

I opened it. An ad, written in Chinese characters, but clearly with the words "Harrah's Laughlin" spelled out in English, for a weekend turnaround bus trip to Laughlin, Nevada, a smaller, calmer version of Las Vegas.

"How'd you get this?"

"Your neighbor, Mrs. Li," she said. "Money is the universal language, baby."

"And?"

"I'm going with Mrs. Li and some of the other seniors from Monterey Park. Leaving this afternoon. Back on Sunday evening."

We'd talked about this gambling thing before. Not that it was to the point of lying, stealing, or heavy borrowing to cover basic expenses, but I didn't want to see her spending up all her extra money and never getting anything out of it. It had been a concern for the last couple years, and I'd hoped getting her away from the gambling scene of Detroit and Windsor, Ontario, Canada, would help curb the itch. Not that L.A., just a hop, skip, and jump from Las Vegas, was any better. If she'd been adventurous, she could have found a map and gone ten minutes south on the 710 Freeway for smaller local casinos.

"And did you plan on telling me?" I asked. "Or just having me show up at an empty house wondering where you were all weekend?"

"Stop tripping, young man. Who's the mom?" she said and laughed. "Nothing excites me more than the cha-ching of the machines. So you'll have the place all weekend for yourself and Jeremy. Not that I would ever invade your privacy on a date. I know my place is in the back house."

"So now you think I should see him?"

"Nope. I'm just putting a thought in your ear."

"So you can go do what you want, Miss I Have an

Agenda," I said. "I don't want this turnaround thing to become a habit, like the road trips to Detroit or Canada."

"Don't you want some alone time with Jeremy?"

"I can have alone time with him anytime I want," I said. "That has nothing to do with this trip to Laughlin."

My planner beeped. It was time to leave for the university.

"This is it, Ma," I said and wrote out a check for two hundred dollars. "Have a good time, but if you blow it all on games, that's it. No more turnarounds. And I won't be happy with you."

Hoped we both would have fun weekends, and that we'd both be able to exercise a little caution—Mom with the games in Laughlin, me with the games of a young man in Los Angeles.

Chapter 8

That morning my workday started with a little more bang than I expected. I'd barely sat down at my desk and started up my computer when . . .

"You Kenneth Kane?" the woman asked matter-of-factly, black hair pulled back into a tight bun, her icy blues peering at me like I was a criminal. I knew this look. Another court processor.

I could have said, "Duh, you saw my name on the office door," but didn't. Resigned myself to the continued fallout of DaVon Holloway's indiscretions.

"Yes, ma'am. I am Kenneth Kane."

She handed me a manila envelope, and I saw the familiar Superior Court of Los Angeles County return address.

"Please sign here."

"Can't you serve these papers at people's homes?" I asked as I signed. I knew the answer. Most people being served, or in trouble, avoided home as much as possible. And since most people spent the majority of the day in a nine-to-five . . . the whole process made sense. Just not how I wanted my Friday morning to start. I handed her back the signature roster.

"Thank you, Mr. Kane. Have a nice day." She turned around and left.

I opened the envelope and pulled out the papers. Another court date. Six weeks away. I'd been subpoenaed. The woman DaVon didn't marry, but who had his son nonetheless. A child support hearing in the matter of DaVon Holloway, Kenyatta Abernathy, and minor child, Ke'Von Abernathy Holloway. Always something there to remind me of DaVon's inability to keep his dick wrapped up and at home where it belonged. Hadn't started that way. Kenyatta's husband had died in a fire DaVon had fought and lost. Checked in with her, out of concern, a few weeks after and continued checking in on a regular basis. Just like with Vanessa. Called it consoling a fire widow. I called it adultery.

What would they want me to testify for anyway? It's not like matters of gay and lesbian households were that significant and important in family law. Half the time people assumed the only concerns of the community were drinking, dancing, drugging it up, and doing as many partners as possible. Certainly DaVon Holloway wasn't becoming the poster child for gay family law issues. And most certainly this little Kenyatta Abernathy didn't think she could squeeze any more juice out of DaVon's lemons. Thanks to his trifling bunch of parasitic brothers, sisters, nieces and nephews, DaVon's paychecks never made his ends meet . . . and as a firefighter for the city of Los Angeles, he made a decent paycheck and benefits. Which is why I never asked him for rent, utility, or entertainment money. Let him leech off me for six years, but at the time it was more leeching out of love. Now, I just resented everything I did for him. And if little Miss Kenyatta thought she was getting her hands on any of my income, she was sadly mistaken.

I folded everything back into the envelope and stuffed it in my bag. Logged on my computer and clicked to open up e-mail. Scrolled through and saw two messages from Jeremy, sent at 7:45 and 8:11 in the morning, among the other business and university-related e-mails. Opened up Jeremy's first note. Phone rang.

"Kenny?" It was DaVon. Didn't even wait for me to do my standard work greeting.

"Yes."

"You got served?"

"Yes."

"Sorry about that. It's just some little misunderstanding. I don't think it'll even go to court."

I let DaVon continue on with his explanations and excuses. Scrolled through Jeremy's e-mail. More of the same. Excuses. Everyone had excuses. It was only 8:40 in the morning. Wished I could be at happy hour. Needed to find an excuse to get there early.

To: *Kenneth.Kane@cuelamail.edu*
From: *BrOwNcHiLd1986@e-mail.com*
Subject: Executive Suite

What's up buddy? I don't know what happened to me last night. Well, I know what happened—I didn't eat anything since lunch and drank too much. Sorry I got so fucked up and that you had to babysit. It was nice of you. It was nice of you to show up and surprise me. Sweet. I'll make it up to you. Promise. Swear.

Lata,
J

Opened the second message from Jeremy.

To: *Kenneth.Kane@cuelamail.edu*
From: *BrOwNcHiLd1986@e-mail.com*
Subject: Date

Hey again, it's me. Just wanted to know if you got plans tonight and this weekend. Maybe we can do

> something like hit up a movie, get some grub, or just chill at your place and do the movie and grub there. Whatever you want to do. Let me know. At work until 2, then getting a haircut. Hit me back. My work is 323.555.8085. My cell is 323.555. 0513.
>
> J

". . . once I talk to the attorney and the people at the court," I heard DaVon continue.

Had no idea what he was talking about, but I remembered something I'd been meaning to ask DaVon about.

"When are you paying back the twelve hundred dollars I loaned you to get your place, DaVon?"

"That was a gift, I thought."

"A loan."

"I don't remember it that way."

"Yeah, you gotta have your version of every story, huh?"

"If you hadn't kicked me out, I wouldn't have needed to get my own place."

"I guess it's all my fault that we broke up, huh? Fuck off, DaVon."

I hung up, printed the e-mails, and hit reply to *BrOwNcHiLd1986*. Planned to take him up on his first date offer, despite the previous night's episode. Mother gone. DaVon's latest fuckup. Friday. Left me feeling a little vulnerable and restless. Even though I knew I should be looking to other sources for entertainment . . . and love.

"Knock knock." I heard the southern Texas voice before she came walking through my office door. Allison. My new boss. Well, two months new. Since January. "How are you? Just wanted to let you know I'm back, sweetie."

Great. More good news coming to my office door. I minimized the computer window with Jeremy's e-mail. In case Allison got a case of the nosies, as she often did, and came around to my side of the desk to see what's up on my computer screen. She called it checking up on workplace productivity. I called it invasion of privacy and personal space. Either way, I didn't want her knowing I was an on-line buddy of a twenty-one-year-old going to school down the street from CUELA. Didn't want her to know much about me at all, except what she needed to know for work.

"Glad you're back," I lied. "You look rested." Tried to figure out what she'd had done. Skin peel? Electrolysis? Wrap? Botox? Not Botox . . . face not paralyzed.

"Thanks," she said and walked around my desk. Computer check. Forced me to swivel to face her, unless I wanted to continue talking with my back to her. She continued, "I have a billion e-mails to read through, too. Hey, I ran into some of your friends from USC and Cal State L.A. at the conference."

"That's nice."

I learned early on in my university career to keep my answers to professional questions short and personal questions shorter. Especially when it came to colleagues you didn't know or trust. Mom's white-lady-law lessons. Allison sported the "Perez" by marriage only.

"They had some interesting things to say about you."

"Really?"

"Very interesting."

"I'm an interesting person," I said. Smiled. In my mind I added a quick roll of the eyes, twist of the neck, much like Drucilla Winters would on *Young and the Restless*.

"That you are," she said. Winced her eyes at me, like she was trying to read my mind. Felt like minutes passed in the ten seconds of silence.

"So?" I prompted.

"Why didn't you tell me about the situation? DaVon? The multiple affairs right under your nose? The kids? The paternity suits? You don't even seem like a man scorned by his partner of six years. You could have come to me. I'm here for your personal and professional development, sweetie."

"Happened before you worked here," I said. And wanted

to add that not even my mother called me sweetie and that she should nip the habit in the bud, but instead just said, "I try to keep my personal life personal."

"And to think he left you for a woman," she said. Stared at me. Like she wanted the full Channel 2 Eyewitness News Special Report on who, what, when, and how it all happened. "I also saw and heard the woman serving you court papers and your conversation with DaVon just now. Your door was open, sweetie."

"Sounds like you got an earful."

"That I did," she said. She turned away and retreated toward the door. Guess she knew I wasn't planning to make her my new confidante. Already had crossed that line once, with Carlos, and though it brought me a genuine friendship, it also brought me DaVon and my own personal *Days of Our Lives*. I was sure she was on her way down the hall to Carlos's office. I'd have to give him a warning call. Make sure his morning on-line shopping spree was temporarily halted. "One more thing, Kenny."

"Yeah?" I looked up. Thought she had left unannounced as she often did. I heard my cell phone beep. A message. But didn't take it out my bag.

"I'm going to announce this at the directors' meeting on Monday," she said. "If you or anyone on staff have problems with my leadership here, you need to make that statement by leaving. Resign. Be a man or woman of your word. Good day, Kenny."

Could Allison have been any more *Dynasty*? My God! All that was missing were monstrous shoulder pads, heavy makeup, and dramatic music striking up when she turned away. All I knew was that if I followed my heart and started that community youth center space I'd always wanted to, I could really resign and start a new career away from the university. One that didn't involve a so-called caring and concerned boss, who hadn't had the slightest idea her husband had been out cruising in a gay bar the night before. That would be saved . . . for later.

Grabbed my phone from the side pocket of my bag. Red light blinking. A message. A text from Jeremy:

WHERE RU? CALL WHEN N 323 555 8085 *BESOS*

"Office of Admissions and Enrollment, Jeremy Lopez speaking," he answered, sounding all professional and without the hip-hop edge of the previous nights. Sounded as proper as his morning e-mail to me. So he did master the King's English and could use it when necessary. Another tip from the white-lady-law manual. Know when to switch it on and switch it off.

"Jeremy, it's Kenny."

"Dude, I thought you was tryna ditch a nigga." The edge came back. "Where you been? What's crackin'?"

"Crazy morning. You don't wanna know. But I'll tell you later."

"You can tell me now," he said. I could hear the music go up in the background and the boisterous conversation of young men—probably his boys—continue. Sounded like they'd hooked up a PlayStation in the office. "It's kick-back city with the boss gone today, but I had to open up and gotta do a campus tour at eleven."

"Is your boss Marisela Rodriguez?"

"Dude, how you know?"

"I work in Student Affairs, too. It's a small world. We know everybody."

"Don't rat me out about kick-back city Friday," he said. "Mari's a bitch."

I suddenly felt like a nosy neighbor who controlled whether or not some kid on the block could get in trouble with one word from me. Decided to change the subject before my age and professionalism showed, and I ended up looking like the bad cop. Jeremy's boss, Mari, was a good friend and colleague I'd known for years. Years before Jeremy was part of the picture. Probably would be long after the picture.

"I got an e-mail this morning from this guy I'm talking to," I said in a singsong, happy voice. "Got a text, too."

"Oh, yeah? Someone tryna press up on you, huh?"

"Yeah. He asked me out."

"And what you tell him?"

"Haven't decided yet."

"You tell him you taken?"

"Nope."

"Then you got no choice but to tell him, 'Hell yeah.' "

"You think?"

"Believe me, Kenny. I know."

"I guess," I said, still playing the silly hard-to-get phone game. "Depends on what he wants to do."

"If I were him, I'd take you out somewhere nice like Sizzler or Red Lobster, go to the latest action movie at the mall, get some Boones or 151 and cola, whatever, and kick it at your place after. That would be my ideal date, but then again . . ."

I'd have a lot to teach Jeremy about the world of cuisine, liquor, and independent art-house film if we were to start this going out thing. Not that I was that many years or generations from mainstream taste myself. I could still dabble in a Friday-night splurge at the poor man's steakhouse and enjoy myself every now and then. But . . . you learn things with education and age and experience.

"I think I'm gonna go out with him, then."

"Cool," Jeremy said. "Sounds like a date."

Waited to see if he'd take the initiative on the when and where of the date, but he didn't make a move during the pause in conversation.

"How about seven?" I asked.

"Sounds good, Kenny. I'll be waiting in front of the crib."

"Cool." I guessed it would have to be cool. He hadn't offered to swing by my place to pick me up. Which really made me wonder if he had his own ride. Not that I had or needed my own when I was a college student at Northwestern or Indiana. And not that I minded being the primary mode of transportation so far. But still . . . you needed a car to have any sort of life in L.A. Sad, but true, necessity of life in SoCali. "See you then."

"Can't wait to see my Kenny," he said. And I could almost visualize the smile on his face, in his voice. The giddiness of a first official date. "I'll call you back at your office when my tour is over."

"Good deal," I said. "Can't wait to see you, Jeremy."

"Lata."

He hung up. I smiled. Opened and read his e-mail messages again. Created a new folder on my computer to save them in. Added our photos to my screensaver slide show. Imagined there'd be many more to come.

Chapter 9

After a fresh taper cut, a three-mile run around the track near my house, and hot shower and facial, I was on my way to pick up Jeremy for our first date. Seven-thirty. Our first official date, away from the club scene, away from friends, and without alcohol playing a factor. Had never interacted with him without either of us drinking, and thought it would be a nice change of pace. Like, real adult. Thought it would give us a chance to have conversation and get to know each other. Maybe see if I was dealing with the real thing, a real man, or just some young boy running game on me.

And with this being my first official date since my breakup from DaVon, and with six years of *Sex and the City* training behind me, I'd made a backup plan with Carlos. Just in case.

"I could be your mom or dad who got sick," Carlos said over the cell. "A neighbor noticing something suspicious at your house. Or just me, concerned that you forgot to turn on TiVo or something."

It was an old-fashioned and tired trick. The one-hour 9-1-1 phone call. To check in on the status of a date, and to feign an excuse if it wasn't quite working out. Not that I'd thought an excuse would be needed.

"You need to have a backup," Carlos said and laughed. "But I bet one hour into the night, you guys will be in your bed. How long has it been?"

"Months," I said and turned off Atlantic to enter Jeremy's hood. "Because I didn't give it up to DaVon at all during all the paternity test crap."

"You must be aching to get you some," he said. "Remember to wrap it up. Use condoms. You don't know what ponds Jeremy's been wading in. And you're not a monogamous couple yet."

"A lot so-called monogamy did me with DaVon," I said. "I've got just one more test to go next week and I'm in the clear. Maybe Jeremy and I can go get tested together."

"Maybe, but don't scare the kid on the first date with test talk," Carlos said. "He's twenty-one. Keep it light. In fact, you two shouldn't even be talking sex-talk on the first date."

"I know," I said. I got to Jeremy's street and turned right. "Damn, there's no parking on his street tonight. I'll call you later."

"No, I'll 9-1-1 you and see if you need an out."

We hung up. I continued driving down Jeremy's street. Looked cute in the dusky sunset light. Cute, working-class houses of various pastel colors, with the famous and necessary burglar bars over the windows, and iron gates closing the driveways off to traffic. The past couple nights there'd been open spots at or near Jeremy's house. Not that I really needed to park this night, since it was a quick pickup and then movies and dinner. Or dinner and a movie. Whatever the order. The usual Ford or Chevy pickups had disappeared and were replaced with younger, hipper Accords, Acuras, and Scions. All with East L.A./Monterey Park–style racing enhancements. The type I'd seen many times in the CUELA student parking lot. All surrounded by the types of young men I'd seen at CUELA. The young, college-age, multiethnic groups of guys who looked . . . very . . . similar . . . to Jeremy and his friends. The multicultural pack of go-getters thinking they ruled.

I double-parked, turned on the hazards, and lowered my window. Jeremy jogged over, big grin on his face, hair freshly cut, eyebrows newly threaded and shaped, looking even younger in the sunset twilight. Looking real Daddy Yankee. I knew I was about to be handled by this young, hip-hop pretty boy. Could just feel it, but it was too late to make the 9-1-1 call to Carlos.

"What up, boo?" Jeremy asked and blew out a cloud of smoke in the opposite direction. "You ready?"

"Yeah. Are you?"

"Yeah, in a minute," he said and leaned in the window. Kissed me. Short peck on the mouth. At least he wasn't shy about his feelings or attractions or intentions. Especially in front of his boys or his neighbors. Boy's got balls. Thought most boys in the hood would shy away from public displays of affection. Had to check myself on that stereotype. "There's a little change to the agenda, Kenny."

In the background I heard someone yell, "Whaddup, Kenny?" I backed from Jeremy's face.

"Is that Nacho?"

"Yeah, that's the change," Kenny said. "We got invited to this party that I totally forgot about. So I thought we could all roll up there together. How's that sound?"

"I didn't think our date was going to be a party . . . with your boys."

"If it's not cool, I'll just tell them and we can do something on our own," he said. "I just flaked and forgot. It's our honor society frat."

"A college party? I'll be the oldest one there, Jeremy."

"Chill, Kenny," Jeremy said. "They all think you're twenty-five, remember?"

"Well, whatever, that's still old for a college party," I said. Felt a little anxious and frustrated. Not expecting a change in plans. "It's only seven-thirty. It's early for a party, isn't it?"

"Yeah. We'll chill here for a coupla hours. I got drinks, but maybe we can hit the liquor store on Beverly?"

In the background I heard Nacho yell, "Whaddup, J? We kickin' back here or what?"

"Whassup, Kenny?" Jeremy asked me. "Your call. I'm down for whatever. I just wanna spend some time with you, whether it's alone or with you getting to know my world a little."

I hated being put on the spot like this for kid games. Part of me was pissed off that our first date plans got totally changed and planned without me being consulted. That I was thirty-three and being manipulated by a twenty-one-year-old, and worse yet in front of his friends. That whatever call I made would be both good and bad for me, Jeremy, and his boys. I could have ruined their night. Ruined mine. Or compromised. But the compromise would have given Jeremy the upper hand. Or maybe have earned me "cool points" with Jeremy's boys. Either way, I couldn't analyze, pontificate, and do a pros/cons SWOT chart. Besides, I didn't have the luxury of time. A couple cars were blowing their horns behind me. I was blocking traffic trying to get through Jeremy's street.

"Yeah, let's hit the party."

"I love you, man," he said and kissed my cheek. "Just pull into my driveway. I'll open the gate."

Jeremy backed away and looked at Nacho and his other boys. Gave them the thumbs-up sign and flashed his infectious smile. I rolled up my window, parked in the driveway behind a red Honda Civic with expired plates, and took a breath. Wondered why I was putting up with Jeremy's college-boy drama. He hopped in the passenger side and I knew why.

"Come here," he said and grabbed my head toward his. Planted one of his fast, wet, sloppy kisses on me until I slowed him down. Our tongues met, danced in each other's mouths, signaling to the other in what direction the night might turn. He pulled away and traced my lips with his forefinger, lightly darting it in and out for me to play with. Showed him how much I might be able to please him if he played his cards right. Went back to kissing, making out, and creating steamy windows in my truck. Until we heard the tapping outside Jeremy's side and pulled away.

"Oh, shit," Jeremy said. He wiped a small circle of steam away. "Nacho."

I hit the button that lowered Jeremy's window a little.

"J, we need your money to get the shit," Nacho said. "We gonna jet to the store."

"Bitch, my wallet in the house. I'll pay you later."

"We won't have enough without your part."

I chimed in, "Here. I got it. How much you need?" Reached into the center console and grabbed my money holder. Handed over two twenties to Jeremy, who handed them to Nacho. "Here's our part."

"Cool," Nacho said and did a double take at the cash. "Back in about an hour."

"Thanks," Jeremy said and turned to me. "We should probably go inside before the cops come knocking, huh?"

"Yeah, probably."

"At least we got some alone time," he said. Infected me with his smile. "Get to know my Kenny better."

And I realized that though Jeremy and I had been touching base, e-mailing, and running into each other in clubs these past few days, we'd really not known or learned a lot about each other. That we'd gotten connected through flirting and kissing, but not by really listening and sharing verbally with each other.

The inside of Jeremy's house reminded me of the working-class home I'd grown up in back in Toledo, Ohio. Small and overcrowded with too much stuff. Lots of browns and beiges, wood tables, plastic covers, throw rugs, knickknacks, religious icons, and generations of faded family photos on the walls and available mantel space.

"My grandparents on my mom's side, who stay in TJ," Jeremy said and pointed out the picture. "That's where everyone is this weekend. Mom gets her asthma medicine there cheap."

"I didn't know people really lived in Tijuana. Wow."

"Yeah . . . here's the rest of my rainbow coalition family . . . my oldest brother, Froylan, who died when I was sixteen, about five years ago. Police mistaken identity. He'd be almost thirty if he were living . . . My Dominican cousins and grandparents back in New York—we don't get out there too much to see them in person. The brother above me, Angelo, who is in Arizona. Got a baseball scholarship, but got some white girl pregnant in college and got stuck, married to her and her family . . . My mom and dad with all of us when we were kids. My dad is dark as you, see? That's me in the middle with my buck-ass teeth before braces . . . José Luis is my age, but ten months younger, but into all sorts of speed, weed, coke, dope. People get us mixed up all the time. He's out there wherever, doing whatever. Shows up whenever to see his baby girl who stays here . . . My youngest brother, Eric, who's been in Iraq since after high school. He's so cool and my best friend. Just turned twenty. I hate that he's stuck there, but he didn't want to hit the books like me, so he's paying the consequences . . . My only sister, Yadira, she's sixteen going on sixty, the way my mom has her taking care of Jose Luis's baby and Froy's kids. Froy's wife, Tuong Van, stays with us and their three Hapa slash Lat-Chino kids. That's all the screaming you probably heard in the background on the phone when you called."

"Wow, you got a lot of people staying here," I said. And realized I probably sounded judgmental, but it was true. There couldn't have been more than three bedrooms for a dozen people in the house. "Thanks for sharing about your family and the pictures. You and your brothers look alike, and everyone looks like they love each other a lot."

"They a'ight," he said, faced and hugged me. "You'll meet them all soon enough. They're a little dysfunctional and do crazy things at times, but I'd do anything for them."

"Cool," I said. "And what's that picture hidden in the back? You and Alex Trebek?"

"Don't ask." He chuckled. "My nerd days. I was on *Teen Jeopardy* back in the day."

"Serious?"

"My mom seriously brags about this picture. I hate it," he said. "Look at those glasses. Those train-track braces. That greasy hair. Looking like a Mexican Pee Wee Hermanito." Jeremy placed the *Jeopardy* picture facedown.

He didn't ask, but I told him anyway about my mom staying with me temporarily during the winter, about growing up with the basics but nothing more in Ohio, about my family's eighteen-and-out rule and that it was a job and your own place or college at that age, about my younger sisters and their husbands, careers, and kids in Phoenix and Oakland, and that he'd meet them all one day. Throughout this, Jeremy lightly kissed my ears, cheeks, neck. It was hot, getting the kind of attention Jeremy was giving me.

"Cool," he said while grinding against me. "Sounds wonderful."

I looked down. Felt Jeremy growing hard against my leg and asked, "What are you doing?"

"That's the magic stick," he said, raised his eyebrows, and grinned. "Let me show you my room."

"Cool, but remember your boys will be back soon."

"Yeah, whatever. I'm the one on the date," he said. "You want some water or Kool-Aid? The good stuff will be here soon."

"I'm cool."

"You are," he said. Planted a short kiss on my mouth. "You're so freaking cool, Kenny."

Jeremy guided me from behind through the tiny hallways and turned to his bedroom at the back of the house. Hugged and kissed me on the back of my neck until we arrived. The faces of other Lopez relatives and ancestors stared us down from their frames on the walls. Made me feel like I was taking advantage of their younger son, nephew, grandson, though he was twenty-one and very much a man with free choice and a very strong libido. Felt kinda inappropriate, yet flattering, to be hit on and found attractive by Jeremy. Loved the free-spirited, go-with-the-flow, say-what-you-feel nature of youth. Made me feel good being around Jeremy. At his age, he couldn't have had the level of baggage or issues someone my age, like DaVon, would have.

"Damn, Jeremy, this is sweet," I said when Jeremy unlocked and opened his bedroom door, which was unlike any other room in the house. Sleek, modern, clean. Jeremy had definitely raided the IKEA showroom on several occasions to furnish his room, and had taken hints from all the home makeover shows on HGTV in terms of color, style, and space use. The various shades of orange and red and chocolate brown on the walls, candles, bed linens, and art work in the room blended well. Felt warm and homey.

"I did it all myself," Jeremy said as he showed me the walk-in closet he told me he'd designed and built. His clothes organized by genre—hip-hop, business, club gear, preppy—and then by color. His DVDs and video games lined up in their baskets. Belts, ties, and shoes placed in their sections of the closet. "Don't laugh when I show you this."

Jeremy unlatched a panel in the closet that revealed all sixteen thousand romance novels written by Danielle Steel, as well as contemporary black and Latino fiction by Terry McMillan, Alisa Valdes-Rodriguez, Mary Monroe, Mary Castillo, E. Lynn Harris, Carl Weber, and Eric Jerome Dickey. A few nonfiction books by Keith Boykin. Pretty much everything they'd ever written, all in hardback. Mint condition.

"You read all of these?" I asked.

"Yeah. Got started on Danielle Steel when I was eight, and would sneak them from my mom and read all night."

"The dirty parts, right?"

"Nah, those I got from other books like my brothers' porno stashes," he said and put his arms around me, pulled us waist to waist. "Learned how to slow motion real good."

"Oh, yeah?" I said and smiled.

"Yeah." He winked. "I'll show you my skills lata."

"Thanks," I said and pulled away. Turned to look around his closet. Impressive. "I never would have pictured you reading Danielle Steel. Or being on *Teen Jeopardy*."

"No one does. That's why no one will ever know," he said and closed his miniature library. I kept it open when I saw one more thing that interested me.

"You like Maurice Jamal's films?" I asked and ran my finger along two DVDs on a shelf.

"You know about Maurice Jamal?"

"What black gay person doesn't know about *The Ski Trip* or *Dirty Laundry*? I really loved *Dirty Laundry*."

"He spoke at this film festival last fall in Hollywood," Jeremy said. "I went for extra credit, but it was real impressive. Gave me copies of both films, after I disclosed the *Jeopardy* thing in an audience icebreaker. Real silly how it opens doors."

"You shouldn't be embarrassed by the *Jeopardy* thing," I said. "That's really impressive."

"Thought you might appreciate it, since you're all educated and book smart."

"That's debatable."

"A sexy, fun, young-at-heart, professional man. Not a boy, like these other foos out here."

"Anyway, this ought to be your major," I said, wanting to get the attention and compliments off me, and pointed around the walk-in closet. "Forget the college counseling blah blah blah. You should think about architecture or engineering. You have an eye for space and design."

"An eye for fine men, too."

He scooped me by the small of my back to him. Soon, we were like two sixteen-year-old boys sneaking a make-out session in the back of the family house during a family holiday visit. Except that night, we were not sneaking and were definitely communicating we wanted to move beyond first or second base action.

"How you get down?" Jeremy whispered against my neck.

"I do everything," I whispered back.

"Damn, Kenny. That's hot."

"You a taker or a giver?" I asked.

"Both. What are you into?"

"Both," I said as he continued kissing my neck. "Been tested?"

"Last month at school. Clean."

"Same here, but I have an ex who cheated. Still testing."

"Me, too. Cheating ex and testing. Gotta test all the time these days anyway."

"Well, only if you run your bedroom like a fast-food restaurant. Over a billion served."

We laughed a little.

"That's funny, Kenny."

"You got condoms?"

"Hell, yeah, gotta use condoms," he said. "Magnum man here."

"Oh, yeah?"

"Feel." Jeremy placed my hand on his zipper. Squeezed my hand so that I could get a handful of him. Put my thoughts of violating the twenty-one-year-old out my mind, as I saw that he was both a willing and experienced seducer.

"Feels nice," I said and unbuttoned his baggy denim shorts. They fell and revealed boxers being held up only by the justification for the magnum. Unbuttoned the boxers, held my breath as I snuck the first look. The first look was always the moment of anticipation, and could determine long-term lover, friend, or forget it. "Nice."

"Let me see, Kenny," he said as he undid my jeans, lifted my T-shirt. Thank God I ran and did crunches today. "Niiiice."

We leaned against the wall, touching each other, kissing, breathing hard, stroking until one or the other decided to make the move south. Had to happen eventually. It was the game men liked to play. Who was going to go down first? And whoever did go first had better be damn good, or else there'd be no moving forward to the next level of bedroom play. Checkmate. Jeremy made the first move, as he held me, kissed my neck, left hot saliva on my chest and nipples, tickled my navel with his tongue, and tasted me with his lips. Worked me like I was the source of life. Like I was his man. Like the way I would relax DaVon when he came home from work when we were together. The way partners are supposed to. Let my mind shift back to the delicious tickling, tugging, and tonguing by Jeremy, heard his light moaning and groaning, did the same as he drove me crazy, leaned my head back against the TV screen on the dresser, whispered a few four letter words—compliments to the giver of a job well done.

Some song by Nelly blasted from Jeremy's phone, which hung from the pocket of his shorts on the floor. He pulled off and away from me.

"My stupid ex."

My phone buzzed. Carlos's 9-1-1 call. Perfect timing.

"My friend."

We both fumbled to grab our phones. I picked up. It was Carlos. On schedule. Watched Jeremy slip into his closet with his phone, his magnum still at attention against his stomach.

"How's everything?" Carlos asked.

"I'm cool."

"How cool?"

"Real cool," I said. "Just kicking back at a friend's place."

"You're being a nasty ho, huh?"

"A little bit."

"You better turn that homie-vato stud out. And make sure he does the same for you."

"No doubt."

"Is he a giver or taker?" Carlos asked. "Fuck, never mind. Not my business. I'm just a married voyeur. A happily married, yet bored, voyeur."

"Whatever," I said. "Uh. Both."

"Good," he said. "I'll let you get back to Jeremy. Need a follow-up call?"

"I can talk for a minute," I said and saw Jeremy peek out from the closet. "He just got a call from an ex."

"Wow, something you both have in common. The ex factor."

"We haven't talked about it," I said. "But I do know his ex cheated, too."

"That's what twenty-one-year-olds do—look for new pieces," Carlos said. "Not that I'm psychic."

"Gee, thanks for the prediction."

"I didn't mean it like that."

"Sure. I'll talk to you later."

"Well, be careful. Have fun. Call me. Ricky's working all weekend. I'm bored and home alone."

"Will do. Thanks."

I hung up. Started feeling a little chilly, being all seminaked and exposed, and pulled up my boxers and jeans. Straightened out my T-shirt and sat on the bed. Could hear, but tried not to, Jeremy's conversation with the ex. Jeremy the prep could turn gangsta and vicious in a heartbeat, as he let loose a string of expletives that would make a raunchy-mouthed comedian blush and run for cover. I picked up an *Entertainment Weekly* that was sitting on the bedside table and leafed through, seeing all the latest in the world of Paris, Jamie, Lindsay, Vivica, and Ricky. Got so caught up, I didn't hear Jeremy come back in the room.

"Let's roll," he said and grabbed his boxers and denim shorts off the floor.

"What about Nacho? Your boys?"

"They'll meet up with us there."

"Cool."

He went into the closet. Came out with a fresh wife-beater T-shirt, which showed off shoulder tattoos I hadn't seen before, the silver chain with cross pendant, and added bling to his ears. Put on a denim jacket. Looked me over, head to toe, said I looked good—I was wearing new Diesel jeans and shoes, and a black fitted T-shirt with some Chinese-language symbols—and kissed me.

"My ex is so drama," he said. "I know you overheard us."

"Not really," I said. Lied. I'd heard most of it. "Mine is drama, too. We'll compare notes."

"At the party," he said and kissed my cheek. "Or after the party."

We laughed. He spritzed us both with Issey Miyake, gelled and finger combed his hair until spiky and stiff, and went to wash his hands. Returned. Pulled out the phone. Picture time. We posed at least ten different ways together—silly, serious, lovey-dovey, crazy—and kissed in between each photo.

"Just make sure to e-mail them to me," I said.

"Sure," he said and looked at me like he had a quid pro quo demand in return. He did. "If I can ask you a favor."

"Hmmm, what is it?"

"Can I drive the X5 tonight?" he asked and gave me puppy-dog eyes, while nodding his head up and down yes. "I just wanna show them how we rolling together."

My truck was a no-no, even to my mom. I'd gotten her a rental so she could get around town when I wasn't home. Too risky letting someone else get behind the wheel, whether you knew them or not. But then again, everything else about my meeting Jeremy was unconventional. And unexpected. Much like my answer to him.

"I'm trusting you," I said and tossed the keys to him. "You're taking care of my baby tonight."

"Most def I'm taking care of my baby."

Chapter 10

We could hear 50 Cent blasting halfway down the block as we walked toward the house where Jeremy's honor fraternity was throwing a party. We were in Highland Park, a city known for its quaint Craftsman-style houses, narrow streets, and where professionals and yuppies lived side by side with the working class and poor folks they were trying to buy out. It was also a place that had been in the news recently for Latino gangs targeting violence at African-Americans in certain parts of the city. That worried me a bit since Jeremy had to park my baby two blocks away from where we were going. It gave us some alone time before the party, and I was depending on Jeremy to watch out for me.

"My ex might be here," Jeremy said. "If I get in a fight, you got my back?"

"You serious?" I asked. "I was going to say the same thing, with all the news about the violence up here toward black people lately."

"Yeah, but it's kinda exaggerated, I think," he said. "But my ex—the bitch is crazy."

"Does the bitch have a name or description?"

"Nah, I don't wanna jinx it," he said. "Just stay close and hugging up on me all night. We'll have a drama-free night. I promise."

"So I take it your frat knows about you? Dating men, that is?"

"Half of 'em you saw out with me at Metro when we met the other day. Nacho, Tony, Daniel, Slimer . . ."

"Slimer?" I asked and made a face.

"You'll know it when you see him eat."

"Ewww."

"It's funny. But everything will be cool tonight. We'll kick it for an hour or so and head back to my crib."

"Cool. I just wanted to spend time with you."

"Come here," Jeremy said and stopped in front of a darkened house. Flipped his L.A. hat to the back, his biceps looking nice and firm in his wife-beater, moon reflecting in his dark eyes. Sat on the stone wall, pulled me to him and kissed me. A risky move, but I felt confident in his arms. "I'm so glad I met you. You're one of the best things to come into my life."

I wanted to say, "After two days, you know this?" but kept my mouth shut, smiled, and then said, "Thanks. I'm glad I met you, too."

Not that I was cynical about our attraction, but I wanted to stay grounded and real. Two days couldn't have given Jeremy that much to feel. But it was nice to be with someone who could be open and truthful with their emotions. Maybe that's the luxury of youth—living life as a permanent freshman year of college, where everyone was a potential best friend or lover.

"That means a lot to hear you say that," Jeremy said. "That's another one of the problems with my ex. Never shared his feelings."

"I'll be sure to be open and free with—"

"The booty," Jeremy interrupted and laughed. I laughed. He put his hands into my back pockets. "Just kidding."

I could hear 50 Cent transitioning into some serious reggaeton music, which made Jeremy and me sway on the stone wall.

"We better make our entrance before we start something out here on the street," I said. "Or find ourselves in trouble."

I saw Nacho and a couple of Jeremy's other friends walking up the street, and we waited for them to catch up so we could make our entrance together. Like the nontourage we pretended to be. Me, the thirtysomething professional, with a bunch of college students, including a sexy twenty-one-year-old masquerading like we were boyfriends, who could have been my own students at CUELA. All the same boys I'd seen at Carlos's party the other night when Jeremy and I first met. We did the customary fist knocks and hand slaps. Met Nacho again. Tony. Daniel. Slimer. Some other guys I remembered seeing at Metro and at Executive Suite, but could not keep track of their names. They were passing around a bottle, a joint, and insults about who looked the best and worst of the bunch. I passed on all of the above, but noticed Jeremy didn't. Made a mental note to ask for my keys back. No accidents or tickets wanted here.

When we walked in the house, it looked more like a prison-release party than an honor fraternity college party. Through the hazy, red lights, I could see everyone in a standard white top—whether it was a wife-beater, an undershirt, an oversized button-down—and dark bottoms—creased Dickies, baggy jeans, sagging three-quarter-length shorts. Bling for days. Around the neck. In the teeth. On the earlobes. Circling fingers. Everyone was tatted up, shaved down, goateed out. The smell of incense and weed overpowered the small living room of the house. All eyes were on me, the lone guest not in uniform. Or was it that I was a stranger? Or one of a few black guys in the mostly Latino crowd? Was I on the wrong turf? Or, God forbid, the oldest-looking one in the room? In Diesel that actually fit and formed on my body, it couldn't have been the latter, but then again, you just never knew.

Jeremy grabbed my hand, which I was reluctant to hold on first glance at the crowd, and we went to the kitchen area where the host, Ramon, someone Jeremy introduced as a classmate, was tending bar at the sink. Ramon offered us both a jungle juice concoction he'd been specializing in all night, and Jeremy grabbed my free hand and took me to the side door. Outside the kitchen window, I could see dozens of the uniformed guests shaking and swaying on the concrete dance floor—the driveway—in front of the garage and back house. Looked like fun. Felt like throwing my hands in the air for a minute or so. Was sick of, but still loved, that Daddy Yankee song from a few years back, "Gasolina."

"Me and Tony and Slimer have something to take care of right quick," Jeremy said. "You'll be cool?"

"You don't want me to go?"

"Well, I can't give up all my secrets yet," he said. Toasted his drink against mine. "Back in about ten minutes."

"So what? Just stand here?"

"Come on, Kenny. You're smart. Work with students all day. I'm sure someone will be all over you. But don't forget you're mine."

Jeremy looked around and kissed my cheek. He, Tony, Slimer, and a couple other guys walked through the dancing crowd and to the apartment above the garage out back. I could see the silhouettes of partygoers through the apartment's sheer curtains, bottles flailing in the air, hands passing around cigarettes and pipes, bodies becoming one. I wondered what business Jeremy could have that would take him away from his date with me. Sipped on the sweet and potent jungle juice and stood in the kitchen. Seemed the safest place. Living room was full of potheads relaxed and numbed to the world. Dance floor would have been nice with a partner to actually dance with. Kitchen was the best. People looking for drinks and small talk. Something that would pass the time while I was waiting for Jeremy.

"Oh no you ain't here." I heard a familiar voice and turned toward it. Jabari. Even he, who was more of a Ben Sherman or FCUK guy, was in white and blue baggy gear.

"You just closing in on all my turf. First the clubs, now my parties."

"Jabari, thank God you're here." I smiled. Tapped glasses.

"What are you doing here?" Jabari asked, with a hint of annoyance in his voice. "Shouldn't you be at home, watching *Murder, She Wrote,* knitting sweaters, or making soup? Stay on the freaking D-list with the adults."

"I got invited, thank you very much," I said. Smiled. "I still make the guest list."

"Damn, word gets around about our parties," Jabari said. "Soon you'll be stealing my men."

"Please," I said and clinked my plastic cup against Jabari's. "I didn't know you were in this frat. Is everyone here gay or what?"

"It's an honor frat, doesn't count much, except for the parties and except that most of us are gay or bi." Jabari looked around and past me, I assumed for one of his friends in the dancing crowd. "How'd you get invited?"

"A friend," I said. "The one I was supposed to meet at Executive Suite the other night."

"So a younger man?" Jabari said. "Well, younger than you. Sweet. Just leave one or two for me."

"Oh, please, this is definitely your turf," I said. "Where's Blake?"

"On a date," Jabari said and continued looking around. "I'm out cruising for one. Or at least wanna make sure my ex isn't here. He supposedly met some hot new boy on the scene that no one's seen before."

"And you wanna see if the rumors are true?"

"Damn straight," Jabari said. "I want to see if this bitch was worth him getting over me."

"I'm sure he's not," I said. "But if I were you, I'd find someone new and even up the score."

"True," he said and clinked his plastic cup against mine. "He's probably up in the den of sin, as we call it. Silly crack addict."

Jabari pointed up to the apartment above the garage. I knew Jeremy was up there, but didn't want Jabari knowing my date was in the so-called den of sin, too. So I played it off, stayed calm. Didn't want to get a reputation at the university for dating younger crack addicts, though Jeremy didn't seem the type.

"What goes on up there?" I asked.

"Everything and anything," Jabari said and rolled his eyes. Looked around the crowd some more. "Stuff you bust students for at school."

"Like?"

"I don't know if I want to get into it with you. Are you friend, foe, or administrator now?"

"I'm here and talking to you. What do you think?"

"Cool." He tapped his drink against mine again. "Initiation activities. Sex, drugs, rock 'n' roll. As much of it, any way you want it, pretty much. Our chapter sometimes comes over here to party with the ELAJ chapter when we get busted at CUELA."

I appreciated the information, and probably would have offered some administrative words about the initiation activities, not necessarily warnings, but the jungle juice had me buzzing and relaxing. Like I was one of the students, though not dressed in the prison gear attire of most of them.

Jabari continued, "But you didn't hear any of this from me, friend."

"It's our secret."

"So where's your boy?" Jabari asked. "Betta not be playing around on your ass already. Some fine-ass muthafuckas here."

"He's around somewhere talking to some friends." Wasn't going to admit to Jeremy's den-of-sin action. Wasn't even going to mention Jeremy's name, just in case Jabari got in the mood for some I-told-you-so conversation about his crosstown frat brother.

"Well, he's gotta be special to snag you," Jabari said. "Me,

Blake, and all the boys in the gay group at school all wish we could get with you."

"Is that your liquor talking?" I rolled my eyes and smiled. "Get with me? No way."

"I wouldn't lie to you, Kenny," Jabari said. "You're like a big brother to me. A sexy big brother."

"You're joking, right?"

"My lips to God's ears . . . or your, hmmm . . ." Jabari looked down below my waist and smiled mischievously. "Damn, if I got a hold of that."

"Thanks."

"If he hurts you, he's got to answer to me."

"You're sweet, Jabari."

"Don't let him go out and treat you like the fireman did."

"I got it, Jabari."

"Don't let him treat you like my ex did me, silly crack addict."

Jabari finished the last of his drink. Asked if I wanted a refill, which I declined, and he sashayed out the side door of the kitchen with full drink in hand toward the den of sin. Got stopped by two of Jeremy's friends on the makeshift dance floor and they moved to the newest Missy Elliot creation. Jabari pointed to me and did a come-here sign, as in join him and Jeremy's friends on the dance floor. Small world. I smiled, put my hands up and nodded. Declined this dance, but would do the next one after going to the bathroom. Wanted to wait for Jeremy, but didn't want him thinking I was out meeting and dancing with other guys on our first date.

The bathroom line inside the house was seven people long and at least an hour wait, suspecting the kind of action going on in it. The out-of-it guys in front of me passed the time taking group photos with their digital camera, even grabbed me for a few of their pics. Kinda like the party pics I'd posed for while in college in the Midwest, but different. No one smiled in these, and I was missing a drink or, in some of their cases, a blunt. The school administrator and a bunch of shaved-head cholos, urban preps, and Latino hip-hoppers at a college party. If they could see me now.

I knew the next best place for a man to relieve himself at a party was outside, near a dark house or alley, and I walked through the smoke-filled living room out the front door and a few houses away from the action. Called Jeremy's cell, but got no answer, and left a message telling him I stepped out front for a minute in case he looked for me. Found an unlit space between two dark houses halfway down the block and did my business. Quick.

"This is LAPD, place your ID on the ground in front of you and put your hands up."

I heard the echo of several police voices over loud horns, music stop, people murmuring. Sounded like a party raid. I zipped up and stepped back out to the sidewalk. Looked to the right and saw the party house illuminated, police helicopter overhead beaming its concentrated lights, red and blue flashing across the night shadows. Saw a few of my white shirt, blue pants picture buddies being pulled out in cuffs. Thought about Jeremy and the so-called den of sin. Called his cell again, but got no answer. With the popos in everyone's faces, he couldn't have answered. Didn't want to abandon my date, but figured it wouldn't do any good for me to get mixed up in the raid. Turned left and headed toward where my X5 was parked.

"Excuse me, sir," came an authoritative voice from the middle of the street. Light shined in my face. "Can I see your ID?"

"Why? I'm just going to my car."

"Where are you coming from?"

"I was visiting a friend and now going home, if you must know."

"You have your ID?"

"Yeah."

"Take it out. Slow."

"Get that light out my face so I can see you," I smarted

off. Mom would chide me for violating the white lady law, especially with the police. Would say no matter what kind of education or proper English I spoke, I shouldn't even try to get over the law.

The officer turned the light off and walked toward me. I took out my ID. He started laughing. When my eyes adjusted I saw one of my former students standing before me, dressed as one of LAPD's finest. He still looked the same as he did at CUELA—walnut-colored skin, just under six feet tall, wide smile, chiseled jawline, and expressive dark brown eyes—except his physique looked buffed under the light blue shirt and dark blue slacks, no doubt an effect of police officer training. Who knew he'd grow up to look like this after college?

"Just kidding, Kenny."

"Omar Etheridge," I said. "Fuck, you had me scared. What are you doing?"

"I'm a rookie on the force." Omar pointed to his silver badge and supply holster around his belt. "Making sure these little kids don't try and escape the raid. Got a complaint from neighbors about noise, drugs, public sex, you name it. Not the first time we been here."

"Crazy."

"Some of them are from CUELA, I heard."

"No way."

"Yeah, but anyway you go on home," Omar said. "We'll be here for a while. There's gonna be some arrests. Drug possession, underage drinking, possible hazing activity. Your favorite stuff. Might end up on your desk on Monday if we find CUELA students here."

"Great. More work for me."

"Good thing you were just visiting a friend." He smiled and winked. Like he knew what was up.

"Yeah."

"See you later, Kenny. I'll be up to visit campus sometime," Omar said. "Heard you're single, just word on the street."

"True."

"I better get back to work, Kenny. I'll holla at you later."

"See you later."

I continued walking up the street to my truck, thinking about how I used to have the biggest crush on Omar when he was a student at CUELA. One of the quietest, yet most effective student leaders to grace the campus and my office. I whispered another "thank you" into the air and picked up my pace. Two blocks later, saw Jeremy sitting on the curb behind my truck. Cigarette in one hand. Cell in the other.

"I need a soldier," Jeremy said, smiled, and put his cigarette out on the curb. Stood up and walked toward me. Tossed me the keys. "Can you handle it?"

"Where the . . . ?" I asked, but didn't know where quite to begin. "What happened?"

"Don't trip, Kenny. Just take me home and let's handle some business."

"Jeremy, why are the police at your frat's party?" I asked. "What's going on here?"

"The less you know, the betta," Jeremy said. "Don't want you mixed up in their party."

I pressed the keypad to unlock my baby. Stood at the back of the truck with Jeremy. More questions on my mind. "How'd you get away? I was scared that you were going to get arrested or something. What about your boys?"

"Aww, you care," he said as he leaned in for a kiss under the moonlight. Managed a quick peck. "Your place or mine, mister?"

"Let's get you home."

"So we gonna handle some business?"

"Let's just get you home first."

"I like you, Mister Kenny. You're so freaking cool."

"Stop it," I said and smiled. "Thanks."

I couldn't help but laugh a little at the cute puppy-dog face he made. Gave him a hug and told him to get in the truck. I could tell he was under the influence of something, but didn't ask. That would wait until the morning.

* * *

"You can't go already," Jeremy said as we sat in his driveway. This, after another ten-minute make-out session, and after his explanation of how he escaped the party raid—slipped out a hole in the fence behind the backyard, jogged through the alley and around the block, managed to stay out of view of LAPD's best. "Our first date isn't over yet. I've got more planned."

"We've been through enough to last ten dates," I said. "I'm not sure if this . . . I just don't know."

"You mad?" he asked and caressed my face. "I'm sorry, Kenny."

"No, not mad, but want you to be straight with me about the party," I said. "I just don't know how you can be so calm."

I knew why. He was twenty-one. Didn't have a care in the world, or all the hang-ups and baggage that come with post-college life. I'd been the same way at one point, before maintaining a professional life, paying mortgages, and helping exes out of their legal problems.

"Because we freaking got out of the raid of the decade," he said and smiled. "Do you realize the kind of trouble we'd be in if we stayed?"

"I know. And I *don't* know. That worries me."

"So this is it, Kenny? Wanna call it quits?"

"We never even called it starts," I said. "Maybe I should quit while I'm ahead."

"But I know you don't want to," Jeremy said. Smiled. Nodded. Forefinger teased tip of my nose.

"Stupid," I said and smiled back. "You confuse me."

"You confused about this?" Leaned in and kissed me. Smiled. "You make me wanna shoop."

We broke apart and laughed. "You are so silly, Jeremy."

"Just giving it to you old school."

"I like that you make me laugh," I said. "You're fun."

"See, you can't call it quits, then," he said. "At least not yet. The fun and games are just beginning."

"Right."

"So let the games begin and come on in, baby," Jeremy said and grabbed the keys from the ignition. "No one's here at the candy shop. We'll be alone finally. Pweese?"

"Gimme the keys."

"Pweese?"

That sad puppy-dog face and his warm hand squeezing mine made my answer come quickly.

"All right."

Jeremy locked the truck, and we walked through the side fence and into the house. He and I kissed from the side door, through the kitchen, living room and narrow hallway, dropping a jacket here, a shirt there, finally depositing pants and boxers just inside his bedroom door. He grabbed a bag of sex essentials and tossed it on the bed. We kissed more, our tongues slow dancing with each other. His light brown skin pressed against my dark brown skin as we stood in the middle of the bedroom and explored each other's bodies in the darkness. I let my tongue drift lightly up and down his neck until I heard him gasp as I found his weak spot. Grabbed my ass tighter and backed us up to his bed. I fell on top of him, still working the same spot on his neck, his legs spreading wide and wrapping around me. Bedsprings creaking, singing in response.

"Damn, Kenny. You. Feel. Good."

"You. Too. Baby."

We kissed more. He loosened his legs. Hands on my shoulders and a slight push. An invitation for me to go down, move south, taste him like he'd done me before the party. I moved lower over my new young lover, gave each essential part of his body a slow kiss or lick of the tongue, loved the salty taste of his skin, hovered over his magnum and blew warm air from my mouth over it. Watched it twitch and rise higher as his hips and hands worked in tandem to feed me. Held my head steady and continued moving lower. Not ready to give him the pleasure he sought yet. Massaged his right foot, kissed the bottom, slowly took in a toe and sucked. Watched his eyes close, his mouth making an O, his hips writhing, him grabbing his magnum.

"Shit, Kenny."

"Relax. I'm just starting."

Moved up to his ankle, kissed the tender ticklish spot behind the knee until he cried and moaned, massaged and kissed the insides of his thighs until I was close enough to smell the delicious, musky scent of his love. Grabbed magnum and kissed everywhere around but magnum himself. Jeremy's hands massaged the back of my head and neck, trying to force me to put magnum in my mouth. Finally gave in, kissed the tip and just underneath. Heard him shudder and moan as I slowly let him disappear into my mouth and tongue. His warm hands on my shoulders, one leg folding up to give him a better angle in. Let him descend slowly and disappear again. Loved hearing his profane approval for a job going well. One hand on magnum, one hand squeezing his nipple. Sweat. Saliva. Salvation.

"You want me to come?"

Pulled off. Whispered. "Yeah, but not yet and not in my mouth yet." Continued my work. A little faster to get him more excited. Growing larger. Ready. To. Explode.

"Stop, stop, stop," he whispered. "I'm really close. Damn."

Pulled off. Super slow. To savor it and drive him crazy. Whispered again. "I love it." Blew more warm air, ran my tongue underneath the entire length of magnum.

"Damn, you're good."

"You were good earlier."

"Want more like earlier?"

"Yeah."

Kissed the sloppy, savage way lovers do when not caring about anything but getting each other off. His tongue ring clinked against my teeth. Loved the fierceness of his lips.

"And then you wanna handle business?"

"Yeah."

"You make me hot, Kenny."

He flipped me over onto my back, mirrored every move and kiss I made on him, sucked until I got really close and made him pull off. Started pulling on himself.

"Doing you like that really gets me turned on."

"You wanna come?"

"I'm about to."

"Me, too."

We lay side by side, jerking, tugging, kissing occasionally, moaning, whispering more profane approval, and just as we both were ready to release, Jeremy moved on top, grinded against me until both our stomachs were coated in ourselves. He looked into my eyes, kissed me slowly, eyes on me the whole time. Kissed me long and hard again, and we lounged in each other's arms ten minutes in our sweat and warmth and release, good exhaustion keeping us from moving.

"That was freaking good."

"Yeah, it was."

"Look at the mess you made, Kenny."

"Such a pretty mess," I said and smiled. Somehow I didn't think Vanity's song from the eighties made his iTunes. "You probably don't even know that song, huh? This singer named Vanity 6. She's real God Squad now, I think."

"Uh, nope," he said.

"Anyways, it's been a minute since I was with someone."

"Since the ex?"

"Yeah," I said and realized I didn't want to be thinking about DaVon at this moment. "You know how to work it, Jeremy. You're good."

"You, too, Kenny," he said. "I love it. Fuckin' turn me on."

"Me, too."

"Can't wait to ride my Kenny and have Kenny ride me."

"Sweet," I said. "Can't wait."

"It's getting cold," he said. "I'll be right back."

He got up, ran to the bathroom, ran the faucet, and came

back. One warm and wet towel he used to clean us off. One dry towel to dry us down. He tossed them to the side of the bed, crawled next to me, put one leg and an arm over me.

"You staying?"

"You want me to?"

"Hell, yeah."

It was always an awkward moment, the first time being physical with someone. Was it a one-nighter? A hit-it-and-quit-it, fuck-and-chuck situation? Worthy of staying overnight for seconds or thirds in the middle of the night or first thing in the morning? Was it a prelude to a possible long-term relationship? I had a million questions and no answers. Certainly, I liked Jeremy. There was some kind of chemistry between us, even though we'd known each other just a few days. But I didn't know anything major about him, except that he liked to party, was a student, ten-plus years younger, from a loud and large Dominican-Mexican family, had baggage from a recent breakup, and had some sketchy friends and acquaintances. He didn't know much about me either, certainly not about my baggage with DaVon, my professional life, my family's issues, or how I like my eggs in the morning. Together, all we knew were each other's bodies, and that would suffice for the moment.

As I looked in Jeremy's eyes, and felt his hand rubbing my shoulder, I could tell that he was serious about the invitation. That he didn't want me to leave. That the night, with all its drama and surprises, was the beginning of something new. And even though I'd just finished having sex with a twenty-one-year-old, and felt like I was lying on the right side of the wrong bed, I was surprised that I wanted to stay.

"Okay, I'll stay."

"Cool," he said. "Most guys just eat and run."

"I'm not most guys."

"I know. Thank God you're not."

"You been hurt, huh?"

"Who hasn't? You?"

"Yeah."

"I promise not to hurt you, Kenny."

"I take promises seriously," I said. "I won't hurt you either."

"Trust."

"Should we play twenty-one questions now or in the morning?"

"You mean figuring out all the stuff we have in common?" he asked and looked at me. "We have forever to figure all that out, as far as I'm concerned. I'm playing for keeps, and you know I've got to be serious when I say that. I came already."

We kissed. Jeremy wrapped his arms around me tighter and closed his eyes. I looked up at the ceiling. Felt Jeremy's heartbeat against me. Felt so innocent, pure, and right. At least for that night.

Chapter 11

"You dirty slut," Carlos said. "Four times in one night? Kaiser running a special on Viagra?"

Carlos and I were stretched out on ledges in the sauna at our gym, staring face-to-face across from each other. Had the steam and heat all to ourselves. I called Carlos as soon as I left Jeremy's place around noon. Met at the gym for some serious weights and a run on the treadmill and rewarded ourselves with the sauna afterward. Our way of keeping ourselves soldiers in the battle against the thirties.

"I'm not ready for the nursing home yet," I said. "I can still hang. Thank you very much. Why you keep bringing up the four-times deal?"

"Sorry to offend," Carlos said. "I'm a married voyeur, I told you already. Ain't getting it from no one but Ricky."

"No offense taken. Still . . . you're thirtysomething, too. Everything works on you, right?"

"For sure. Ricky, too," Carlos said and got quiet before asking, "So what's it like to sleep with someone barely out of high school?"

"It was better than I expected. Jeremy's got a lot of practice under his belt, or been watching a lot of porn."

"Better than DaVon?"

"Jeremy's very good at what he's doing, surprisingly," I said. Thought about DaVon just a couple times in between lovemaking with Jeremy, and both times thought about what Jeremy did and how he moved was ten times DaVon's best. And I never had a complaint about DaVon in bed. "Never been kissed or touched so good. I mean, DaVon was good . . . *really* good, but Jeremy is just fucking off-the-hook nasty, uninhibited, energetic, willing and ready . . ."

"Okay, don't get me too turned on," Carlos said and made a face toward the sauna door. "Not seeing Ricky until his weekend shift is over tomorrow afternoon."

"Most definitely," I said. "I hated sitting around, being bored, horny, and waiting for DaVon to finish his forty-eight-hour rotation."

"So what else?"

"I don't know," I said. "I had so much fun with him and his boys. The party. The after party. The drama in between."

"I'm a little worried if Jeremy's crowd gets their parties raided."

Knew I should have kept that little piece of information to myself. Not that I didn't want or appreciate Carlos's opinion, but it was too early in this thing Jeremy and I had to be raising other people's red flags. Wish I'd gotten the same kind of red-flag alert from Carlos or Ricky, especially Ricky, the best friend who knew that DaVon had started stepping out on me with his firehouse widows. That kind of compassionate conservativism would have saved me two years and twenty thousand-plus dollars in legal fees and support for the kids. Not that I was counting or dwelling.

"It was just a little misunderstanding," I said. "No biggie, I'm sure."

"If you say so, Kenny."

"I say so, Carlos."

Of course, the thought went through my mind very briefly that Jeremy's friends had some shade and drama going, but I wanted to also have faith in his innocence and naiveté. Was sure he wasn't totally like the company he kept. A little bit in hip-hop taste and style maybe, but definitely not in substance.

The decorating skills. Danielle Steel and other books. *Teen Jeopardy*. Concern for his little brother in Iraq and family in general. Definitely, the more I thought, someone with depth and an interesting mix of characteristics.

"So what's next for you and Jeremy?"

"I don't know," I said. "I wasn't expecting to meet anyone so soon after DaVon. Especially someone so young. And we're different ethnicities, not that it's that big a deal. I always saw myself with other black guys and definitely not in their early twenties."

"The kids fall in love quickly. I hear them in the cultural center on campus all day. Always in love, always breaking up. Always meeting someone new on MySpace."

"Jeremy's a grown man, though, not a kid."

"Okay, twenty-one," Carlos said. "But they think after one fuck they're in love, married, and ready to commit for life."

"That's a stereotype," I said. "Though he said he's a long-term kinda guy."

"Or maybe since he's so experienced in lovemaking, he's a player and trying to get every kind of notch filled on his belt. The old, the young, the rainbow coalition, whatever's clever."

"Whatever, Dr. Phil," I said. "Don't read too much into it yet. It's just a couple of e-mails and one date."

"And sex."

"Sex, yes," I said. "And who knows. He's supposed to call later today. Maybe we'll talk."

"Hope he calls."

"I'm sure he will," I said. "I think I like him."

I couldn't believe I said it out loud. I couldn't believe I meant it. I liked Jeremy. Started to fall and it was less than a week of knowing each other. Call it my own personal Stella-groove-back moment, a leap into the unknown after dealing with DaVon's mess, stepping out on faith. Whatever. This kind of emotion was for the movies, not a thirtysomething and twentysomething living *la vida loca* in L.A.'s San Gabriel

Valley. I'd always criticized other people for falling so soon, for sharing their giddiness for every little thing, when I knew it would be just another movie-of-the-week date. Things had started fast and furious with DaVon all those years ago, and we lasted six-plus years. But I knew I was different, that I could judge character better than others.

"Good for you, Kenny," Carlos said. "I hope this puts closure on DaVon."

"Well, I got another court subpoena, but that's another story for another time," I said. "Jeremy's a good kid."

"Cool. You should let me and Ricky meet your new friend."

"Why? So Ricky can go straight to DaVon? Or so you can tell me everything you see wrong with Jeremy?"

"No, just a simple dinner," Carlos said. "You know how Ricky likes to cook those big portions for the firehouse. And I promise, no critiques."

"Good," I said. "Because there'd be a lot more happy couples if they had someone like Jeremy in the mix."

"What? A student? Broke? On work study? No car? Living at home with the folks?"

"Very funny."

"Just giving you a hard time," Carlos said and laughed. "I support you. Hope Jeremy does you right."

"I hope so, too."

"So dinner tomorrow night? My place? You, Jeremy, Ricky, and me."

"As long as Ricky's not too tired from his work."

"I got that covered."

Thought it was an even exchange. I'd met Jeremy's friends the nights before. Now it was his turn to meet my best friend and his partner. Knew these meetings generally cemented the fact that you were a couple, or at least talking and moving toward couplehood, and looked forward to dinner. Looked forward to the day when we'd be known collectively as Kenny and Jeremy, and all our friends would accept us—differences, flaws, and all.

Chapter 12

Felt like a college student, one who'd just come out the closet and didn't know how to deal with the excitement of a new relationship, of finding the one you thought was "the one," yet found oneself alone, sitting and waiting for a phone to ring on a Saturday night that wasn't ringing as expected.

Passed the rest of the afternoon, after working out with Carlos, being productive. Did a movie and bookstore run with my kids from Big Brothers/Big Sisters. Cleaned and dusted the main rooms in the house. Ran to Home Depot for sink washers. Picked up dry cleaning. Restocked my and my mom's refrigerators. Spent a billion dollars at Target on CDs, DVDs, toiletries, and some snacks for my office. Found a romantically cute card and new games for Jeremy's Game Boy Advance. Just because.

I lay down for a quick nap, waiting for Jeremy to call. On one hand, I was super excited to be starting something new with someone so new, fresh, and different than I'd dealt with before. On the other hand, I was trying to get my emotions in check and intellectually think about why I, a thirty-three-year-old man, with degrees, a profession, and a very good personal platform, wasn't aiming my sights on someone with similar characteristics. There really was no way to explain it. Who really knows why we fall for who we fall for? All I could do was hope and pray for the best with whoever fell into my life. At the moment, I was falling for Jeremy Lopez, brown, beautiful, twenty-one, and in process. That was a positive thought to sleep and dream on for a few hours.

Found myself at nine-fifty at night. Finally awake from the nap. Alone. Weekend. No phone call, texts, or voice mails. No plans. Still waiting for Jeremy to call. Two homemade apple martinis into a buzz. Thinking the thoughts that come with dating someone new, someone younger: they're out with someone else; they find you a bit too outdated to keep dating; they're just not that into you; they got what they wanted in bed and that's that.

He said he would call.

Found myself calling the cell from my house phone. Calling the house with my cell. Just to see. Mechanical errors? None. Did I pay the bill on time? Never a problem with auto pay. Did I change my number and forget to tell him? No way. Crazy thoughts.

Started feeling horny. Thinking about the first time with Jeremy. Everything worked. Turned Jeremy out four times already. Mechanical errors? Didn't think so. Got plenty of compliments. Made him come. That wasn't pretend.

Made a third apple martini. Definitely the last before going to sleep. Tried to remember the conversation before I left his house—his parents' house—in the morning. He's too young and unestablished to own his own house, remember that, Kenny.

"So let's do something tonight, if you're not busy or too tired."

"Sure. We'll talk."

"I'll holla at you."

"Or I'll call you."

"Well, either way we'll talk sometime today."

"Mos def."

Went something like that. I think.

Maybe something came up. An emergency. The family had

car problems on their way to Tijuana or something. Maybe he's in the hospital. That's crazy talk, Kenny. He would have called if something like that came up. Well, what if he couldn't talk? How could he tell me. Come on, Kenny. It's rare that people go mute or get mouth paralysis. He's too young to have a stroke. Get a grip, Kenny.

Clicked a few times on the computer until I was at my work's e-mail system. Just to see if Jeremy decided to reach out and touch electronically, instead of by phone. A bunch of spam and a few work-related messages that could wait until Monday. Opened up the first message Jeremy sent a few days earlier. Looked at our pictures together in front of my truck. Box popped up, indicating new mail had arrived. Bingo! A message from Jeremy. Opened it. New pics of us. Our *America's Next Top Model* poses before the infamous party. A couple of couple shots of us at the party. A short message: "I'm feeling so good. All because of you, man. Holla back at your boo sometime. J"

Thought maybe Jeremy thought I was flaking on calling him. Had I said I'd call? Or Jeremy? What the fuck? Not like we were kids or playing games. I'm the adult, er, the older one. So I called his cell. Picked up on the first ring.

"What happened?"

"Nothing . . . yet. What's up with you, Jeremy?"

"Just chillin' on-line, fixing up my MySpace page," he said. "I just sent you an e-mail with some pictures."

"I got it, that's why I called."

"Why'd you wait so late to call?" He sounded annoyed. "I've been waiting all day for your call."

Maybe I had said I'd call first, and left Jeremy hanging all day. Maybe Jeremy was running game on me. Mind games. Not really sure anymore. Apple martinis had blurred my thinking. But made me feel a little flirtatious.

"Sorry, babe," I said. "Wanna do something now?"

"It's too late. I already made plans."

Oh no he didn't. So I said calmly, "What are you doing?"

"Going out with my boys."

"Oh, yeah? Where to?"

"Not sure. Either to The Catch or Chicos. Maybe the mansion party at the Hayworth."

"All are good tonight. Or so I hear," I said. "I'm just chillin' at home, got an apple martini, thinking about you."

"Apple martinis?"

"Yeah. Got a whole bar, well stocked," I said. "And I'm thinking about magnum."

"Oh, yeah?" Jeremy said, his voice lowering a bit. "That's kinda hot. Magnum misses you, too."

"So you wanna come?"

Knew one way to a twenty-one-year-old's heart was through a six-pack, a joint, and the hint of a blow job. Learned a few things working at a college on the ways to pique a college boy's interest. Free liquor and sex. Sad, but true.

"Maybe me and my boys will stop by for cocktails," Jeremy said. "If that's okay."

"That's cool. I'd like to see you."

"I'd like to see you, too," he said. "Sorry if I seemed pissed off. I thought you wasn't feeling me or something. I been sitting around doing nothing all day. And you know I don't have a car."

"I thought the same thing when I didn't hear from you."

"Awww, I love you, man."

"I love you, man."

Laughed. And laughed. And laughed. As if we could really love each other so soon after a date and making each other come. The silly way new people who are dating get over every little cute thing. Every. Little. Thing. Smile.

Gave Jeremy my address. He told me what he was wearing, red Puma jacket and red-and-white Puma sneakers with jeans, and instructed me to find something in the same color, style, and genre. Said we were going out tonight. Me, him, and his boys. Nacho. Daniel. Tony. Slimer.

Ran to the shower. Got out the best, most trendy athletic

gear I had in my closet. Mixed a less potent cocktail. Waited for Jeremy and his boys.

And waited.

And waited.

And waited.

Two more cocktails and two hours later, I heard the gravel driveway crunching and a car engine, saw the security light out front turn on, and heard the knock on the door. Just after one in the morning. Leaving less than an hour to party at most L.A. clubs and bars, unless we did Catch's after hours. Kept my cool. For appearances in front of company.

"Come on in," I said.

"Whassupers, Kenny?"

The crew poured into my living room. Got introduced again to Nacho. Daniel. Tony. Slimer. Pointed to the hallway through which the boys could find the den and the bar. Made sure the giant-screen TV was turned on to one of the music video stations for their entertainment. Jeremy looked good in his red athletic wear, complemented my black-and-white Puma gear, and kissed me. Breath smelled and tasted like he'd just come from Woodstock and smoked an orchard of doobies and drank a few dozen forties. Not that I'd objected to anyone's occasional use, not that I'd tried anything since being an adventurous undergrad in college, but still . . . It just wasn't one of the ingredients I necessarily wanted in someone who was a potential mate.

"You look good, man," Jeremy said, eyeing me from head to toe. "Look so fucking good to be so fucking—"

"Careful."

"Mature," he said, after a slight pause. Laughed. "I'm the luckiest fucker in the world. You know that?"

"Oh, are you?"

"Hell muthafuckin' yeah," he said and crashed on the living room sofa. "I'm so fucking high and drunk. Come here and hold me. I just wanna crash with my Kenny tonight. I love me some Kenny."

I sat on the sofa next to Jeremy, and he stretched out. His legs on one end, his head in my lap. Closed his eyes and I looked down at his face. So beautiful. So young. Could be a model if brown faces were mainstream faces in the fashion industry. I ran one hand across his chest, straightened out the collar of his jacket, which had gotten frazzled in his fall to the sofa. Saw the signs of a man who hadn't been sitting home all day doing nothing. Two half-dollar-sized raspberry-colored marks on the far side of his neck. The spot I knew he loved, that I loved, that I'd been careful not to leave hickeys on.

"What did you say you did today?" I asked.

"Nothing. Chilled at the house. Thinking about you, man."

"You sure?" I said, and rubbed my middle finger across both spots on his neck. "Nothing else?"

"Dude, you tagged me," Jeremy said, opened his eyes, and looked into mine. As if I were the D.A., he was the defendant, and was trying to convince me he was a credible witness. "Don't trip."

"I don't tag or get tagged," I said. "It's tacky to me."

"Well, you must not remember how crazy you got on me in bed," he mumbled and put a finger over my lips. "Shhhh, don't talk, baby. Just hold me and enjoy the moment. Don't be a hater."

"But," I said and tried to move his finger.

"Shhhh, don't speak. We're vibing right now."

Tapped his finger away and said, "Houston, we have a problem. You have hickeys that I know I didn't make. Now either I'm crazy. Or I'm extremely forgetful. Or you're not being honest. Don't bullshit me."

"Dude, would I be that stupid to display the evidence and then come kick it with you?" Jeremy said. "Hell muthafuckin' no. Case closed. End of discussion. Now lean down here and kiss me, nigga."

Felt stupid. Felt lied to. Felt played. Could see my mother making the miniature violin motion with her fingers. Wondered how those hickeys got on his neck, because I hadn't put them there. I *know* I hadn't. Thought getting tagged was tacky, especially since every teeny-bopper fast-food worker seemed to think it was cute and classy to display. Thought about what my mother had said the other morning, and basically all my life: people tell you about themselves without saying a word. At this point, I knew Jeremy was telling me he'd been with someone else within the same twenty-four-hour period he'd slept with me, and that he didn't intend to tell me the truth.

And then I thought about how stupid the whole situation was. I was thirty-three. He was twenty-one. I wouldn't be having this conversation with someone my age or older. We'd be arguing over something more significant: our next vacation, stainless steel or marble, tax deductions, which foster kid to choose, upgrading to a larger home, whether or not the paternity tests and accusations were true. Not some juvenile, third-grade, hickey action. I wouldn't be hosting a bunch of his community-college, frat-boy friends in my house, when, now that I thought of it, we were all supposed to be going out to some club or dancing. Last time I'd checked, I wasn't the promoter of Club Kenny.

Heard a glass drop and break on the tile, where Nacho, Tony, Daniel, and Slimer were. Like the chaperone I was feeling like, I told Jeremy to chill and I'd check on the boys. That this conversation wasn't over. He said it was. I said it wasn't. He said it was. I heard Nacho's voice yelling for towels and a bandage. Let Jeremy's head slide back onto the sofa and ran to the den. My den of sin.

Nacho'd cut his finger on the metal cap of a rum bottle and dropped it. Glass and liquor over the floor in front of the bar. He was fending for himself. The other guys, supposedly Nacho's friends, were flipping channels, sipping drinks, passing a blunt (obviously didn't know about my no-smoking-in-the-house rule), and paying Nacho no attention. I turned into Scout Master, Big Brothers/Big Sisters mode.

"Daniel, broom's in the kitchen next to the stove. Slimer,

mop's in the closet. Tony, get the trash basket by the fridge. I'll fix up Nacho."

No movement, just a few "uh huh"s as they continued lounging, motionless, on the sofa.

"Now!"

They sprang into action, and I heard little comments like, "He's not my dad," "Party pooper," "Such a freaking hater," "Why doesn't Jeremy have to help?" as I took Nacho to the bathroom to clean his cut and bandage him. Really wasn't that bad. More annoying, he said, than painful. But it gave me a chance to be alone with Jeremy's best friend. To talk. Maybe hear what Jeremy's intentions were. To see if there was an off chance one frat would rat out his brother. The chances of that were slim to none. Still.

"Hold still," I said and tweezered out a small sliver of glass. "That hurt?"

"Nah, it's cool."

"What's up with your boys?" I asked. "They don't know how to help a brotha out?"

"Shiiiit, Kenny, we're all faded," Nacho said. "Jeremy got some strong shit from one of his neighbors. It's like the freaking bomb."

"Hmmm. Like the freaking bomb, huh?"

"You wanna light up with us?"

"Nah, thanks," I said. "I don't use. No offense or judgment."

"Cool, more for us," Nacho said. "You letting us crash here?"

"Guess so," I said and swabbed some disinfectant along the cut. He winced. "It'll be okay. I don't think you need stitches."

"You know everything, huh?" Nacho said. "Jeremy says you're the freaking bomb, too. And, if I say so, you look freaking good for your age."

"Oh, yeah," I said. Smiled. Didn't know if the age comment was a true accolade, or a little dig at me or Jeremy, but whatever. Got back to being miniature ER. "What's he say about me?"

"Dude, can't let all Jeremy's tricks out the bag," Nacho said and laughed a little. "That's my boy since fourth grade."

"Whatever you say."

"But all he talks about all day is 'Kenny's my man,' 'Kenny's done this, done that, got this, got that,' 'Kenny's a hundred times better than Jabari.' It's like the freaking Kenny Show or something. I don't know what you put on him, but you got my nigga the fuck in love with you."

Flattered with all the compliments and declarations of Jeremy's feelings, but cut to the more important question in my mind.

"Nacho, who's Jabari?"

"Kenny's psycho ex," Nacho said and used his good finger to circle in the air around his ear. "He's two cans short of a six-pack."

"It's not the same Jabari who was at the party last night?"

"Bingo. The crazy bitch from CUELA."

I wondered why Jeremy never said anything about his ex being a student at the place he knew I worked. And what about Lalo, the ex Jeremy had mentioned on that first night we met and ate our post-club tacos? Was Lalo just a code for Jabari? Had Jeremy known Jabari was a student of mine and just changed the name? Certainly couldn't expect to get the answer from Nacho, but could find out one other important fact that Jeremy omitted from our conversation.

"They still see each other, don't they?"

"Not my place to tell," Nacho said.

"We talked about it," I lied. "No labels or ties yet between Jeremy and me."

"Well, they kicked it today," Nacho said and examined the bandage job I did on his finger. "Only because Jabari decided to give back the things Jeremy left at his apartment."

"And are they just kicking it like exes? Or *kicking it* kicking it?"

"I probably said too much," Nacho said. "I like you a helluva lot better than Jabari. But talk to J if you want to know more. I shouldn't say anything else."

"I think I got my answer."

"Don't tell him I said anything. He's really digging you."

Nacho excused himself from the bathroom and left the door open.

Sat on the edge of the tub, listened to the boys making plans for a quick exit from my place despite the fact they were drunk, high, and not in any condition to drive anywhere. Felt responsible for them, and yelled from the bathroom that I'd pull out the sofa, blow up air mattresses, and bring in extra comforters for them to crash overnight in the den. After a few minutes of wrangling, they decided to stay, and I brought them everything they needed for their sleepover.

"And I'm sleeping with you," Jeremy said and snuck up behind me, his body pressed to my back. "You foos be careful and don't break any more of my man's shit."

Jeremy followed me through the long hallway to my bedroom. I slammed the door behind us and watched Jeremy's lean body come out of his clothes. Dropped everything on the floor. Naked. Magnum growing to full attention as he plopped on top of the bed.

"Jeremy," I whispered forcefully. "I wasn't going to embarrass you in front of your friends, but this is your first and last night staying overnight here."

"Why? Whassup, boo? Talk to me, sweetie." He motioned for me to sit next to him on the bed.

I dropped my clothes to the floor, but left on a tank top and boxers, and climbed under the covers, turning my back to him. Thought about making him stay in the den with the rest of the boys, but wanted answers instead.

"You still sleeping with Jabari?"

"We messed around today, but haven't *slept together* slept together in a couple weeks," Jeremy said calmly, as if nothing. Climbed under the covers, too. Pressed magnum against my ass, put his arms around me. "So you know? Who told you?"

"Yeah, I know now," I said. "Thanks for telling me yourself."

"Shhhhh." He kissed the back of my neck. "Don't get all upset. Me and Jabari are over for real now. It's all about you now. You and me."

"He's my student."

"I'm your man."

"Are you? I don't think so."

"Hell, yeah," he said and slid his hand under my tank top to rub my chest and stomach. Pressed even harder against me, grinding, kissing my ears. "I'm all yours. In bed and out."

"It's been less than a week," I said. "We shouldn't be talking about being each other's man yet."

"Well, we're on our way, right?"

I lay still, enjoying the warmth of his hard body against mine, and while I loved the idea of this fantasy man in my bed—the kind the sorority girls on campus would catfight over, and the boys in the gay group at school would drool over—and knew that our sex life was hot, I felt conflicted. I never got a straight answer from him about anything. Seemed like there was always something on the edge of trouble with Jeremy. Liked him and despised him at the same time. Closed my eyes and decided to open up.

"Jeremy, my last relationship lasted a little over six years. It just ended five months ago. DaVon cheated. Not once. Not twice. But dozens of times. The first one I accepted, stupidly, as his first strike. We worked through it. Or so I thought. Until he got served with paternity tests from various women in L.A. accusing him of fathering several babies. Two were true. God knows how many more women he had unprotected sex with, and God knows how many more children will show up. I spent thousands defending him in court, defended him to my family, and all along DaVon knew the accusations were true. He made a fool of me. He made a choice to lie, by sleeping around and by keeping his children a secret. I don't like being made a fool of. It makes me feel stupid, and like I was a fool for trusting and giving myself. I'm taking a risk with you, Jeremy Lopez, getting involved with you so soon after DaVon. We're sleeping together and don't really know each other. This is not how I expected my next relationship to start off. A lot of sex, a lot of lies, and me sleeping on the right side of the wrong bed. Maybe we should just go our separate ways in the morning. I'm too old for you anyway."

Jeremy pulled at my shoulder until I turned toward him under the covers. "I'm sorry you've been hurt. And I'm sorry I lied to you about these hickeys, and that I didn't tell you about Jabari. Honestly, I had no clue you knew him."

"But you knew I worked at CUELA."

"Big campus," Jeremy said and rubbed my cheek. "But that's not the issue. I was not honest with you, and I should have been. Regardless of your past relationship history, I owed you that. You're so freaking awesome, Kenny. You're open-minded, you accept me for my ghetto-ass problems, my smoking out and getting a little crunk, and for all my other faults. And fuck the age thing. You're what I want. I wouldn't have stepped to you if I didn't think you were fine. You know you fine, don't you?"

He leaned in and kissed me.

"No more lies or omissions?" I asked.

"None," Jeremy said. "I'm sorry if I added to your hurt."

"Mean it?"

"Yeah."

"Because one more strike and . . ."

He smiled and giggled. *"¿Papel o plastico?"*

"That's *my* line, paper or plastic."

"My mom uses it all the time with me and my brothers."

"Funny."

"Not funny is this," he said. "I'm freaking turned on and horny as fuck. You are, too."

He grabbed at my boxers and rubbed until I came alive.

"You're bad," I whispered against his ear. "Really bad."

"Just good and good at it," he said. Moved lower. Tickled me with his tongue on my stomach. Stripped me naked under the covers and teased my penis with his tongue. "I want you in my mouth."

"Take it," I moaned as he did what I told him to. Sucked good. Eyes rolled back. "Shit."

Could feel magnum rubbing against my lower leg as he worked me. All lips and tongue, no teeth. So warm. The best. One hand on his hair, the other pulling the bedsheets out of place. My mind drifting in the warmth and wetness of his mouth, thoughts going everywhere, melting into the bed.

"Slow down," I said and pulled Jeremy off me. Panting. Quivering close to the edge. I wanted to prolong the experience for both of us.

"What's wrong, baby?"

"Nothing's wrong. Feels too good."

"Oh, yeah?" He gave me a sloppy kiss and slid magnum from my leg to navel. Loved feeling my penis sandwiched between our stomachs. Grabbed his ass. Kissed. Grinded. Kissed more. Heat rising from our friction. Like we were already inside each other. Dug his face into my neck, kissing and sucking. "Want some of that ass."

Hell, yeah, I wanted to say, not knowing if he was asking or stating. Managed to moan, "mmm hmmm." Wanted to feel him inside. Wanted to be inside him. Either way worked for me.

"Got condoms, Kenny?"

"Yeah."

"Feel like fucking."

"Me, too."

"Wanted to fuck you when I first met you."

"Have at it," I said. "I'll get mine next."

"So freaking hot."

Before the night was over, we depleted my lube and condom stash as we took turns giving and taking with each other throughout the night. Took each other to the best physical highs we could experience together. And, I guess, with our emotional sharing about past hurts, coming clean about lies, making promises about what we wanted the future to look like, took our relationship to another level as well.

Chapter 13

"You running a day care around here or what?"

I couldn't believe my mom was standing just three feet over us, cigarette in one hand, rubbing the invisible miniature violin in the other. Saw she had on another one of those tacky T-shirts she'd probably picked up at a truck stop on the way to or from Laughlin: MY OTHER GRANDKIDS BOUGHT ME A CAR. I hadn't heard her come in my bedroom, until the sound of her voice stirred Jeremy and me from our sleep. Deep sleep from a long night of adult activities. I looked at the digital clock on my nightstand. Two-thirty in the afternoon. Way past my normal wake-up time.

"Ma, don't you know how to knock first?"

"I did . . . several times," she said and gave Jeremy the eye she usually reserved for me, Tonya, and Cecily when we were up shit creek. "Apparently y'all were too knocked out. The boys out there made a mess of your kitchen. I'll be damned if I'ma clean it up."

"I'll help with the cleanup, Kenny," Jeremy said and pulled the covers over his head. "Just let me sleep some more."

"Good," she said and rolled her eyes at the lump in the bed that was Jeremy. "Because this ain't no hotel or hostel for wayward boys, and I'm *not* Florence the maid."

"Ma, could you give us a minute to get proper and I can talk to you in the living room?" I asked.

"I'm your momma; you ain't hiding nothing I ain't seen before," she said. "But this little one here, I hope he lived up to the size thirteens sitting over there by the doorway."

"Ma," I said. Totally embarrassed. What would she know about thirteens? Ewww. "Please."

"Must be Jeremy, right?" She walked over to the other side of the bed and lifted the covers off Jeremy's head. Greeted him. "I'm Kenny's mother, Mrs. Kane-Butler. If you stick around long enough, you can call me by my first name, Gladys."

"Good to meet you, Mrs. Kane-Butler," he groaned. "I'm Jeremy Lopez."

She covered Jeremy's head again. "Ooh, and he's got manners, too."

"I'll meet you in the living room, Ma. Okay?" I said. Embarrassed that my mom was in my bedroom, just hours after I'd had sex with Jeremy. Certainly she knew. So much for her respecting my privacy.

"Alone," she said, pointed to Jeremy's side of the bed, and did the miniature violin hand gesture. "Got personal stuff to talk about anyway."

"Thanks, Ma."

Watched her leave my bedroom and shut the door. We'd slept longer than I expected to or thought we did. Hadn't planned on doing any family introductions yet. Though we'd started to open up and communicate about our expectations and possible direction, family meetings were an indication that things were moving to something long-term. That wasn't in the plan for a long time.

Grabbed my robe from the closet and tidied up the room. At least all the sex leftovers that I'm sure my mom had seen. Soiled, crusty towels. Used condoms. Slimy lube bottles. Feather duster. Baby wipes. Hand sanitizer. Private things I hadn't really wanted her or anyone else to necessarily see other than the person sharing my room. Wondered what my mother must have thought, coming into my house and seeing Jeremy in my bed, and his frat brothers and friends lounging around my kitchen and den. Knew I'd be getting a strong talk from her. Probably get compared to Tonya or Cecily and the choices they had made in their lives. Not that they'd made any particularly bad choices. But a lecture was not what I'd looked forward to.

Mom was smoking a cigarette and looking out the front window at Mr. and Mrs. Li's house across the street. Her Laughlin gambling buddies. She was nervous about something. Remembered seeing the same nervousness as a child, and coming of age in the early eighties, when money was tight, every other year either my mom or dad was laid off from their auto plant jobs, and the choice between skipping a bill or buying groceries was the sixty-four-thousand-dollar question. Though my parents and stepdad had eventually retired from their auto industry jobs, and made decent pensions, I knew that money was still tight for them. And being over two thousand miles away from home in Ohio, and still trying to manage the household from long distance, was not the easiest thing to do.

"Ma, what's up?" I asked. "Did you talk to your husband? Or talk to my dad?"

"No, it's nothing like that," she said and took a drag of her Kool. "So that's Jeremy, huh? Making butt babies already, huh?"

"Ma, stop."

"Well, he's cute, I'll give you that," she said. "Young, but cute. Like that boy on *Saved By the Bell* you and your sisters used to watch. The one who did *Dancing With the Stars*."

"Mario Lopez."

"You loved you some Mario Lopez," she said and laughed. "Never understood what made you so color struck. Liked Mexicans, them Arabs who owned all the gas stations in Toledo and Detroit, the mixed and mixed-up-in-the-mind kids, always after those light-skinned types."

"DaVon was far from light-skinned. Neither was Will or Kevin or Rodney before DaVon."

"True," she said and giggled. "You and your sisters always brought home fine, chocolate brothas. Don't know why all of a sudden *you'd* throw away a good track record for some kid who could be on those Sally Struthers commercials. The kind that need a sponsor."

"I hope you're not being racist, Ma."

"Not at all. Just saying."

"Jeremy's family has worked hard to be here, and they all work now, and his dad is Dominican from New York originally. They're as American as the rest of us, if you can really call *us* American. But that's not the point."

"Then what is?" She put out the butt of one cigarette and lit up another. "Since you know it all, Mister College Boy."

"What happened in Laughlin?" I asked. "Because you're awfully concerned with what's up at the Lis' house. You haven't even looked at me during this conversation."

She turned in my direction. Gave me the eye and said, "You not Judge Judy, Kenny. But if you must know, we had a horrible weekend in Laughlin. The Lis are cheapskates. I'm sure she'll be over here later today asking for her money back, so you better get those boys out of here before Nosy-Miss-Busy-Body-Connie-Chung comes and starts more gossip."

"You borrowed money to gamble?"

"No, Kenny. She gave it to me when she saw I was running short."

"How much?"

"I didn't tell her to give me fourteen hundred," she said, puffed on her cigarette, and chuckled. "I told her at most four, five hundred at the most. Her English not too tight. Not my fault."

I looked at her and rolled my eyes. Couldn't believe this was the same person who'd raised me all my life. Borrowing money from my neighbors. Bringing her drama into my home. Making racial epithets.

"Ma, you don't borrow money from people you don't

know," I pleaded. "You wouldn't even borrow money from your friends when we were growing up. And back then, there were days we really needed it. You remember the strikes and the layoffs at the auto plants? When we had lights cut off a few times?"

"Times are different."

"Regardless, Ma, I don't have that kind of money to waste on nothing. Not after all DaVon cost me," I said. "I gave you enough money to take to Laughlin. You didn't need more to have a good time."

"Two hundred dollars, big whoop," she said and looked around the living room. "Please, Kenny, I know you got more somewhere. Sell one of them paintings or borrow more off your retirement. Remortgage your house. You're young, still."

"That's not the point."

"Don't you get all huffy with me, son, because I wanna have a little fun and you up here running Neverland Ranch with your stable of boys. We both got our weaknesses."

"Stop. Two different things. And it's not even close to the same. Don't even go there."

"And don't you go there either, Kenny," she said and put out her cigarette. "If you need to lay down the rules, and act like you the parent, then I will just pack up and head back to Ohio. Or maybe go to Oakland with Cecily. She could use the day care help anyway."

"With what money?"

"It's called open-ended ticket, baby boy, or I'll charge a cheap ticket on Southwest," she said.

"No need for all this drama," I said. "Things have been great with you here. I'll call Dad or Stepdad and get money from them. Or I'll just pay Mrs. Li back."

"Now, if you wanna upset your dad or stepdad, then go right ahead. But I'm leaving. I see I've worn out my welcome."

"Ma . . ."

"And don't come begging me back after the new boy toy dumps you," she said. "Did enough counseling sessions after DaVon left you."

"I put *him* out," I said.

"Whatever."

She stormed through the hallway and out the back door of the kitchen. By this time, our voices had raised to a point where I knew we'd given Jeremy and his friends quite a show. I couldn't believe that what had started out as a beautiful night-slash-morning with Jeremy by my side had turned into such a disastrous afternoon with my mother. I didn't want to drive my own mother away, much like I'd driven away, I mean, put out DaVon. Made me wonder if I was a formula for disaster, and if, in just a matter of time, I would do the same to Jeremy.

Chapter 14

Mom left L.A. the next day. Planned to stay with Cecily and her family in Oakland for a few weeks. Then Phoenix to visit Tonya and her family for another few weeks. Got an earful from both Tonya and Cecily as to why and how I'd let Mom leave, because of what they interpreted as an argument merely over my choice of romantic partners.

"I can't believe you'd let some man come between you and Mom," Tonya said. She'd put all the Kane siblings on three-way from her phone in Phoenix. She'd dialed me just as I was leaving from a Big Brothers/Big Sisters volunteer meeting. "You don't make your own mother kick rocks."

Obviously Mom had already spun her own public relations version of our discussion with my sisters, and I was the bad guy. Definitely not a role I wanted to take on, but at various points in our growing up and adult years, Tonya, Cecily, and I took turns as the alleged bad guy in the Kane family. We were close, but could also have our falling-outs.

"Tonya, you need to chill out. I wouldn't kick her out because of a dude."

"What do you think, Cecily?"

"Sixty-four," Cecily said. We used that word, short for the game show *The $64,000 Question*, when we could respond only with a "yes" or "no." That usually meant somebody, namely one of our parents, was nearby and being nosy.

"She's sitting right there listening, huh?" I asked.

"Yeah, that's right," Cecily said. "That's the Michael Baisden show in the background."

"Funny, Cecily. Well, tell her to tell you about the money she borrowed from my neighbor," I said. "All fourteen hundred dollars. When she's done listening to Michael Baisden."

"If it's just money, I'll get Dane to write a check," Tonya said. Her biggest talent these days was spending her anchorman husband's money.

"Whatever, Tonya," I said. "Are you gonna ask her, Cecily?"

"I will take care of that later," Cecily said. "We just got out of baggage claim and are heading toward the freeway. Lots of traffic."

"Stop pressuring her, Kenny," Tonya said. "It's bad enough you're making her cramp Mom into her small place with the babies. But I'll take her in in a couple weeks."

"Great. Make me out to be the bad guy," I said and heard my phone beep. Thank God for small miracles. "I gotta take this call. The whole thing is blown out of proportion. But we'll talk later. Love you."

"Love you."

"Love you."

I pressed one button to end the call with Tonya and Cecily. Pressed another to start a conversation with my best friend.

"I'm so glad you called, Carlos," I said. "My family is stressing me out."

Explained to him the weekend visit from Jeremy and his posse, and the argument with my mom over her Laughlin trip. Told him I needed some days off from work to get my head together. Figure out if I would rent out the back house or use it for something else. Think about the state of my relationships with Jeremy and my mom.

"You need to come over for dinner with me and Ricky, since you flaked on us this weekend and bailed on work lately," Carlos said. "Bring Jeremy, too. We can make our foursome complete again. Like the old days. Except it's Jeremy, not DaVon."

After the scene with my mother, Jeremy and his friends made a quick exit from my house. Hadn't heard from Jeremy since. Three whole days. *Nada.* Had left a couple messages on his cell and house phone, and hoped that he hadn't gotten scared off by the Kane family drama. Jeremy's disappearing act I kept to myself. Kept the Jabari thing to myself, too. Didn't want to share it with Carlos and get an earful from him.

"Dinner would be nice," I said. "Anything interesting at work this week?"

"Something top secret with the president's office has been taking up Allison's week, which is fine with me . . . don't need her all up in my face," Carlos said. "But on another subject, Ricky says DaVon's trying to get the goods on you and if you're dating anyone new, and if you're official with Jeremy."

"Let him keep guessing," I said and laughed. "It's none of his business who my boy is."

"So you and Jeremy are official?"

"Not at all," I said. "It's been barely a week. Exactly a week."

"Still, you've seen each other most of that time."

"Anyway, let's change the subject," I said. "You want us to bring anything?"

"Just yourselves and some wine."

"Cool. Let me check with Jeremy and see if he's free. What time?"

"Seven-ish. Ricky should be awake from his post-work nap by then."

"If I hear from Jeremy, we'll be there," I said and saw my

elusive boy in the distance as I turned the corner of my street. "Speak of the devil. I'll talk to you later. Bye."

Pulled into my driveway to find Jeremy sitting on the hood of the red Civic that had been in his driveway. He smiled as the hood of my baby met his. Looked quite L.A., East L.A., with an oversized white T-shirt that went to the knees, and jeans, Dodgers hat, fresh pair of Nike sneakers, and the setting sun giving his golden brown skin a nice glow. Took off his sunglasses and nodded.

"I was just thinking about you," I said when I got out my truck. "We got a dinner invite from my best friend."

"Good, 'cause I'm hungry," he said. Eyed me up and down with that look new lovers give and learn to read with each other when they're ready for a little bedroom play. "Hungry for your co—"

"Stop," I said and smiled. Flattered to be wanted and desired by him. "Where you been? I thought you were going AWOL since you never returned my calls. Been too many days."

"I'm full of surprises," he said as he scooted off the Civic hood and walked to me. "Got something for you, boo."

He handed me a jewelry box, which was obviously not from a name-brand store. It was plain and white, in a swap meet kinda way. Opened it. Loved it. One of those army-looking chains and dog tags with one of our couple's shots electronically watermarked on it.

"Thank you, Jeremy."

"You gotta wear it, like I'm wearing mine," he said and reached into his shirt to pull his couple's shot tag out. I noticed no new hickeys, and the ones from the other night had faded away. Put his hand out to tap fists, the inconspicuous way friends and lovers could show love in public. "I kicked it at the Pico Rivera swap meet this weekend with Nacho and them, and then Mom made all this food for us. That's where

I was, just kickin' it at home. And the other days, school obviously."

"You don't have to give me a play-by-play of your week," I said. "I just wondered where you were. Thought my mom might have scared you off."

"I don't know whose mom is more drama. Yours or mine."

We laughed, and I asked Jeremy to help me bring in a couple bags of dry cleaning from my truck. Noticed scratches on the passenger side of his Civic when we walked to the front door of my house.

"Nice ride, Jeremy. But what's up with the door?"

"Jabari."

"Serious?"

"It had to be."

"What about Lalo?"

"There is no Lalo," he said. "Jabari is Lalo."

"Huh?"

"Stupid nickname he uses on his MySpace," he said and rolled his index finger in the air around his ear. "He's not too bright. Tries to fool guys on-line into thinking he's Latino or something mixed, when he's black as Africa."

"Okaaaay," I said and wondered why the kid deception games, on Jabari's part or Jeremy's. What other mysteries could this guy hold? Hung the dry cleaning bags on the foyer coatrack. "I think we need to talk about this Jabari situation."

"Yeah, we do, but later," Jeremy whispered and pressed himself against my hip. Kissed my temple, cheek, ear, just below the ear. "I need to ask you a favor, Kenny."

"Besides taking care of this?" I grabbed at magnum through the fabric of Jeremy's T-shirt and baggy jeans. We smiled. He grabbed at my zipper for a quick second.

"I need to keep the car over here, maybe in the garage or behind the back house."

"You in trouble or something?" Years of working with

college students, at various levels of development and disciplinary cases, told me Jeremy was in a situation.

"It's a long story, can't really talk about it," he said. "Just gotta trust me."

"Jeremy."

"Kenny," he pleaded back. Puppy-dog face. "Please? I wouldn't ask if it wasn't important. And it's really important."

Told him it was fine. Knew it was probably not the smartest thing, and that I was probably setting myself up for trouble. Like the kind you see on *Cops* or something. Or the kind where I'd come to the rescue, once again, for a partner who found himself in a jam. Wondered if it was my destiny to always be the one who saves everyone else. Like it was just my life's karma to be the rescuer, the lifesaver. Knew these were the kinds of details I couldn't or wouldn't share with Carlos or anyone in my family, because they were the kind of details that would lead to questions that would make me look and feel stupid, gullible, a pushover, and like I'd been wrapped around Jeremy's finger in such a short amount of time. I mean, I'd heard of quick starts and love at first sight, and Jeremy and I had certainly matched those labels plus some. But I was also far from stupid, gullible, a pushover, or wrapped around Jeremy's finger. I was just enjoying the ride for as long as it lasted.

"So keep it here," I said. "But I don't like secrets, lies, or hidden agendas."

"None here, promise," he said.

"We still don't know each other . . . really. And I have a bunch of questions, or just things that confuse me about you."

He chuckled. "Kenny, I'm horny. Can we talk about this later?" he asked and started hugging and tickling me. Wrestled to the floor of the foyer. Lifted his T-shirt. Undid the button and zipper of his jeans. Kissed the soft trail down to magnum. Squeezed the back of my head. Worked him the way a twenty-one-year-old wants to be worked. On his back. On my knees. A delicious quickie to lighten his load and ease his tension before eating another meal, a real meal with real calories, at Carlos and Ricky's.

Chapter 15

Carlos and Ricky were one of those picture-perfect super couples that other couples and single people looked at in awe, wonder, and envy. Considered such not just because of their enviable looks and personalities, Carlos and Ricky's seven plus years together had been considered the paragon of what relationships between male couples could be. They had well-paid, professional jobs, enjoyed an active sex life exclusively with each other, supported each other's interests and hobbies in and out of the relationship, and, despite the conservative and traditional upbringings each had as a child, had the unyielding support of their families.

The family support translated itself into equally supportive friendships. For Carlos and Ricky, most of those friendships were mainly with other couples, including DaVon and me. One of the things I had missed most from my breakup with DaVon was the camaraderie developed with our circle of friends. We had the Stentorians, the black firefighters association in L.A. And we had the gay firefighters and law enforcement professionals and their partners. Other couples who had together withstood buying homes, adopting kids, managing careers and households, developing meaningful relationships with each other's families, and other conflicts and ups and downs of relationships. When you're a firehouse spouse, there are certain things you just know and worry about. Accidental deaths or injuries from fires or related illnesses. Accidents with speeding or slow cars. Accidental outings of your sexuality in a typically male and stereotypically even more male profession. Accidents with equipment. Accidental or actual sabotages from fellow competitive firefighters. These were the things that bonded our circle, and kept Carlos and me close as colleagues and friends. When DaVon and I broke up, it didn't necessarily break up the circle of friends. It just made things a little awkward. There are no rules for who gets custody, and as a single person, your status among the couples is seen suddenly as a threat or, at the very least, something that makes you an outsider. That Carlos was reaching out to Jeremy and me, as a couple or whatever we were, meant a lot.

As Jeremy and I pulled up in Carlos and Ricky's driveway, I gripped his hand and he gripped mine tighter. He was nervous, I could tell, even though I'd tried to reassure him on the ten-minute drive over that everything would be okay, and that he had nothing to worry about with Carlos or Ricky.

"Hey, Kenny," Carlos said as he greeted us at the front door. He was holding a black dish towel and oven mitts in his hands. I knew the real cook in the household was Ricky, or the local Juan Pollo restaurant Carlos liked to frequent, so the attempt at a domestic greeting didn't fool me. "And this must be Jeremy? Good to meet you. I've heard a lot about you."

"Same here," Jeremy said and held out a hand. Gone was the playful, down-for-whatever tone he usually spoke with. "I hope it's all been good stuff you've heard."

"Most definitely," Carlos said. "Come on in. Ricky just got out the shower and is getting dressed. I'm watching *Ugly Betty* on DVD waiting on you guys."

Jeremy and I followed Carlos to the kitchen, where he had a pitcher of margaritas and a tray of appetizers waiting—hummus, pita chips, and mini-enchiladas which all looked like they came directly from Costco. We sat at the small table, and Carlos "tended" to the meal he'd "prepared" at the stove. I poured two drinks and knew it would be any second before Carlos and then Ricky would start their inquisition of Jeremy.

"So, Jeremy," Carlos asked as he ran a dry ladle through a pan of rice.

"So, Carlos," Jeremy interrupted. "What version of my life you want? The X-rated or PG-13 version?"

We all laughed. Ice broken.

"Whatever version you wanna give is fine. But if the X-rated version is good, we might end up having a four-way orgy tonight."

"A little group action never hurt nobody," Jeremy said and laughed. Swallowed down his margarita like it was a shot. "*Pues,* I figured you guys already got your questions lined up, so I came prepared like Antonio Villaraigosa."

Jeremy charmed Carlos with stories of growing up in East L.A., updated him on youthful trends and must-haves, and talked about his goals, desires, and how he wanted to get there. All the standard things we'd talked about in the previous week of hanging out.

"You're bringing Jeremy to the annual Vegas trip, right?" Carlos asked. "Everyone would love him. It's our clique of gay firefighters and partners, and we do little trips together."

"Ooh, Vegas," Jeremy said. "I'm all in. Double down."

"We didn't talk about it yet," I said. "But I think it would be cool."

"I love me some Vegas," Jeremy said. "Pai Gow Poker is my game."

"Mine, too," Carlos said. "You can play nice and long, and not lose as quickly like on the slots."

It was nice seeing Jeremy "on" and enjoying the company of my best friend, and that Jeremy was deemed good enough to go along on the Vegas trip our firefighter couple crowd did every year. Granted, I was no longer with a firefighter, but I could still be part of the circle. That felt nice. As for the small talk with Jeremy, it was a little on the superficial side and conversation stayed light. What didn't come up were all the red-flag items Jeremy and I had yet to delve into: Jabari, the party, the regular use of alcohol, pot, and who knows what else, and the car I was now keeping in my backyard, among other subjects.

Once Ricky joined us, we continued having a fun, lively conversation. Mostly about pop culture—films, music, television. Stayed away from politics. Didn't want Ricky's compassionate conservatism coming out. The night reminded me a lot of the days when DaVon and I would join Carlos and Ricky for dinner. We drank more margaritas, ate the restaurant-bought homemade meal of roasted chicken, pinto beans, and salad, and had coffee and flan for dessert.

After dinner, while Jeremy stepped into the rest room and Carlos put dishes into the washer, was when Ricky approached me in the living room. A rerun from the first season's *Noah's Arc* was playing on Logo, our post-dinner entertainment. We were loving the antics of Noah, Chance, Ricky, and Alex on the show. For the moment.

"Something about him looks real familiar," Ricky said. "I can't quite put a finger on it."

"He looks like most other twenty-one-year-old L.A. guys, duh," I said. "And even that's being stereotypical."

"Nah, it's something else," he said. "I feel like I know him from somewhere."

"He was at your birthday party," I said. "Otherwise, you're thirty-five, he's twenty-one. No way you guys travel in the same circle."

"Ha ha. Funny. Look who's talking."

"Anyway, I heard DaVon's asking about my love life," I said.

"He still cares," Ricky said. "He's human."

"Tell him he doesn't have to care," I said. "And that I'm seeing someone new."

"Well, let's see something more permanent before you go

advertising your new relationship," he said. "Shit goes down in flames sometimes before you get a chance to admire what you built."

"Thanks for the vote of confidence, Ricky," I said. "I think I'll get it right this time, since I discovered Jeremy on my own and not on your referral."

"Defensive," he said. "I'll keep quiet, then."

"Just saying," I said. "Sorry for snapping."

"Yeah, right," he said. "I'm just trying to look out for you."

In one of those soap opera-ish moments, Jeremy walked in during Ricky's line.

"Look out for Kenny for what?" Jeremy asked and put his arms around me.

"Oh, it's nothing," Ricky said and picked up the television remote. Flipped to ESPN to watch NBA highlights. "It was good meeting you, Jeremy."

"Same here," Jeremy said and looked at his watch. "But I got class and work in the morning. Gotta earn that paper and graduate . . . like you old-timers did back in the seventies."

"Very funny," I said and grabbed on to his arm.

"Guys, don't go yet," Carlos said as he walked into the living room. Put his arms around Ricky's waist. "It's not that late."

"Yes, it is," Jeremy said. "Especially for you all in the Geritol generation."

We laughed, exchanged a few more pleasantries before leaving, and Jeremy and I were soon in my truck to drop him off in East L.A.

Part of me was a little angry with Ricky and his digs, suspicions, whatever at Jeremy. Knew there would always be some tension between us, with him being the one responsible for bringing DaVon into my life and maintaining contact with him after our breakup. Jeremy fumbled with the radio, opting not for his usual hip-hop station, but for KJLH slow jams. My girl Tammi Mac was keeping us company with her "Back Seat" radio show.

"So what did you think?" I asked.

"Your boys are interesting," Jeremy said. He started scrolling through missed calls and text messages on his phone. "Guys in their thirties have fun in a different sort of way, huh?"

"Just a little tamer than your crowd."

"I'm not the biggest fan of Pollo Loco or Juan Pollo chicken."

"You could tell, huh?" I asked and smiled. "I thought it was just me."

"Even a blind man could tell," Jeremy said and continued manipulating his phone. "Fuck."

"What?"

"Jabari blowing up my phone like it's Baghdad."

"We gotta do something about that," I said. "I won't be able to keep a straight face at school when I see him."

"You ain't gotta tell that bitch nothing," Jeremy said and turned his phone off. "But what else did I think about tonight?"

"Yeah, did you have fun?"

"Carlos is cool," Jeremy said. "Ricky can suck my left nut."

"What?" I asked. A little surprised. Ricky hadn't confronted Jeremy directly. "Where'd that come from?"

"I don't get a good vibe from him, that's all," Jeremy said.

"What's up with that?" I said. "Some of your friends I . . . just know are part of your life."

"And as long as you and I are kicking it, I don't want to be around him. Kept looking at me funny all night."

Jeremy grabbed my hand that rested on the center console.

"First of all, Jeremy, you won't dictate who my friends are and aren't," I said. "Ricky's kinda part of the package. Can't be with Carlos without Ricky coming along. You don't pay my bills and you don't pick my friends."

"Ain't got time for fake-ass white-acting *pochos*."

"So . . . what?"

"We can kick it with Carlos, but fuck Ricky."

"But . . ."

"Just like you don't want me around Jabari, I don't want Ricky in our mix. Deal?"

"No deal," I said. "Jabari's your ex. Ricky and I have never been anything but friends. It's not the same."

I let his hand loose and changed radio stations from my steering wheel. We'd just turned the corner near St. Stevens, the Catholic parish a couple blocks from Jeremy's house. Driving to his house helped me avoid answering his demand directly. One week, and already issuing demands and conditions. Damn. But I knew we'd have to confront a lot of other things head-on pretty soon. Especially if we were planning to take this relationship beyond the one-week kicking it stage.

"Gimme a call tomorrow after work and school," I said when we pulled in front of his house. "Besides this picking friends thing, there's a lot we need to iron out once and for all."

"Fine," Jeremy said and opened his door. No kiss, or even a hug, as we had usually ended our nights. "Talk tomorrow."

Slammed the passenger door and walked up the driveway without looking back. Wondered if I had done something wrong standing up for myself and my friends. Wondered if I had done something wrong by asking that we clear up all the mysteries, questions, and issues that remained between us. As I drove away, I knew my desire for answers was normal. That it was normal to want to communicate with someone you were starting to care about. Even if it had been just a little time since you met.

Chapter 16

"So no court action this morning, Kenny?"

Allison Perez, my compassionate conservative Texan boss, laughed as she swept unannounced again into my office. I'd missed a lot with my weekend and days off from the job, apparently, as her Kelly Ripa blond bob had been transformed into a Katie Couric cut and color. Even with the hair makeover, the Ann Taylor look remained—lilac sweater set, pearls, and black slacks. And so did the usual mode of conversation between us.

"You're welcome to watch *Court TV* on the digital cable piped into your office," I said. Closed up the photo slideshow on the computer of me and Jeremy. Didn't want small talk with Allison, or even her fake interest in my personal life. Just the facts, ma'am. "What brings you by?"

"Do I need a reason to see my favorite director?" Allison sat down in the chair across from my desk. Quite a change from her usual routine of looking over my shoulder to see what's on my computer screen. "Enjoy your days off?"

"It was okay," I said. "I was dealing with family issues. Personal stuff."

"Well, we got a little problem with some of the boys in the honor frat," Allison said and slid a file across the desk to me. "Take a look at this, Kenny," she said and smiled. Like the cat with a canary for breakfast.

"What's this got to do with me?" I asked. Somehow I just knew, but needed to ask.

"Seems they were involved with an illegal party this weekend. Freshman boy in a coma. Alcohol poisoning. Evidence of sexual assault, but won't know definitely until he wakes and talks. Or any of our students talk."

Shit, I thought. I'm toast.

I opened the file and saw a dozen or so pictures from the same party Jeremy had taken me to over the previous weekend, some reports from LAPD outlining underage drinking, the presence and sale of narcotics, hazing, and lewd acts that allegedly had taken place on the night in question. Several names of students involved in our various student organizations and leadership positions were mentioned in the report, and one in particular stood out. Jabari Nelson.

I wondered if she knew I had been there. If she did, she wasn't letting on. Remembered Mom's white-lady-law codicil: Don't admit anything, even in a casual, friendly context. It'll pop up again when you least expect it, and it'll be blown out of proportion.

"So what does this have to do with me, Allison?" I asked again for clarification, but mainly to stall, think, worry. What does she know? "Well, besides the obvious that I oversee student organizations."

"I knew that master's degree kicked in every now and then, Kenny." She chuckled in that way people who think they are being cute and humorous, but aren't, do.

"I've had rare occasion to use it in recent months," I said. Wasn't letting her get the last snap, boss or not. "Anyone can be trained to follow a predictable to-do list. But anyway, I'll follow up with the group. Is that it?"

"Of course not, darling," she said. "This party is a serious matter. Some of our students were arrested, a student is in a coma, and too many other unmentionables happened there. Thank God LAPD's turning everything over to us and keeping this out of the press for now."

For once, I agreed. Obviously Omar had done his part to make sure this party and my attendance were kept on the low. I'd have to thank him for his help. And pray extra hard the student made it out of his coma.

"So, Kenny, I need you to throw the book at them," Allison continued. "No matter how harsh or unreasonable it seems, but within university protocol of course."

"Yes, this needs to be addressed, Allison," I said. I didn't necessarily think it deserved "the book" as Allison suggested, unless the student in the coma didn't survive. The party wasn't even thrown by the CUELA chapter of the group—it was ELAJ's—and it was held far from the CUELA campus in Highland Park. "I'm on it like yesterday."

"Now don't blue-state out on me and get all flip-floppy, Kenny," Allison chuckled and then quickly gained composure. "They're lucky the president's office intervened. He can't have this affecting our outreach and recruitment efforts. So go after all of them involved. Especially that little Jabari Nelson boy. Smart-ass boy is a little too sassy and doesn't know his place. Isn't he the president of our chapter and of the gay group?"

"First, he's not five," I said. Felt weird attempting to defend Jabari, after learning he's Jeremy's ex and hearing about some of his childish antics. Then again, none of it was confirmed. Just hearsay. Like the reports in the folder from Allison. "Anyway, I'll keep you posted on how my meetings turn out."

"Let's be quick and decisive. Need to show we take illegal parties and hazing seriously, if this gets out."

"Like Texas justice, right? Fry 'em, then try 'em after the fact?" I chuckled and gave a fake smile. Not at the situation, because I worried about any student who would drink so much as to end up in a coma. But more at trying to annoy Allison, who did everything she could to annoy me.

"If you say so," Allison got up to exit. Pulled her typical *Dynasty*-like turn at the door. She's always ready for the last line. "Don't let this drag out like your own legal dramas with DaVon."

"Meaning?"

"Oh, nothing at all," she said and smirked. "Have a good day."

She got me good with that one. I could do one better. I knew secrets about her husband and his night retreats while she's away at cosmetic, er, professional obligations.

"Rolando enjoying his job and life in the executive suite?" I asked. "Playing top dog with the big boys?"

"Meaning?"

"Just making conversation, Allison," I said. "I'm sure it's hard for your husband being the only man of color in an executive position at his firm. That's all." I turned toward my computer.

"For your information, Rolando and I have the kind of marriage where we don't see color," she said.

I wanted to turn toward her and make some remark about her husband not seeing his wedding ring or his marriage vows or his declared sexual orientation while she's out of town either. But kept that to myself. Played with the computer mouse like I was beginning to start work. Really just thinking about how complicated things could get if I had to go after Jabari like my boss implied I should. Jabari was a good student, reminded me a lot of myself when an undergrad, but had a big mouth when he felt wronged. I'd seen it, or rather heard it, in his visits to my office when he'd bitch about other students trying to usurp his power in his student organizations, or how he'd go up the chain of command of an academic department to get a grade changed, or which new relationship or breakup he was going through. How we never got around to Jeremy's name coming up remained a mystery. And now, I found myself trying to make sense of so many questions. Questions about how to handle the missive from Allison. Questions about Jeremy's everything. Questions about why I was throwing myself so quickly into a relationship with him, or whatever it was we were doing. It was really not in my agenda at all—a relationship—but it was developing, and the connection with Jeremy was definitely solidifying.

When I sensed Allison was no longer in my doorway, I picked up the phone for the first of two calls I needed to make. One to Carlos, to share my newest work assignment and to confess everything going on with Jeremy and me. But before that, to the man who probably saved my life and, for the time being, my career.

"This is Officer Etheridge speaking."

"Kenny Kane from CUELA here."

"Mister Party Animal," Omar said. His voice lightened up, became less formal. "Hold on. I'll call you from my cell."

Five minutes later, my cell rang.

"How'd you get this number?"

"I'm a cop. I can find out anything I want," Omar said and laughed. He sounded more relaxed and playful now. "Anyway, figured we should make this call off-the-record and off company phones. Know what I mean?"

"Most definitely, though *your* president might be listening right now to our conversation," I said. "Thanks for keeping the situation quiet. Well, as quiet as you could about me anyway. How's the student in the coma?"

"He was in bad shape," Omar said. "The doctors think he'll pull through. But it could be days. You never know about these medical mysteries and comas. He might have been sexually assaulted, at least that's what it appears. Various objects. We just need someone to talk."

"That's terrible," I said. "I had no clue all that was going on, and under my nose. I was invited by someone."

"The reports didn't mention you being there," Omar said. "Know what I mean?"

Felt relieved for the moment, but knew it wasn't long before someone talked about seeing me at the party. "Omar, if there's anyway I can repay you . . ."

"Don't trip, Kenny," Omar said. "You didn't throw the party and you wasn't there. You saved me so many times when I was in college. The loans for lunch, or books, or even hooking me up with DaVon, who got me in with his friends at LAPD."

"Well, DaVon's history in terms of being my partner, but I do appreciate this," I said. "My boss wants me to lay down the law on the students. They all saw me there. Someone's going to talk if I have to pursue this case."

"I'm sure."

"But that's my problem, not yours, Omar."

"Maybe I can help," he said. "Let me take you out for dinner. Talk strategy. Got a lot of inside scoop being on the force, you know?"

"I should take *you* out, Omar," I said. "You name the time and place."

"I'm down for tonight."

"Well," I said. Hesitated. What if Jeremy wanted to do something? Nah, he was probably still mad. But regardless, I needed to have a talk with Jeremy about the party and any involvement he might have had in the student coma case. "I gotta check in with someone first."

"The ball and chain?" Omar laughed a bit. "I thought you and DaVon were history."

"We are, but there's someone I'm kinda hanging with," I said. "The reason I was at the party."

"Going gangsta now, huh?"

"I guess. Kinda."

"Be careful. I don't want you ending up in some file. As a cold case or something else."

"He's a good guy, for the most part, but I just don't want issues," I said. "You know how people get jealous."

"Well," Omar said and paused a bit. "We haven't done anything yet. Maybe a little jealousy will make things exciting . . . for all of us."

"Excuse me?" I thinketh the copeth doth flirteth. And I

kinda liketh. Not the time to even be thinking about picking up or flirting back.

"Don't trip, Kenny," Omar said. "So I'll pick you up. Six-thirty?"

"Perfect. I guess you already have my address, too?"

"Yeah," he said and laughed. "I have a lot to talk to you about. Good thing we ran into each other at that party."

"I guess so," I said and smiled. Flirting or not, I loved the ease of our reunion conversation. Wondered what Omar had to talk about. "So thanks again, Officer Etheridge. I owe you."

"Hmmm. This is gonna be fun."

"What?"

"Being in the driver's seat," he said. "Four years ago it was a different story."

"We better stop this conversation before . . . I have work to do."

"Six-thirty. I drive a black Durango."

"Cool. Later."

Put the cell back in my bag and picked up the office phone to dial Carlos. Two rings in, Carlos waltzed into my office carrying his portfolio. Slammed the office door closed. Looked tired, like he'd been up all night, yet seemed wiry like he'd drunk a pot of coffee by himself. Wasn't even dressed professionally—or at least hadn't thrown an iron on his shirt this morning.

"Ricky told me you and he had words . . . about Jeremy," Carlos said and sat down in the chair Allison had just exited minutes earlier.

"Don't worry about it, it's nothing," I said. "It's funny, though, because Jeremy wasn't really feeling Ricky. I don't know what's up with that. Some kind of vibe, I guess."

"I think it's a little more than that." Carlos opened his portfolio and pulled out a sheet of paper. "Ricky had this faxed over to the house after you guys left. I couldn't sleep after seeing it, but decided I had to tell you . . . in person rather than over the phone."

Carlos handed me the fax, on fire department letterhead: "WANTED for suspicion of arson." Sometimes DaVon would bring these types of signs and pamphlets home, for distribution in the neighborhood or at CUELA. Most had anonymous sketches of men accused of various crimes, mostly fire related or crimes covered up by fires. None had ever had sketches of men I knew. Men like Jeremy. Though it was still an anonymous sketch, there was no doubt of what Carlos, Ricky, and now I saw. Jeremy's face, sketched in black and gray. Description of his height, weight, and skin complexion very similar to Jeremy's. Wanted for the suspicion of arson in several abandoned and occupied homes in East L.A., Boyle Heights, and other locales just east of downtown. The clincher: a late-model Civic was seen in the area or leaving the scene at each of the alleged crime scenes—fires dating back over the last year and a half. The Civic that was now sitting in my backyard, away from Jeremy's house, hidden from the world. Or was it?

"Why are you giving this to me?" I asked and handed the bulletin back to Carlos.

"Duh, why do you think?" Carlos said. "You're my best friend. You're dating an arsonist."

"Allegations," I said and waved him off. "And it's just a sketch."

"Kenny, you're not stupid."

"No, I'm not."

"So?" He raised his eyebrows, moved his head side to side. "What are you going to do?"

"Nothing," I said. "What's there to do?"

"Confront Jeremy," he said. "At least let him know what we think."

"So this is what Ricky meant when he said Jeremy looked familiar?" I picked up the paper again, looked at the sketch and description. "Jeremy's in college, Carlos. He works to support his family, a family he loves very much. He was on

Teen Jeopardy and reads romance novels, for God's sake. He's not an arsonist."

"I'm just telling you what Ricky suspects. It's too close of a match and coincidence."

In my mind, I knew. We always know. The lover, or wannabe lover, about whom there are too many questions and not enough answers. When loneliness and being single seem less desirable than being with the wrong person. And when we don't want our friends or family to know everything negative that's happening in our relationships, even though coming clean is exactly what would help. Still, we hold on to our pride rather than share what's really going on.

"Carlos, I don't mean to sound rude, but Ricky's judgment hasn't been the best when it comes to the men in my life," I said. "He thought DaVon was perfect, but of course, we know that wasn't the case."

"This is different," Carlos said. "Adultery . . . arson. Way different."

"Of course you'd defend Ricky," I said. "You're a happily married voyeur. No one else has the right to be happy, so of course you'd defend Ricky."

"And there's no reason you should defend Jeremy," Carlos said and gathered his portfolio. I grabbed the announcement before he locked it away. "You've only known him mere days. Me, for seven years, Kenny."

"I'll talk to you later."

"What should I tell Ricky?"

"I'll talk to you later. Okay?" I said. "I've got work to do."

"Allison got you on the party case, I heard," he said. "Afraid your skeleton's gonna surface?"

"I'll deal with it if it comes to that," I said. "I haven't even talked with Jeremy yet about it . . . the coma or sexual assault allegations. Just found out I'm on the case."

"The boy's trouble, and is going to drag you down,"

Carlos said. "You should give him the boot now before you're too involved. Ricky's ready to turn in Jeremy."

"He'll do no such thing," I said. Raised my voice, and realized I was ready to pounce on my best friend. "I've got a million things on my list from Allison, my family stuff, and other things I don't want to talk about. I want to at least talk to Jeremy first. Is that cool?"

"Whatever, Kenny. But the more you delay . . . people could be in danger, including you."

"Jeremy's harmless."

Carlos rolled his eyes and left for his day of meetings on campus. Didn't get the dramatic response I'm sure he expected. Not that I planned to flinch from my poker face or let him know that his doubts about Jeremy were just adding to and confirming the questions and doubts I already had.

Dialed Jeremy's cell. No answer. Maybe he was still mad from last night's disagreement over Ricky and ignoring my calls. Knew he'd be in class and giving campus tours part of the afternoon, but didn't care how many missed call messages, or texts, or e-mails I had to leave for him to know it was urgent we talked.

But I knew in just a few short hours, I'd have some of the answers I wanted. Whether it was directly from Jeremy, or from another source who could find out anything he wanted. On the record or off.

Chapter 17

"You want me to do what?"

Omar put his fork down. Took a swallow from his water glass as if he were shocked at my suggestion. Especially after the direction our conversation had turned.

"You heard me, Omar," I said. "I want you to check out Jeremy Lopez's background."

Maybe I'd seen too much daytime television, both drama and talk shows, in my day. Or maybe I'd listened to too much of the Morning Home Team on KJLH—or rather their listeners—and heard too many horror stories of people getting burned badly by lovers, spouses, and friends whom they thought they'd known, but didn't. And in this case, getting burned was no laughing matter. The arson allegations. Starting a new relationship that had the potential to be more dangerous or dramatic than anything DaVon could have put on me.

Maybe I was the one being overly dramatic. After all, boys who read Danielle Steel and who appear on *Teen Jeopardy* don't do bad things. Do they?

"I can do it, Kenny," Omar said, matter-of-factly, without flinching. Such a cop. "A basic check of public records, or go a little more in-depth with sealed and private records. Maybe even check out some of his friends and acquaintances and family, too."

"Whatever it takes," I said. "I just wanna know what I'm dealing with."

"Kenny, after all you've done for me in college, it's a done deal," Omar said and grabbed my hand. Squeezed. We were sitting in a gay-friendly restaurant and bar in West Hollywood, The Abbey, and though Omar had never given any indication of his sexuality . . . okay, maybe I was just reading too much at this moment. He let my hand go. I *was* reading too much. "I can get you a basic rundown of his life in a couple days. More in a week. But I gotta wonder something."

"What's that?"

"Some of the lessons you taught us in leadership classes," Omar said. "You know, 'People with real money don't brag about it,' or 'If you've got doubts, follow your instinct.' I wonder if your situation with Jeremy is already doomed. I mean, these should be things you guys should be talking about instead of going behind his back to investigate."

"Point taken," I said. "I know exactly what you're saying. We *should* be communicating about these issues, but I just need reassurance. And Jeremy doesn't have to know."

"Is it even worth it? How long you known him, a few weeks? You feeling him that much already?"

"Omar, I'm sure you've had that feeling from meeting someone new," I said. "You're all over the place after a breakup."

"Just asking," he said. "Because I get these requests a lot. And most times people say they want this information, but then when it comes it's a whole 'nother story."

"I appreciate the concern," I said and gazed a little long into his eyes. Thought he'd be the perfect replacement for a guy like DaVon. He looked like a younger version of DaVon. But he looked away from my gaze. I guess the flirting was just my imagination. Back to business. "Don't say anything about this to anyone, okay? About the background check."

How our conversation had moved to such a comfort level was beyond me. Until I ran into him outside Jeremy's fraternity's party, it had been at least two years since seeing Omar. He'd always been one of my favorite students. One of my favorite straight students. Quiet, with strong leadership qualities. Popular with peers. President of Black Student Union for a semester, and active with student government after that. Always open-minded and outspoken for underdogs and those who couldn't speak up or have their cases heard, whether it was the socially inept or those socially cast aside because of whatever race, class, or gender categories made them considered undesirable at the moment. Omar, dark, tall, strong inside and out—the kind Destiny's Child praised in the song "Soldier"—was the kind of guy one wanted around as a friend, advocate, or more. Now, he would be helping me with the most important questions and issues related to Jeremy.

"No one has to know," Omar said. "It's our secret."

"Thanks. And thanks for keeping the whole party thing, at least my being there, out of the report. The stupid things I do for Jeremy."

"We all do stupid things for someone we're into," Omar said. "But I gotta ask, or say rather, that things can't be too great if you're having your so-called man investigated. Just an observation. Maybe you need more time to get over DaVon or find someone more situated and stable. Take it for what it's worth. You can do better, Kenny."

"Sounds like you've been talking to my mom, Carlos, and Oprah."

"Maybe I have."

"Right," I said. "I know I'm probably fishing at the bottom, but when you get to a certain age and think your glory days are winding down . . . you grasp at what's reaching out to you. It's a gay thing, you wouldn't understand, Omar."

"Funny you should mention that," he said and finished the last of his coffee. A signal that our dinner and evening reunion would soon be over. "But honestly, I always thought you were an admirable, strong black man. I don't know everything that happened with DaVon, just the basics, but

Jeremy sounds like a scrub barely skirting the edge of trouble. If I kicked it with dudes, which I don't, I'd kick it with you."

"That's funny and flattering, Omar," I said. Felt open enough to give him my confessions. "Because I had a big old crush on you when you were at CUELA, but I don't kick it with students."

He chuckled and said, "But I'm not a student anymore."

"And you don't kick it with dudes."

"Right."

"Right."

A few seconds of awkward silence. We gazed at each other. Smiled.

"Anyway," he said.

"Anyway."

"I should get you home now," Omar said. "You got CUELA drama. I got the courtroom first thing in the morning. If we delay much longer, who knows where we'll end up."

We zipped up Santa Monica Boulevard to the 101, connected with the 60, and were soon speeding up Atlantic to my house. Funny how cops can get away with violating the speed limit. Must be the law enforcement sticker on the back window. Needed one for myself. We pulled into the driveway. Lights illuminated Jeremy sitting on the front porch stairs.

"That's Jeremy," I said. Hadn't expected to see Jeremy for a minute, especially with our latest tiff over Carlos and Ricky, and also his busy school schedule. "Goodbye needs to be quick."

"Not like we're giving him a show, but I feel you," Omar said and reached into his wallet. Pulled out a card and scribbled some words on it. "This is how you can reach me, twenty-four-seven."

"Thanks."

"You sure you gonna be okay?" Omar asked. "Kinda late for visitors, isn't it?"

"He sometimes stays overnight," I said. "I guess tonight is one of those nights."

"Jealous."

"Jeremy's not that type. To get jealous, I don't think."

"I'm talking about me."

"Stop," I said and smiled. Omar had turned into quite a confident flirt and charmer since leaving college, but what good would it have done to flirt back. Boys like Omar had a way of charming, and confusing, everyone. "Thanks for everything. I'll talk with you later."

"Yeah, later. At least I got a mental picture of the boy we're dealing with."

Jeremy watched me get out Omar's Durango, his infamous puppy-dog eyes illuminated by the porch light, his book bag sitting by his foot. Omar backed out the driveway and sped off, and Jeremy looked like he wanted to cry.

"I was about to leave," Jeremy said.

"I didn't know you were coming by," I said. "Didn't hear from you all day."

"I know," he said. "I was fucking pissed off about our fight."

"Yeah, we need to talk about that. And other things."

"I *was* going to apologize for blowing up about Carlos and Ricky, and say that I blew it out of proportion," he said. "But I see you just got over it, and started kicking it with new dudes already."

"Omar used to be a student of mine and works for LAPD," I said and put my key in the front door. It was already unlocked. "But that's beside the point. Why's my door open?"

"I've been here since seven," Jeremy said and got up. Slung one strap of his book bag over his left shoulder. Walked in the house behind me. "But you got someone new already. It's all right. You're over me. I see how it is."

"Jeremy, please."

"I thought I'd come and make up for my attitude," he said. "I made you dinner."

"Thanks, but I had dinner with Omar," I said. Jeremy looked sad, like I'd let him down. "I appreciate the gesture. It's nice of you. We need to talk about the party you took me to."

"Later," Jeremy said and smiled. Gave me that seductive look, the wanting-and-needing-sex look that I'd grown used to seeing during our time together. Grinded against me, whispered hot breath against my neck and ear. "After I let you take care of the magic stick."

"No. Be. Serious." I pushed him away.

"Fine, I see I'm not wanted," he said. Pouted. Walked away. "I'll put the key back under the mat and go."

"Don't. Go. Jeremy."

I pulled Jeremy's shoulder. He didn't resist. Turned around and kissed me. Pushed my back against the hallway wall. Warm hands everywhere. Hot kisses everywhere else. Pinned my shoulders against the wall. Kissed, licked, bit my neck, ears, cheek. Ripped buttons on jeans and boxers, loose fabric and threads dangling. Grabbed one leg to wrap around his waist. My back, head banging against original artwork.

"Don't. Fight. Me. You. Love. Me."

"Mmmmmm . . ."

"Say. You. Love. Me. Kenny."

"Mmmmmm . . ."

Turned me around, left cheek pressed against abstract green and red objects on canvas. Force. Anger. Passion.

"You. Love. Me. And. No. One. Else."

For the moment, my mind voided itself of the questions, suspicions, concerns I had of Jeremy. Knew that I might hate myself in the morning, or this weekend, or next week, when Omar came back with his report, or when or if the freshman student came out of the coma or worse.

But I was, once again, going to give in to Jeremy tonight.

Chapter 18

Somewhere in the middle of the night, when all lovers are supposed to hear are the sounds of light snoring, and when all they're supposed to feel are warm arms and legs against each other, I heard Jeremy whimpering and felt him thrashing around in the bed next to me. First thing I thought was a seizure, for some weird reason, because of not really knowing Jeremy's medical history. Called out his name. Gave him a tap on the shoulder, called him again, and turned on the lamp on the bedside table. His eyes opened wide, looked at me and around the room, and he grabbed on to me with his sweaty hands and arms.

"Bad dream, Kenny," he whispered and put his head between my neck and shoulder. "Hold me for a minute."

"It's all right. I'm here."

"It was my brother, Eric, in Iraq," Jeremy said. "Weird. He was telling me he was about to die, and gave me instructions on how to look after the family and keep my life right. And then he ran into a burning school building to save kids, and I tried to run after him to stop him, but I couldn't. It felt really hot, so I didn't go in. I was trying to yell his name, but I couldn't get my voice to make noise."

I ran my hand against the back of his head as he rested on me.

"You're okay, Jeremy," I said, trying to comfort him. "And I'm sure everything is okay with your brother."

"It was so real," Jeremy said. "If anything happened to Eric, I'd die. He's my boy. I already lost one brother for real, and another one out there doing who knows what."

"Wanna talk about it?"

"Nah, not really," he said. "Just gonna e-mail Eric and hope he calls home soon. Wish his ass didn't sign up for the stupid military. He actually had options, like community college at least, unlike some of the people who . . . whatever. Forget it. Just gets me mad and sad he's over there."

He pulled away from our embrace and leaned back on the sheets. Stretched out. Stared at the ceiling. Asked me to turn the light off, and said that he'd be okay.

"Kenny, it's so weird, but in the dream Eric said I better not fuck up the good thing I got with you."

"Serious?"

"Yeah." He pulled me closer to him, put his arm around me. "I know I'm drama, Kenny, but I'm young and I'm trying. This is new for me. These feelings. I can't explain."

"Yeah, I know."

"Do you? I mean, you're older, more stable, sexy as fuck, and could probably find someone with less issues than me."

"You're just mysterious, that's all," I said. Hoped this would open up our communication, so that I could call Omar off the case. "But there's a lot about me you don't know either."

"But you know about Jabari," Jeremy said. "You know something's up with the car I asked you to store in your garage. You know I like to party, and drink, and smoke a little herb. You know I flake on you, and I don't really like your friend Ricky. If I were you, I don't know if I would put up with all my shit. You must really like me . . . or DaVon just put you through so much hell that my shit is like heaven."

"The things we endure for love, huh?"

We laughed and hugged. His hands slid down to magnum and brought it to life again. He looked at me and smiled.

"I'm sorry about that hallway wall scene last night," he said and kissed me. "I don't know if I was just horny, jealous seeing you with that brotha with the phat ride, or what. That's not me to force you . . . and sex, you know? We were role-playing, right?"

"Role-playing," I said. Question or statement? Not exactly sure how I meant it. "I don't know what it is . . ." Not sure exactly if my ambiguity was about last night's sex, or answering his question as to why I like him. Either way, Jeremy had me confused, yet turned on and attracted at the same time.

"Or is it that I can put it down in bed, and make you feel like you're twenty-one again?" Jeremy asked and laughed. "You're in it just for the sex, huh? Probably got you praising my name to Carlos and Ricky, huh?"

"Nah."

"Dirty old man," he said and laughed. "You got your Blatino boy toy and can call it a night, huh?"

"It's not just the sex," I said. "And I'd never call you a Blatino boy toy, because I don't see you in those terms. Unless you're looking to be exoticized."

"Then what is it?"

"I just like you. Hard to explain. Something about you, Jeremy."

"And this." He pulled my hand to magnum. Laughed. Even in our mature and private sharing moments, I was reminded that Jeremy was still developing into the man he was going to be. And that maybe years from now, he, or we, would look back and laugh at the fiery and confusing way we started out. "Wanna talk on the mic again?"

"You're bad," I said and tugged on magnum. "Of course I do."

"If I lived here, we could be like this all the time," Jeremy said. "That would be off the hook, huh?"

Uh, definitely not something in my plan. Living with another man, especially so soon after getting DaVon out my system. And even though my mom had left for Oakland, I hadn't grown so lonely that I needed constant companionship at my home. Moving in with someone required a little more feeling, and definitely a lot more time than Jeremy and I had known each other. Not gonna make the same quick move-in choice like I did with DaVon. And this wasn't a decision to be made in the middle of the night, when both of us were clouded by being horny and about to have sex again.

"You're kidding, aren't you, Jeremy?"

"What did you all say in the eighties? I'm serious as a heart attack," Jeremy said and chuckled. "Actually, it wasn't my idea. It was the other thing Eric said in the dream. That I gotta get away from the family and house in East Los for a while. See if I could move in here, to give you and me a chance. A *real* chance."

"Eric's quite the oracle, huh?" I said. "What he tell you about the party? The guy in the coma? Is everything going to work out?"

"We'll holla about that lata," he said. "But I know you must like being all independent, the got-yourself-together career man. It was just a thought—the moving in together thing."

"A serious thought from a prolific dream, huh?"

"Then I thought we could rent out the back house to my boys," he said. "But that's for thinking about later."

"Right," I said, feeling for the moment that I was dealing with a salesman, rather than a loverman. A defendant, rather than an almost boyfriend. "You think a lot in the middle of the night."

"Weird brain chemistry, I guess," Jeremy said. He kissed my forehead, cheek, neck. Magnum against my hip. Leg thrown over my hip, preparing for takeoff. Definitely trying to persuade me with the most primal incentive. "But at least think about it, boo."

"I'll think about it when you're ready to talk about the party," I said. "I have to deal with this at work, you know?"

"You sexy when you mad, Kenny," he said and kissed me.

"I never want you to be mad." Kiss. "Just let me love you." Kiss. "Is that all right?" Kiss. "Pweese, can I just love you and feel it back?" Kiss. "No questions?"

I glanced over at the digital clock on the nightstand, while Jeremy rolled on top of me. Almost five in the morning. Let myself be kissed, tasted, and desired by Jeremy for the next hour, both yelling out each other's names as the alarm clock went off and the KJLH Home Team greeted us with the early morning headlines, including another arson fire in East Los Angeles, authorities looking for a suspect (fitting Jeremy's description—sounds like a thousand other men in East Los) wanted in a dozen or so other mysterious fires in the area. And one more headline. This just in: Deathbed confession from CUELA student in coma.

Chapter 19

"Well, I think it's fucked up that you'd rat me out, Kenny, when you were at the same party."

Jabari wasn't having it.

Five minutes into the conversation, in which I was supposed to discipline him and his honor fraternity, Jabari rolled his eyes, laughed, and got up to leave.

I hated Allison Perez for putting me in this situation. Having to come down hard on one of my favorite students. Having to be a hypocrite. I was at the same party as Jabari and several other CUELA students, and they all knew it. So did Omar. But up to this point no one'd ratted me out or said anything about my presence. Not like I was an active participant. I was merely a guest of Jeremy's.

Besides, a student had died, and university administration had a lot of questions. And I was the one designated to get answers, and get them quick, before LAPD got involved. Allison had phoned me, well, warned me, in the morning, while I was dropping off Jeremy and before I'd arrived at the office. Once the case moved out of my office, and into the hands of legal authorities, there was no telling how big this would get. Luckily, Omar's intervention had kept my name out of everything. And the intervention of the president's office had kept the case and story out of the view of the media. For now.

"Jabari. Please. Sit."

"I don't want to sit."

"Jabari," I said and raised my voice.

I had thought Jabari of all people would be able to separate our professional relationship with me as advisor and staff member, from that of mentor, big brother, friend. Thought he'd be able to see I was just doing one aspect of my job. Yes, an aspect that he hadn't been on the receiving end of—discipline—but an important part of my job that he'd known and heard about. Gossip spread fast on campus, and especially among student organizations, when something went down with one of their peers. And now, sitting before an angry Jabari, I could imagine how quickly word would spread that I was suspending Jabari's group's recognition for the rest of the academic year, a crucial time with the spring budget and funding requests coming in a few weeks, and possibly for several years now that the CUELA freshman pledge had died. This suspension, no matter how long, would render Jabari's fraternity useless, null and void. Without university funding, which student organizations relied on, his group would struggle—even with membership dues coming in from new recruits and established members.

"I don't wanna sit, Kenny," Jabari said and ran his hand over his brand-new frohawk.

"I think you should," I said. "We're still in an official meeting."

"I thought we were boys," he said as he sat back down in the extra chair behind my desk, the one where he'd normally sit and dish with me, and not in the meeting chair across my desk where he was moments earlier. "You been there for me through everything since I been at CUELA."

"Look, I'll see what I can do to make this easy," I said. "But one of our students died, one of your brothers, and someone needs to talk. Before LAPD takes over. And they will."

"Ain't gonna be me," Jabari said.

"Jabari, I know it wasn't a party planned by our chapter, so that's a good thing," I said. "I just need to know what happened, and to what extent CUELA or your honor fraternity was involved. Besides, what would it hurt to talk? You'll be gone and out in the real world in a few months."

"Why don't you ask your boyfriend who brought you to the party?" Jabari said. "You can't make me talk, or punish me for the same thing you done. I could go straight to your boss, Allison, or to the president's office if I wanted to."

"You could."

Shit. Jabari was the type who would and could. He knew how to work in the system and, in turn, make it work for him. Such a miniature version of me, when I was a Northwestern undergrad. But I knew he wouldn't go to Allison or the president's office. I was Jabari's mentor, friend, and he had to know I was only doing my job. He was intelligent and knew how the system worked. Had to know how it was being under Allison's looking glass. Maybe not.

"And get that cheesy picture of me off your computer slide show," he said while glancing over my shoulder at my computer screen. Last thing on my mind. My brain was on getting Jabari and me out of this jam. Wasn't even prepared for what came next. "What *the fuck* are you doing with JJ?"

"What?"

"You and JJ? There." Jabari pointed at the screen. Mouth stuck in an O, eyes wide open.

I'd forgotten about the pictures of Jeremy and me by my truck the night we met at Ricky's birthday party, in Jeremy's bedroom before the frat party, at the party, that I'd saved on my hard drive. Pictures that automatically became part of the screensaver slide show on the computer monitor when there was no computer activity for several minutes.

"What are you and JJ doing together in those . . . Fuck, you are *not* the bitch JJ left me for," Jabari said and got up for a closer look at my computer. I jiggled the mouse so that the slide show would end, but it was too late. Jabari had gotten an eyeful of Kenny and Jeremy in all sorts of couplehood bliss. "You are one fucking hypocrite, Kenny."

Busted. Knew Jeremy and I needed to come clean to Jabari before Jabari found out. Didn't want this to come out as a surprise. Especially at an inopportune time . . . like this.

"Cradle-robbing hypocrite," Jabari shouted. "JJ is my *boy*friend."

"Your boyfriend? Impossible."

"You. Are. So. Busted." Jabari said, mouth ajar, almost forming a smile. "This is laughable. Where are the hidden cameras? I can't believe this shit."

I put my head down. Nodded. Felt bad. Knew nothing could remedy the situation.

"I found out after Jeremy and I got involved," I said. "I'm sorry, Jabari. I never meant—"

"You *are* sorry," Jabari said. "One sorry piece of shit who'd sell out one of his own students for a piece of ass. Befriend us all so you can wait in the wings to steal our boyfriends? How sick, you dirty old man."

"I had no clue you and Jeremy, JJ, whatever you call him, were together," I said. "You never mentioned a name."

"Right."

"He told me his ex was named Lalo," I said. "I didn't know Lalo was you. You running around like you're on *Alias* or something?"

"This is classic and oh-*so*-funny," Jabari said. "What else did he tell you? About me."

"Nothing."

"I'm sure he did. JJ's a fucking exaggerator and lying piece of shit. I'm sure he made up some story about how bad I was to him."

"No, not really."

"Yeah, right."

"I'm serious, Jabari. I didn't know about you and Jeremy."

"He tell you how he cheated on me over and over?" Jabari asked.

"No."

"How he gave me an STD?"

"No."

"More than once?"

"No."

"How he charged up all my credit cards to get his crazy-ass gangbanger brother out of jail?"

"No."

"He tell you I was crazy?" Jabari asked. "More like crazy for staying with his ass after he hit me. Crazy for putting up with his violent mood swings. Crazy for believing that he'd keep his dick in his pants. Crazy for staying with him after he forced himself on me time and time again, when I didn't want sex. Couldn't even wait to complete his STD meds before trying to sleep with me again. He tell you that?"

"Just a little bit," I said. "We never really focused on you. He said he was over his ex."

"He tell you how he fucked me hard the other day? The day after the party? How we laughed at how we helped each other escape the cops?" Jabari said. "How I put it on him good. I know you saw the hickeys. I. Did. That."

"Okay."

"I still turn him the fuck on," he said. "Just one word and I got him. Whenever I want."

Ouch. That hurt. I thought it was just some innocent making-out session, not full-on sex, when I confronted Jeremy about the marks on his neck.

"We need to calm down, Jabari," I said. "This meeting is not about Jeremy."

"It's exactly what this meeting is about," Jabari said and shoved the file of pictures and reports about the party off my desk and onto the floor. "So coming down on my group is more about you getting back at Jeremy's ex—me—than exhibiting sound judgment as a university administrator? I see how it is."

"These are two different things."

"I should kick your ass up and down this hallway," Jabari said and stood up in front of me, as if he were threatening me. I stood and faced him. Would defend myself if needed if he struck me. "But I'm not crazy, contrary to what Jeremy might have told you. I'm not getting kicked out of school for fighting you on university property. And my organization is not getting disciplined. We're not responsible, and I'm not taking the rap for that kid dying."

"It's my job."

"You should have *thought* about your job when you let yourself get sprung by Jeremy Lopez," Jabari said. "You should have *thought* about your job when you showed up at that fraternity party in Highland Park. I'm sure one of my boys got pictures."

"We're friends, Jabari."

"Think again, buddy." Jabari put on a fake smile and headed toward the door. "I can make lives and I can ruin them."

"Stop being so dramatic, Jabari. Let's talk this out."

"Fuck you, Kenny," he said. "We've got nothing to talk about. Unless you're talking about dropping this silly farce of a case against my fraternity. Or unless you're talking about giving me back my Jeremy."

"Okay, Jabari, I get the picture."

"I don't think you have the full picture," Jabari said. "But you will if you go forward with this case and try to question people. I know how much your job means to you . . . and from the look of those photos with you and JJ, I'm sure he's starting to mean a lot to you, too. Like you said, I'm graduating and out in a few months. I have nothing to lose."

"So what now?" I asked. "You really want things to go down like this?"

"It's up to you," Jabari said. "You're the adult. Figure it out."

"Jabari. Wait."

"And as for Jeremy, keep his sorry ass . . . for as long as he'll stay," Jabari said. "If he cheated to get with you, he'll cheat to leave you."

And like that, Jabari slipped out my office, slamming the door behind him. The stupid screensaver slide show popped up again, with pictures of Jeremy and me from the past few weeks. What a difference a few weeks had made. A few weeks ago I hadn't known Jeremy, hadn't known the happiness of being swept up in emotions, hadn't known the web of secrets I'd be wrapped up in, or the trouble those secrets could potentially get us into. Damn Jabari. Damn Jeremy. Damn this job.

Damn this job.

Yes, there was a way out of this situation.

I left work early. Told Carlos and my supervisor, Allison, that I wasn't feeling well. I wasn't. Had plenty of sick time to use.

Took a long drive around L.A., freeway hopped, going from CUELA to Hollywood, Hollywood to Inglewood, Inglewood to UCLA. Finally ended up at Santa Monica Pier, walking along the beach. Chilly afternoon. Cloudy outside. Like my mind.

Didn't want to think about Jeremy, Jabari, my job, and the million questions, suspicions, and allegations swirling around me. Not to mention DaVon, the upcoming court hearings, what would happen to my mentoring at Big Brothers/Big Sisters if this got out, and even Omar's investigation into Jeremy. And most importantly, that a student had died, because of being hazed or drinking too much at a party I, too, had attended, though I'd had no clue what was going on in the den of sin. But couldn't help it. Needed to sort through my life. Figure things out. Needed to make sure what I planned to do would be the solution to my problems.

Chapter 20

"I oughta fly back out there and slap you upside your head."

Mom, in her usual off-the-cuff style, thought I was stupid and wasted no time in telling me so. She was probably right. I caught her on the phone just before she was starting to cook dinner for my sister Cecily's family in Oakland. I sat in my kitchen, in front of an empty Styrofoam container of Chinese takeout, staring into the backyard and at the empty back house where my mom had been staying just a few weeks earlier.

"So you don't think that would work?" I asked. "Then what? Things are pretty messed up, and I don't want to get fired."

"I wouldn't quit just to get out of it," she said. "You look them in the eye and deny it. Ain't that what your boy Bill Clinton said back in the day?"

My plan was simple. Resign. Make it effective immediately. Leave the discipline of Jabari and his group to someone else. Maybe he'd rat me out, but by then, I'd be long gone and still have my vacation pay coming to me, even though I might have to answer questions by LAPD. Maybe not, if Omar could keep his colleagues off my back. And I could even cash out my retirement, including CUELA's contribution, and live off that until I found another university gig.

That's if another university would take me on after this scandal. Would also give me time to focus on me, Jeremy, and figuring out if dating him was worth the trouble. Well, I knew the answer. But I still felt something for the boy.

"Obviously you haven't listened to yourself," my mom said. "You better not give up your life over a man, a *boy*, who's done nothing but bring you heartache and pain. Remember the white lady law, Kenny. You're not a long-suffering heroine. You don't have trust funds to support your angst and confusion. You can't afford the luxury of thought."

"I know."

"Then act like it," she said. "I'd expect this kind of poor decision-making from Tonya or Cecily, but not you."

"We all are entitled to one mistake," I said. "Besides, Tonya and Cecily are doing well with their lives."

"One mistake?" Mom said and sighed. Obviously didn't want to get into sibling bashing at this point. Only Kenny bashing. "I told you the first night, when you told me about his drinking and carrying on, that boy was nothing but trouble. I could tell he wasn't worth nothing, how he put the covers over his head like he couldn't even greet me proper. Mama knows."

"At least give him the benefit of the doubt for being sleepy."

"Excuses, Kenny," she said. "And now you're being blackmailed by Jeremy's ex? And you think Jeremy might be an arsonist, or at least connected? And you think he might have been involved in that student's death? Or at least he probably knows what really happened at some stupid kid party he took you to? Kenny Kane, I know you better than that. Is it just the sex? You going through one of those third-life crises they talk about on talk shows? Honey, get help, but don't get sucked in by this Jeremy kid. Hell, with DaVon it was only the women and babies. You were handling that well and put him out anyway. And now you're willing to go through the fire for some boy you barely know? Like I said, I should fly down there and slap you upside the head."

"Well, I better go," I said. Knew she was right in her own way, but something about Jeremy just kept me wanting and hating him at the same time. Actually, wanting more. "I have a million things to do and think about."

"Fine, baby," she said. "Didn't mean to upset you."

"It's okay. It's your job, Mom."

"I'm just saying, it's about equally yoked relationships these days," she said. "One person shouldn't be having all the fun while the other one does all the work and is paying for that fun."

"All right, bye. I'll talk to you later."

"Bye."

Mom had a point. It was something we'd always had instilled in us. That whomever we ended up dating or marrying, it should be someone who's willing to stand side by side, as an equal contributor and equal benefactor, in the relationship.

"Relationships are more than just who looks cute or who is funny," Mom said as Tonya, Cecily, and I sat at the dinner table six months after our father went to Mississippi. I was fifteen, Tonya was ten, Cecily six. "I married your father because he loved to have a good time. And we did have lots of good times before he went back home. Just remember that it's not just about having fun. I know you don't like the nerdy types, but those are the ones you'll appreciate years down the road. Marriage is about long-term investment. Who's going to be there, and give you a good life, for more than a couple months or a few years. You want something equally yoked when you finally settle down."

She ended her first marriage to our father once he moved away, and soon remarried, though now this marriage was facing similar challenges and causing her to travel across the country to spend time with my sisters and me.

I wondered if the equally yoked concept applied to age and ethnicity, too. If I was spending too much time trying to be a teacher and mentor type in both my professional and personal life. If I was a little bit too color blind.

And I wondered, if I was considering such a drastic measure such as quitting my job because of all that meeting Jeremy had brought upon my life, should he be part of the decision making? Should I have him sitting around this kitchen table with me, right now, hashing out everything, from Jabari to the Civic hiding in my backyard, from his drinking and smoking to his sleeping with Jabari recently? And was that allegation they'd slept together, rather than merely made out, just part of Jabari's game to try and gain a mental edge over me in the discipline hearing? And then I wondered, how stupid is it to give up a job to cover up my being a hypocrite and for falling for a twenty-one-year-old? A twenty-one-year-old with charm, looks, smarts, edge, and skills in bed that won't quit. A twenty-one-year-old who could easily have his pick of anyone out on the scene, who didn't need to be saddled down with a thirty-three-year-old unemployed university professional, and who, if he left, would have made all this job-quitting drama worthless. Where was Jeremy, by the way? Hadn't heard from him all day.

And then I wondered why I was confusing the two situations. Jabari's discipline and party situation had nothing to do with my Jeremy situation. That was a manipulation on Jabari's part. They're separate situations, interconnected very loosely.

Continued making a list of the pros and cons of quitting my job, being involved with Jeremy, and committing myself to doing something else. Maybe moving to another city? Starting the young adult community space?

Tired of being the good boy, the logical one, the one who always comes to the rescue for other people, and the one who plays it safe, I knew what I needed and wanted to do.

Quit.

Chapter 21

I arrived at my office a little before six in the morning, racing the sun as it rose over the San Gabriel Valley. Wanted to pack the things in my office, load them up in my baby, and drop off my resignation letter before a lot of students or colleagues came by asking questions.

The students, I would miss. Carlos, too, though I imagined our friendship would continue even though I was no longer part of his professional world. Wouldn't miss Allison Perez at all. At. All. Almost wanted to go off on her Jabari style, but knew I needed to work in this town and in this field, student affairs, again. Couldn't burn the bridge completely, but could loosen a few cables. I knew about Rolando, her husband. Talk about the possibility for a *Dynasty* ending.

My work at the university had always been an important part of my life. Stumbled across student affairs and higher education completely by accident. No one wakes up, say, in third grade, aspiring to be an out-of-the-classroom university professional. When I was an undergraduate at Northwestern, and very much an obnoxious, but with potential, student leader like Jabari, I had wonderful mentors who showed me the ropes of university life and life in general. Found people who took an interest in the working-class black kid from Ohio, who kept me on the right path, and influenced my coming-of-age years in Chicagoland. Started out simply as a floor representative for my freshman residence hall, then on to writing for the *Daily Northwestern*, a stint as a senator in student government, president of the Multicultural Journalism Association, working as an R.A. in the same building I lived in freshman year, and before you know it, four years is almost up, the early career choices you thought were important turned out not to be, and an advisor in the Student Leadership office pulls you aside with an opportunity to go to Indiana University for graduate school, tuition free and with a little bit of pay, if you study higher educational leadership and agree to do similar kinds of work you did as an undergrad, but only on a more professional level, with the undergrads at IU. Well, how cool was that?

And with no real focus or desire to pursue journalism, communications, or teach English literature at a high school level, I went for it, fell in love with the field student affairs, and seven years later, found myself staring at a wall full of plaques, awards, photos of the various student leaders I'd mentored and seen develop at CUELA, and my degrees. Not that I was obnoxious about having Northwestern and Indiana backing up my credentials. More to show faculty, who didn't quite see you as a student, but not quite a professional peer either.

Nonetheless, staring at my office wall and the empty boxes I trudged from my car this morning, I couldn't help but feel a little nostalgic about CUELA, how much my life had changed during the seven years I'd worked at the university, and that I was giving it all up for bad judgment . . . in men? In party choices? In supervisors?

Cue up the violins, rewind the tape, Young and the Restless/*Nikki Newman–style, for a trip down memory lane. Look longingly at each photograph with students, colleagues, and guest speakers you've brought to CUELA, caress each picture slowly, let one tear well up in the corner of your left eye, and remember the great events, the smiles, the milestones, the love and respect that brought you together for the pictures. Wonder why you wore certain outfits or certain hairstyles. Reminisce on the time with Jeremy, the laughs, the kisses, the conversations, the sex. Oh, the sex. Think about the students whose lives you'd affected, the awards ceremonies, the graduations, and how DaVon respected, but never really appreciated all you did in your university career. Wonder if this would be happening had you not met Jeremy, or if you'd kissed up and played white-lady-law politics with Allison.* Not. This was real life and a real decision I'd made. Dramatic, maybe. But definitely not a soap.

It's amazing how long it takes your office to look and feel like home, and amazing how quickly your boxes can be packed, the walls can be emptied, and the computer files of your original work and desktop pictures (those damn desktop pictures Jabari *had* to see and use as leverage against me) can be transferred to zips and memory sticks in the still of the morning, before anyone has arrived or phones started to ring. Cart loaded. Resignation letter done, placed in envelope, and laid on top of the computer keyboard. Keys left next to letter. Lights off. Cart tugged. Note the time. Just before seven.

"You can't do this, Kenny."

Carlos dressed in his overnight sweats, hair untouched by product, grabbed my arm and pulled me back into my office.

"How did you know I was here?" I asked.

"Your mother called me. Don't ask how she found my number. She told me you're quitting your job over that party?"

"Yep. I'm out."

"Kenny, that's stupid," Carlos said. "You didn't do anything. You were there, but you didn't see what was happening with that student. You're not responsible, and it's better you just 'fess up to Allison and deal with the university rather than deal with LAPD's murder investigation, which no doubt this will turn into later today. At least you'd have university counsel on your side to protect you."

"I know. I've thought of it."

"So I don't understand."

"It's just a big mess and I don't want to deal," I said. "Maybe Jeremy's not the best, but he's what I've got right now."

"Reality check, Kenny," Carlos said. "It's been a few weeks since you've known him."

"Whatever."

"Don't put your professional life in jeopardy because of Jeremy."

Explained everything. The good: Jeremy's charm, sex, wit, humor, our chemistry together. The bad: Jabari, the car, the party (at least what I knew), how quickly we'd fallen for each other. The ugly: the murky sex scene the other day, Jeremy's reluctance to open up about his mysteries, how long I could realistically live off retirement savings and vacation-time payout, how much I craved, loved, desired Jeremy's intense attraction for me, and that I needed Jeremy in order to finally move on from DaVon. Because deep inside, I still cared for DaVon.

Somewhere between a romantic caring that was dwindling each day, and a caring for him as a human being. Six, almost seven years, of being with DaVon, knowing him so intimately, loving his positive traits, and respecting his flaws, I wouldn't be human if I stopped caring. He had pride and ambition in himself and his career as a firefighter, and those were two traits I loved most in a partner. Early on, he introduced me to his main colleagues in his firehouse, and then the Stentorians, the L.A. County Black Firefighters Association, and I went to the picnics, community service and career days, and parades along with the other partners, mostly wives, who understood firefighter life. He was proud of his work life and our life together, even when colleagues would give him a blank look when he explained *how* we were partners.

Even in the face of discrimination. Most of all, DaVon stayed. He was the first one who stayed with me, and didn't go away when he got bored with the familiar, like the others before him. Like my father. Not that I was dwelling on daddy abandonment issues. Far from it.

Knew I needed to take the same kind of pride in my career. At least influence the direction it would go, rather than wait for outside forces to guide it.

An hour later, Carlos and I were sitting in Allison's office, with the CUELA president, university legal counsel, and a couple legal representatives and administrators from ELAJ, Jeremy's school. Reluctantly, I shared what I observed and knew from the night in question, but nothing about my dating relationship with Jeremy (not sure how much I needed to confess). Said that I had been only an invited guest, but didn't know I would be attending a fraternity party, never made it to the den of sin, and therefore had no firsthand knowledge of what led the student to overdose on alcohol and eventually die. The CUELA team appeared relieved that the majority of the burden seemed to lie with ELAJ's chapter for planning and initiating the party and the activities that took place, even though our campus took the bigger loss—a student's life—and would have to work with the parents and university public affairs on CUELA image management issues. Meant I could deliver the news to Jabari that he was off the hook for now.

Saw the ELAJ team shuffle through the files and reports again. Their lead legal representative took out five pictures. Nacho. Tony. Daniel. Slimer. Jeremy. Said they'd need to get to the guys before LAPD came knocking. I chimed in that those guys were merely attending the party, but not the planners. Felt stupid when they quoted my words that I'd seen the five of them go into the den of sin. Should have kept my mouth shut. Forgot that Jeremy had escaped out the back fence and alley when the party was raided. Odds were the police had no record of him even attending, since he wasn't part of the group of students arrested. Knew the brotherhood would pull through for each other.

But it was too late to take my words back.

I'd ratted the guys out, but saved my job and professional life in the process.

Chapter 22

Once back in my office, I knew I had to get serious about my job again. At least while I had one. Luckily, Allison Perez hadn't fired me, nor had I turned in my resignation letter, thanks to Carlos. So, while I had a job, I had to deal with business at hand, which meant tending to Jabari and his organization—putting them on temporary probation with the university and helping the members cope with the death of their fraternity brother.

I sent a quick text message to Jeremy while waiting for Jabari to stop by my office: ELAJ LAPD 2 ? U n Boys FYI

Felt that was the least I could do, give Jeremy and friends a heads-up, since they'd probably end up in cuffs, on the six o'clock news, or worse before the end of the day. And then, if Carlos and Ricky were right about the arson allegations, Jeremy'd be in even more trouble before the end of the day. If I'd just kept my mouth shut, not said anything. Too late to turn back now. Knew then I was caring for him just a little too much, what "ride or die" meant, what Bonnie and Clyde syndrome was all about.

"I hear you wanted to see me?" Jabari stood in the doorway. "You figure it out like I said?"

"Jabari. Sit."

Jabari looked around, shut the door, and walked over to the chair across from my desk. "You leaving or something?"

"No," I said. Didn't want to let Jabari know I'd actually considered quitting my job due to his attempt to blackmail me. "Just redecorating."

"Interesting thing to do in the midst of an alleged hazing investigation," he said. "So what's up?"

"I'll get to the point."

"Please do. I have more important things to do."

"Jabari. Stop. Just listen."

I explained the organization would be on probation for a quarter, wouldn't lose its recognition with CUELA, and would be eligible to apply for emergency funding later in the next school year if needed. In exchange for the lightened punishment, the frat would additionally be required to do a couple hundred hours of community service with a community organization focused on alcohol education and youth. He sat. Listened for a minute. Looked at me.

"I know you can do better than this, Kenny."

"Jabari. You lost a fraternity brother. Don't be a . . . You're lucky you're not being hauled off to prison. Or worse."

"You tell them about you and Jeremy?"

"None of your business, but yes."

"And you still get to keep your job?" Jabari asked. "No fair. All of you administrators are the same. Just out for yourselves."

"Don't worry about me right now, Jabari," I said. "How are you guys holding up? Need anything from me?"

"We're fine." Jabari folded his arms in front of his chest. "Don't need your help."

"Talked to the boys at ELAJ?"

"A little. Not Jeremy, but the others."

Felt a little weird, having Jeremy's name come up. The boy I'd "stolen" from one of my students. The boy who got us all caught up in this situation.

"Is this all? I don't need your counseling act, Kenny."

"Fine. Just trying to help."

"You've helped enough."

"You're lucky you're not the ELAJ chapter," I said. "I actually looked out for you. LAPD is following up with them. Doesn't look good."

"Oooooh," Jabari said as he stood up and walked to the office door. "So you'll lose him to the system, rather than another man. How cool is that?"

Watched him walk away. Not the way I wanted things to be between Jabari and me. Tense. Awkward. Feeling like the other was the enemy or competition. Maybe time would help us heal our relationship. But for now, it was stuck and going nowhere fast. Much like Jeremy.

"Knock. Knock."

I looked up. Jeremy. Looking good as always. Nike athletic suit. Sunglasses. Nike hat to the back. Backpack straps over his shoulders. Smiling ear to ear.

"What are you doing here? Did you run into Jabari?"

I walked across the room and shut the office door. Jeremy locked it. Dropped his backpack. Stared at me.

"You're in trouble, Mr. Kane."

"I know. I'm sorry."

"You sold me out."

"I tried to text you to give you a heads-up."

"You have to pay," Jeremy said and stepped toward me. Looked angry. Pushed me on the shoulder with each step he made forward, until I reached the front of my desk. "No one sells me out."

"So what happened? Can I do anything?"

"This."

Jeremy leaned in and kissed me. Pressed against me until we were both pushed up on the edge of the desk. My hands exploring his back, knocking off his hat, running my fingers through his hair, calling out his name.

"You missed me, huh?" Jeremy said and smiled. "And I thought I was the only horny one in this relationship."

"You know you turn me on."

"So why the fuck it's been a minute since you seen me?"

Jeremy said and got up off me. Sat in the chair in front of my desk, adjusting magnum around inside his boxers. "I thought you'd sold me out for that dude in the truck you had dinner with."

"Omar? Please. I told you."

"Or I thought you got scared when I said I should move in with you."

"Jeremy. Stop. Listen." I sat on the edge of the desk in front of Jeremy. "Aren't you the least bit concerned that one of your new pledges died as a result of that party? I thought you were mad because I ended up having to talk about what I knew about that night."

"Which is nothing, right?" Jeremy asked. "I don't know anything. I ain't even see that kid while I was up in the little room."

"Well, LAPD's on the way to ELAJ to question you and your boys."

"Let them question," Jeremy said. "I have nothing to share. But to answer your question, I *am* concerned that a pledge died."

"So you do have a conscience."

"And a heart," Jeremy said. "I know things seem weird. But I care about you, too. Don't ask me why. I want to make things right. Wanna make this work."

I kneeled in front of Jeremy. He pulled on the waistband of his track suit and started to take magnum out, thinking I was about to go to work on him. I patted his hand, shook my head no, and looked into Jeremy's eyes.

"If we're gonna make this work, that's a big if, we need to come clean about everything," I said. "And not just have sex to shut me up."

"That all you think I want? Sex?"

"Sometimes."

"Then you don't really know me," Jeremy said. "But if it's what you want, I'll talk. Tell you anything and everything you want to know."

"Thank you."

"But not here," he said. "Your place. Tonight. After work and school. If that's cool. I'll call and bus over to your place."

"Whatever works."

He pulled my face to his. Kissed slowly. Like I'd taught him. After twenty minutes, felt like we were in my truck, his room, my house, anywhere but my office. Kept it innocent. But soon he left for his day at ELAJ and I continued my workday, confident that Jeremy and I were moving forward once we put the incidents of the past weeks and our rocky beginning behind us.

Chapter 23

When DaVon and I were together, and it was one of his days off, I used to love him greeting me after my workday with a clean house, dinner made, music by one of our favorite old school artists in the background. He'd listen to me vent about my boss-of-the-month, student drama, and politics at CUELA. He'd make me something to sip on before dinner. He'd rub my back, shoulders, or feet. He'd ask me to guess what he cooked for dinner, since cooking was something he loved to do—for our household or the guys at the firehouse. Sometimes we wouldn't even make it to the dinner table. DaVon, like the others before him, could charm me out of my clothes and into bed before I knew what was happening. Had no problem channeling my hunger for food into DaVon. Was willing to break him off whenever he wanted. Loved pleasing him and being pleased by him. Loved our black-on-black love story in L.A. The firefighter and the university administrator. Who'd have thought?

The thoughts of DaVon and me came as quite a surprise. I'd just left a stressful day at CUELA, which included an official discipline letter from Allison Perez—probation—delivered as I was walking out the door, and stopped by Costco to pick up a pizza, a box of Heineken, and a couple new video games for Jeremy's Game Boy Advance. Looked forward to a fun evening, a date, where Jeremy and I would start anew, fresh, like we were strangers and hadn't faced the challenges and situations we had of the past weeks since we met.

Nonetheless, DaVon kept popping into my head as I drove from Costco to my house. Thinking about his hands, dark skin, solid body, and how surprised I'd been when, after our initial setup meeting with Carlos and Ricky, DaVon had called me back for a second date. A one-on-one date. Thought that all my intellectual banter and enthusiasm about my career in student affairs would have bored him—he who had been star athlete and voted most popular and best looking in high school—and never been enough to attract him for a repeat outing. How wrong I was and had been all along. Later, found out that it had indeed been my intelligence, coupled with a little bit of naïveté about the ways of the world and men, that had reeled him in.

Juxtaposed this with thoughts of Jeremy and how once again I'd found myself attracted to and involved with an opposite, but this time with age being added to the formula. My attraction to bad boys, athletic boys, bullies, those who were not quite my equal in some areas, but beyond me in others, was something I never quite understood, even after regular analysis and self-talk.

What I came to understand as I pulled into my driveway was that telepathy was indeed real.

"Your ears must have been burning," I said as I got out my truck. "I was just thinking about you."

I was pleasant. Surprised to see DaVon sitting on the bench of my front porch. He smiled. I smiled back. No need for drama, despite the obvious things he and I could have argued about right away. Kids. Women. Money. Those kinds of things. I hadn't seen him since the night of Ricky's birthday party and his three-in-the-morning visit. The same night I'd met Jeremy.

"I heard about your situation," DaVon said. "Figured you might need a friend. I thought this would be a decent hour to come over."

He stood and walked toward me and my truck. Loved

how he filled out his gray T-shirt with black LAFD logo emblazoned across the line of his well-sculpted chest. Loved the biceps, looking like they'd been blasted in his supersets workout routine. Loved how his package dangled in the front of his sweatpants. I opened the back door of the driver's side, and DaVon leaned in and scooped up the box of goods from Costco in one arm, the pack of Heineken in the other hand. I grabbed the pizza sitting in the back passenger side.

"I'm surprised to see you," I said. "You look good. How's the wife and kids?"

"Uh, a'ight, don't really want to talk about them," he said and checked out my purchases. "Expecting little Ricky Martin?" He laughed as he walked to the front door.

"His name is Jeremy, and yeah, he's stopping by tonight after school and stuff."

"After school and stuff," DaVon mocked. "Cute. Hope the younger, newer model rides as well as the one you traded in."

"I could say the same about Vanessa," I said and opened the door. Let DaVon go in first. "But I am not looking for a fight or anything."

"Good, because I didn't come here to fight," DaVon said as he put the box on the island counter in the middle of the kitchen. "I'm a lover, not a fighter."

We laughed, and I said, "Please, DaVon. What's up? What brings you to the lovely San Gabriel Valley?"

"First, I think Ricky and Carlos are wrong about Jeremy and the arson thing," he said. "I'll give you credit for not getting involved with a criminal, though I've heard about his shadiness."

"Okay," I said. Started putting the beer in the fridge. "You want one?"

"Don't you need it to seduce your boy toy?" DaVon chuckled. "Just kidding. Sure."

"Maybe I'm trying to seduce you and get revenge on Vanessa," I said and chuckled. "Just kidding. Jeremy's going to call when he's on his way."

Handed DaVon two Heinekens and he used the opener at the island counter for his and mine. Put the pizza in the oven. Put the three new games for Jeremy in my room. DaVon's eyes were on me as I walked back into the kitchen.

"You still running?"

"Of course. Gotta keep myself in shape for my young one."

"Looking good still," he said and smiled. Took a long swallow of his beer. "Thanks for the drink."

I sat at the counter next to him. Toasted. "I never expected us to be sitting in the kitchen again. Together. After work. Talking."

"Especially after the 'paper or plastic' incident." DaVon laughed. "I can't believe you put me out."

"You deserved it," I said. "I couldn't take one more surprise. One more baby. DaVon, if you were in the same situation, you'd do the same thing."

"I'm sorry," he said. Looked sincere. "I fucked up. My head was all screwed up. Sometimes still is. I don't love Vanessa, but I love my kid with her. And the kid with Kenyatta."

Rolled my eyes as I thought about being served in my office for Kenyatta's custody and support hearing. I said, "Wrap it up and you won't have these problems with paternity tests and kids popping up all over L.A."

"It's hard," DaVon said. "I loved you, Kenny. I'm not DL. I know I'm bi. I like women and men. I haven't lied once to Vanessa or any woman I've been with. I know I fucked up a good thing with you and I'm so sorry." He finished up the rest of his Heineken. "Can I get another one?"

"Sure," I said. "You know where I put them."

"Still keep my seven and seven ingredients in the family room bar?" DaVon smiled and nodded.

"Yeah."

"I think I'll have one of those instead," he said as he walked over to the family room. I stayed in the kitchen and checked on the oven. Looked at the phone on the wall, pressed to check caller ID. No Jeremy. Made sure my cell was on ring mode, and not vibrate. Started talking to me from the other room, "So I came over to tell you something. I think you'll be pleasantly surprised."

"What's that?" I enjoyed our pleasantries and our drama-free conversation, but knew I'd need some time to shower and clean up before Jeremy. Still waiting on his call. A text message at least.

"Well one, you heard about the individual discrimination lawsuits against LAFD and the city? The one black guy and the black woman who happens to be a lesbian?"

"Yeah. I saw that press conference with the black firefighters association." I hated yelling from one room to the next.

"The Stentorians, right," he said. "Well, I'm joining a class action lawsuit against the city and the department. Racial discrimination. Retaliation for filing a complaint. False evaluations by my supervisor."

"That's big," I said and sipped on my beer. Checked on the pizza. "I remember you telling me about that one supervisor, just before we broke up."

"He's still an ass."

"Are they giving you a hard time on the job because of it? For going against the brotherhood?"

"No more. No less. Nothing that DaVon Holloway can't handle."

"Handle it, DaVon." I smiled. That was one of my favorite lines to DaVon when we were sleeping together.

"Another thing," DaVon said from the family room. "Kenyatta and I settled out of court."

"Really? So all that being served at my office with your court case was for nothing?"

"Don't trip," DaVon said as he entered the kitchen. Made himself a tall seven and seven. Looked more brown than clear. Obviously settling in and getting comfortable, despite my telling him Jeremy was expected over. Took a long swallow before setting it down on the counter. "I got a raise and can send a little more to Ke'Von each month. That's all Kenyatta wanted, a few extra bucks a month. It's cool. You don't have to testify for me. I know how much you looked forward to putting in a good word for your ex." Clinked his glass against my beer, which I hadn't taken but two small sips from. Wanted to save my evening buzz for Jeremy, not shooting the breeze with DaVon.

"Well, that's good news. You could have told me this over the phone."

"Can't I come see you?" DaVon asked. "We spent six, almost seven, years together. You'll always be my boy, Kenny. We're still tight, right?"

"Don't you have a wife and kid to be tight with?"

"You always gotta bring that up," he said and smiled. "I'm here to be with you. Not talk about Vanessa and my babies." He looked down. Swirled his drink around and watched the ice twirl like a tornado. "I miss you."

Not what I wanted to hear. Not wanting a confession like this.

"DaVon," I said. Sounded like I was whining. Just like the night of his surprise visit after Ricky's party. "This is not good. Let's change the subject."

"I miss you. That is a fact that is not going to change, whether I talk about it now or you change the subject."

I looked at the oven. Got up to check on the pizza. "Well, thanks. I guess. You're full of surprises, DaVon."

"You miss me, don't you?" he asked. "Even a little bit?"

"I think about you sometimes," I said. "But I'm in a new situation now."

"With Jeremy? Or Omar Etheridge?"

"Omar? That was just dinner. Jeremy's who I'm with."

"Omar e-mailed me at work," DaVon said and took a swallow of his drink. "Kinda hinted that it might be something more."

"There is something more, but it's not what you think. I asked him to do some work for me."

"Never trust a cop," DaVon said and chuckled. "Isn't that one of your mom's white-lady-law sayings?"

I laughed and took the pizza out. Set it on a cooling rack. "You're funny, DaVon."

"We always had fun together."

We did. True. Before the other women. Before the paternity tests. Before things got crazy. A couple years ago, DaVon Holloway and Kenny Kane were in the running for Mr. Gay Black America couple of the year. Funny how things changed. Now, we were both involved in relationships with people of Mexican descent, though Jeremy was also half Dominican. *So* L.A. and West Coast. He had kids to take care of. I had a kid, so to speak, who was taking care of business. I looked at DaVon across the kitchen and started one of my Nikki Newman/*Young and the Restless*, stroll-down-memory-lane moments, reminiscing on our good times, our laughs, silly times with our couple best friends Carlos, Ricky, and the other firefighter couples, the ways DaVon put it down in the bedroom, his first time telling me he loved me, and other random thoughts of our years together.

"Kenny, your cell." DaVon held up my phone. "Probably Ricky Martin on the line."

"His name is Jeremy, duh," I said and made a face at DaVon and looked at the phone screen. Jeremy. I smiled. "I'll be back. Help yourself to pizza. Can't drink on an empty stomach."

"Don't worry about me. Go talk to lover boy."

Picked up on the third ring. Told Jeremy to hold on a minute. Needed to get situated, which I did. Flopped in the middle of my bed. Set the cell by my right side. Put Jeremy on speaker. Left hand down my pants. Big smile on my face, as my man was finally calling and probably close to my house.

"Hey, sexy," I said. "Where you at? I can't wait for you to come."

"Damn," he groaned. "That's kinda sweet. What you up to?"

"Just laying in bed. Thinking about you. Touching myself."

"Niiiiice."

"So you on your way over?"

"Nah," he said. "Uh, something came up, unfortunately. School. Study group. I forgot."

"Are you serious, Jeremy?"

"Yeah, I'm sorry," he said. Paused. "You mad?"

I didn't say anything for a few seconds. "Not mad. Just disappointed. I was really wanting to see you tonight. I'm feeling kinda like playing with magnum."

"Damn, that's kinda tight," Jeremy chuckled. "Raincheck?"

"Do I have a choice?"

"You always got a choice."

"Miss your sexy body, your fat magnum, wanna feel you come inside."

"Damn, what's got into you?" Jeremy asked, trying to match my voice, slow, sexy. "I can't promise, but I'll try. I'll holla at you in a minute."

"Well, if it's tonight or tomorrow, I'll be here waiting," I said. "Can't wait to see you, pa."

"Mmmmm, this is hard."

"Is it? I bet."

"I'ma get back to the books. Talk later."

"Bye."

"Bye."

Pressed the button to hang up, but had trouble turning off the phone. Apparently the same problem Jeremy was having with his phone.

"Naw, nigga, he believes everything I say. I get over on him all the time . . . That's how it is with old dudes like him. Turn 'em out, make 'em feel young and sexy again, and get what you want . . . Hell naw, ain't looking to settle with any niggas now. It's just a dick thang. I don't feel anything for him . . .

I'm fucking you tonight, nigga . . . Let me call Slimer back and ditch him, too . . . Hello . . . Hello . . ."

"Hello?"

"Oh, shit . . ."

"Oh, shit is right, Jeremy."

Chapter 24

Four seven and sevens, three Heinekens, two slices of pizza each, and a long kiss later, DaVon and I found ourselves in familiar territory that hadn't been explored in almost six months. My bedroom. Our old bedroom.

I'd forgotten how much I craved his L.L.-like body, and his skin the color and sweetness of maple syrup. How he'd eat down below like it was Sunday dinner and I had a nonstop buffet to offer. How much I loved the musky, sensuous smell his body gave when in the middle of making love. How I loved bringing him to attention with my tongue, hearing him moan and feeling him palm the back of my head. How his big hands caressed me gently, and pressed me down against the sheets when needed. How much larger he expanded just a minute before the end came. How he loved me to beg him on harder, to call him every profane and vulgar fantasy name I could conjure up, to dig my hands into his muscular back and shoulders and hold on for life. How, at that moment of release, he could channel the deepness of Barry White's voice, and groan and grunt in pain and agony. How he'd shake and shiver when done. How he'd hold me, kiss me, keep me warm with his body pressed against mine, his arms wrapped around me like he'd never leave me for anyone else. How, sometimes, after we were done, we'd hum along to Anita, or Teena, or Kem, or Sade, or the Isleys before calling it a night.

Those things I'd forgotten until that moment, when I looked up at the ceiling, felt DaVon's hot body on top of mine, light sweat gluing us together, and heard his light snoring begin. What I'd forgotten about being with DaVon, and what I wanted to forget about being played by Jeremy, wasn't a memory. It was my life.

"DaVon, wake up," I said. "You have to get home."

"I don't wanna go home," he mumbled. "I'm staying with you tonight."

"DaVon."

"Kenny, shhhh. Just go to sleep."

"Are you still buzzed? Can you drive?"

"Shhhh. Talk too much. Probably why I'm here and Jeremy's not. You talk the fellas outta your life."

"Fuck you."

"Can I again?" He propped himself off me and looked in my eyes.

"Uh, no. Don't think so."

"You enjoyed it."

"True."

"You missed me as much as I missed you," he said. "And don't blame it on the liquor, Kenny."

"True."

"So just shut up, and enjoy having a real man in your bed again."

"You have Vanessa. I have Jeremy."

"We got each other right now."

He kissed me, a light peck on the mouth. I'd almost forgotten how after waking up after his post-sex nap, he'd roll over to face the window, turn his back to me, and fall asleep again, while I grabbed towels to clean up.

I couldn't make myself remain in the same bed as DaVon that night. Too many memories flooded back to my mind, reminding me of what we used to have, and how tempting it could be to forgive, forget, and forge ahead with a reconciliation. Granted, there were other important factors in the picture—Vanessa, the kids, Kenyatta, Jeremy. But for a moment, I let myself drift into the fantasy of a DaVon and Kenny reunion, until I thought—rebound sex doesn't make for a relationship reunion. No matter how good it is.

Moved to the sofa in the den. Buried myself under a comforter I'd grabbed from a hallway closet. Decided to turn on my cell, check for calls or messages from Jeremy. Wanted to hear from him. Anything. That what I'd overheard was a mistake or a joke. Or he was talking about someone else, some other Kenny. Yeah, right. I'd heard exactly what Jeremy said: *I get over on him all the time . . . That's how it is with old dudes like him. Turn 'em out, make 'em feel young and sexy again, and get what you want . . . I don't feel anything for him.*

And it was obvious from the missed-calls list on the cell that Jeremy meant exactly what he said. No calls, messages, or texts. And it was obvious that he, too, was out committing adultery that night. Just like me.

Chapter 25

"So you getting back with DaVon or what?"

Carlos and I were eating lunch at Happy Family, a vegetarian Chinese restaurant in Monterey Park, not too far from campus. Knew that I had to start getting my life back in order. No time to feel sorry for myself and cry over Jeremy, even though he was in my thoughts like all the time. No need to consume myself with workplace drama, even though the fraternity hazing incident was still a major part of my to-do list. And though I had a million other things to worry about, like my parents, like sleeping with DaVon, like getting Jeremy out my system, I knew one constant that had been around but I'd let get strained was Carlos. Decided to reach out. Make some kind of amends.

"Definitely not."

"It's so obvious you and DaVon still have feelings."

I picked at a couple chunks of fake orange chicken, before replying, "I'll admit it was nice."

"And?"

"You know what else," I said. "He's married. And I can't just turn off feelings for Jeremy like that."

"What's that thing your mom does?" Carlos said and rubbed his thumb and forefinger together. "The littlest violin thing? Not that I'm advocating adultery, but that marriage was a sham from the beginning and you know it."

"True. But, whatever. It's reality now. If DaVon and Vanessa break up, it should be because of *their* problems, and not because of me."

"I'm sure Vanessa had the same amount of concern for you when she was fucking your man when he was your man."

Ouch. True. Carlos was right.

"Anyway, did I tell you I had Omar do a background check on Jeremy? Not that it'll mean anything now since we're not together."

"Did you ask about the arson allegations?"

"No, but DaVon didn't believe it was true," I said. "Anyway, I'll call it off."

"Turn up anything?"

"No report yet."

"Don't call it off. Because if I know you, or if I know how these young kids work, Jeremy will be on your doorstep before you know it, trying to ease his way back into your life."

"I'm through with Jeremy."

"Yeah, right," Carlos said. Sipped on hot tea. "Anyway, DaVon and Ricky talked. DaVon wants you back. Wants you back bad. Just an FYI."

"Uh, yeah, I know. He made that kinda clear when we *slept* together."

"You know how competitive and relentless firefighters are," Carlos said. "He won't stop until he gets you again."

"I know."

"So if you know this, isn't it better to be in control of the getting back together?"

"Carlos, this conversation is going nowhere fast," I said. "I'm through with Jeremy. No DaVon. I wish Omar were on our team because I'd be on him in a heartbeat. All I want is my job, my family back to normal, my friendship with you and Ricky. Back to basics."

"Cheers."

My phone buzzed. Incoming text message. From Jeremy: Miss you. Love you. *Besos*. JL.

"What's got you beaming?"

"This."

Showed Carlos the phone and he rolled his eyes. "Oh, God. Don't be stupid."

"Of course not," I said. "Still, it's flattering."

"You overheard the phone call and what he said about you."

"I know."

"You slept with your ex, after you overheard the phone call."

"I know."

We stared at each other for a few seconds. I could see the concern in his eyes and in his face for me. Felt like the Destiny's Child video, "Girl," with Beyoncé and Michelle comforting Kelly.

"You still want Jeremy."

"I know," I said. "Silly, isn't it?"

"I still think DaVon is a much better choice," Carlos said. "Or no one at all."

"I know."

I couldn't explain it. As hurt as I was by Jeremy's words, as confused as I was over his inconsistencies and actions, as saddened as I was over knowing that both he and I slept with other people, I still wanted the fantasy of Jeremy. I did.

Chapter 26

A few nights later, Jeremy was waiting by my truck when I left the gym for my evening workout. Had his backpack hoisted on his back and overnight bag over his shoulder. In one hand, a single red rose. In the other, a teddy bear, one of those cute, tacky kinds with a picture frame cradled in the bear's arms. The picture frame held a photo of Jeremy and me from our first night meeting at Metro.

"I'm sorry," he said and gave his puppy-dog eyes that always got to me. "You mad at me?"

"Are you stalking me or something?"

"No. I know your schedule. I know you like to keep the body tight . . . for your man."

"Right."

He smiled. So sexy, as always, in his hooded fleece sweatshirt and sagging jeans. Me, not so sexy, in sweaty workout clothes.

"Don't make me get loud and shout to the world 'I LOVE YOU,' Kenny."

"Stupid," I said and looked around. Embarrassed. But smiled anyway at Jeremy's guts and courage, stepping to me in the parking lot of my gym. In front of the security staff, gym jocks, and dinner patrons at the Rafael's restaurant in the adjacent lot. "You're not right."

"You ain't right."

"No, *you* ain't right."

"I can show you how right I am for you."

He eased up to me, backed me against my X5, kissed me slow, like I taught him on our first date, under the lamppost in the parking light.

"You know I'll never be able to show my face at this gym anymore."

"Fuck the gym. Fuck the homophobes. I'll take you fat and at home any day."

"Yeah, right. And I'll be sitting on the couch, eating ice cream, wondering whose bed you're in. Like the other night."

"Total misunderstanding, Kenny. No lie."

"Jeremy. There is no explanation for what I heard you say."

"I'm not lying," he said and gave puppy-dog eyes. "You supposed to trust your nigga, right?"

"That word. It has to stop."

"Sorry."

"A lot has to stop."

"Can we take it back to your place? Since you're all embarrassed to be seen with me here at your gym."

"It's not that," I said. "You know."

"You know I love you."

"Right."

Hated these passive-aggressive games that came with the dating process: I love you; no you don't; I love you; how much do you love me; I love you; prove to me you do. When the words alone should be enough and no one should have to prove anything to anyone. Either it is or it isn't. And you just know. But I didn't know.

I unlocked the doors of my truck, and we put our gym, book, and overnight bags in the backseat and hopped in the front. Jeremy flipped on his favorite hip-hop station on satellite radio.

"You taking care of business tonight?" He pursed his lips in that way he did early on, when I knew he wanted to get it on. I knew one thing. If we were going to make a go of this relationship, drama and all, I'd have to take control of the situation.

"We're not having sex tonight, Jeremy," I said and patted his hand.

"Aaah, no fair," Jeremy said. "I thought you missed me."

"I didn't say that."

"Damn, you all tough now."

"But if you want to talk and do homework, you're welcome to come over. It's up to you."

"If you forgive me."

"Fuck it, Jeremy, I'm taking you to your parents' home," I said. "You're not forgiven."

"Why not?"

"You don't even have enough compassion to put yourself in my shoes," I said. "It hurt to hear you say you had no feeling for me. That I was just some old dude—*your* words—you could get over on."

"I'm sorry."

"It's going to take a lot more than that for me to believe you," I said. "You don't know how much it hurt me. You don't know the half of it."

"I am such a jerk," Jeremy said. "I'm sorry. I'll never hurt you again."

"You said that in the beginning."

"I mean it this time," he said. "I'm trying to be what you need."

I didn't respond. We drove up Beverly toward Atlantic. Jeremy pulled out his Game Boy Advance and started playing in his imaginary world. I saw Target and Togo's. Knew I wanted to pick up a couple CDs and a salad for dinner because I didn't want to cook.

"You coming in?" I asked as I pulled into a parking spot in front of Togo's.

Jeremy jumped out, ran around to open my door for me. Patted me on the butt. Laughed. Grabbed at my hands as we walked through the lot to the store door. In the store, felt like I was with one of my nieces or nephew. Every other word: Can you get me this? Can you get me that? Oh, my God, I've got to get the new thug-of-the-month CD. Can you get me a new iTunes card? Damn, I love that reggaeton remix. Please, please, please. Bought my music and four for Jeremy and walked next door to the sandwich shop, which was empty.

"Whassup? Can I help you?"

Togo Boy, with his spiky hair, shaped eyebrows, goatee, youthful glow, smiled and looked right past me, who was at the ordering counter, and at Jeremy. The occupational hazards of dating a younger man. We placed our orders to go, and I listened to Togo Boy make small talk, flirt talk with Jeremy: you look familiar, you know this person or that person, where do you hang out, you should come hear my band play at blah blah blah this weekend, here's my card. Jeremy's small talk back: you do, too, I'm a XYZ at ELAJ, hang out a little bit of everywhere pretty much down for whatever, I'm always down for seeing a show, thanks for the card, blah blah blah.

Blah. Blah. Blah.

Part of the game. Whatever.

Not part of the game.

"This is my boyfriend, Kenny. He'll be with me at the show."

My ears perked up. My insides melted. I couldn't believe what I'd heard Jeremy say. Out loud. In public. To a stranger. We were boyfriends. Weird, but kinda cool at the same time. And even though I knew we had a million things to discuss, which we were finally going to that night, I felt confident that the conversation would go much better than our previous attempts at emotional intimacy. After all, we were boyfriends. At least, according to his words.

Chapter 27

"So where do you want to begin?"

I was naked. In bed. Next to Jeremy, who was also naked. We'd just finished another round of makeup sex. Our first time as boyfriends. Jeremy was ready to talk after a couple hours of communication with our bodies. It was just before eleven at night.

"You sure?" I said. "I've got a lot of questions."

"Yeah. I'm here," he said and scooted closer. Wrapped an arm over me. "I could have jetted after I came. But I'm serious."

"All right."

"Shoot."

"What's the deal with Jabari?"

"Jabari and I were together for about three months. I met him at a frat party about a year ago, and he was sweatin' me forevers, and I finally gave in."

"Why'd you break up?"

"The bitch is crazy. Possessive. Wouldn't give me space to be myself or with my boys, who were kind of his boys, but you know."

"Did you cheat?"

"Jabari and I broke up several times during the three months, and while we were apart I dated and messed around. No lie. I got needs. You *know* that."

"You give him any STDs?"

"We both messed around on the side. I honestly don't know if it was me or him who brought that mess into our bedroom."

"But you're clean now?"

"Like we talked about in the beginning, as of that time, yes. I'm clean. We can go get tested together if you don't believe me. In fact, since we're boyfriends now, we're going tomorrow and every other month together if you want."

"Okay, let's do it, then. Next subject. The car I'm storing in my garage."

"You sure you wanna know?" he asked. "I don't want you saying all I do is bring you legal troubles."

"Legal troubles?"

"Yeah, if you don't wanna know, I won't talk. We're being honest, right?"

"Yeah."

"Ride or die, right?"

"If you say."

"My brother sets fires. José Luis, the one who looks like me. Remember the pictures in my living room?"

"He's the arsonist they're looking for?" I asked. "Carlos and Ricky thought it was you."

"I know. That's why I couldn't, well can't, stand Ricky's nosy ass getting up in my Kool–Aid and not knowing the flavor."

"You're real eighties with that," I said. "But serious? About your brother?"

"Yeah, but it's not what you think," he said. "It's bigger than you think. José Luis is a druggie. Bangs off and on. No doubt he needs help. He met someone who works for one of the City Council people. Offered José Luis a job assignment. Do the deed. Make it look accidental. When the insurance money comes in, the owners kick some to the council staff and José Luis; then the construction contractors get to bid, more kickbacks to the council staff, and more to José Luis. I found out by accident. José Luis started getting a little careless with his tools. And I already lost one brother to police violence, one to a white trash family in Arizona, one to Iraq, and I'm not about to lose one to the criminal justice system. Not gonna let my mother go through another loss. That's the story."

"So I've got the getaway car in my garage?" I asked. "I'll be damned."

"They'll never find it. Trust."

"We have to get rid of it, Jeremy," I said. "We can't keep it here."

"We?" Jeremy smiled.

"That's what I said," I said. Rued the day I became an accessory, but didn't want to see another black or brown become a statistic . . . especially when it was a crime initiated by politicians trying to lure in the poor and disenfranchised to do their dirty work.

"Okay, we will. You're so cool, Kenny. Thanks. Any other questions?"

"The party?"

"I didn't have anything to do with the brother who died. Didn't touch him, didn't make him drink. I heard about it and knew what was going on, but I didn't have any direct anything with that incident. Remember, it was a last minute plan to go?"

"Yeah, we were supposed to have our first non-club date that night."

"Anyway, when I heard the cops raid, I knew which way to jet. I always have an escape plan, just in case."

"That poor kid."

"I know. I do have a heart."

We kissed.

"You have a heart and another hard-on, mister."

"Any more questions, Kenny?"

"Why did you say the things you did on the phone the other night? I heard it all: 'He believes everything I say. I get over on him all the time . . . That's how it is with old dudes . . . Turn 'em out, make 'em feel young and sexy again, and get what you want . . . It's just a dick thang. I don't feel anything for him . . . I'm fucking you tonight, nigga . . . Let me call Slimer back and ditch him, too . . .' That was like putting the knife in me and twisting it. Did you fuck someone else?"

"Okay, look, I'm sorry for not coming over when I said I was. What had happened was . . ."

"Be straight, Jeremy."

"I met this dude on one of those MySpace or DowneLink sites."

"Was he black?"

"Yeah."

"Was it just sex? Or more than sex?"

"Was less than sex."

"What?"

"Homeboy was dumb as rocks," he said. "Trust. I can't hook up with someone who can't keep educated conversation sometimes. Not after meeting you."

"You guys laughed at me. Or at the fact you were getting over on me. Not cool."

"I know."

"That shows a lack of integrity and respect for me as a human being."

"Sorry, babe," he said and planted kisses over my cheeks, eyes, forehead, ears. "Sorry. Sorry. Sorry. I'll never disrespect you again. But at least I didn't cheat on you."

"Why should I believe you?" Especially when I slept with DaVon, thinking Jeremy had been with someone else.

"Because I'm here," he said. "I could have jetted right after the sex. But I feel something for you and wanna make things right."

"You mean it when you said we're boyfriends?"

"Yeah. If that's what you want."

"I don't."

"What the fuck?" Jeremy leaned up, looked concerned

and disappointed. "I open up to you about everything and you just drop me like that?"

"I don't want to be your boyfriend if you keep shit up like you have."

"No more drama, I swear," Jeremy said. "You're the best thing to happen to me in a long time. I can't imagine my life without you as my man. So . . . you wanna be my man?"

Thought for a second and said, "I do." I smiled. Looked over at Jeremy. Looked up at the ceiling. The same ceiling I stared at while DaVon worked his magic, same spot, different sheets that Jeremy and I were now in. "I need to come clean about something, too."

"Kenny, no need. What I've done is far worse than anything you could have done. So don't trip. Clean slate. We're starting new. How does Jeremy Lopez-Kane sound? Or Kenny Kane-Lopez sound? Stupid, huh?"

"Yeah. The world would trip out, huh, seeing this."

"I know. Especially this."

Jeremy rolled over on top of me. Started heating us up for the next round, our first time with everything out in the open, almost total honesty, and with words that sealed our commitment and our lives together.

Chapter 28

Felt like singing Jill Scott's "Whatever," the next morning and over the next several weeks, as Jeremy and I eased ourselves into the comfort of being a new couple. An official couple. Felt like cooking him fish and grits, or arroz con pollo, every morning, noon, and night. Walked around work, gym, life in general with a smile and lightheartedness that I hadn't felt in a long time. I loved the giddiness of being in a new relationship. At least one where I knew the feelings were mutual and equal. When every little word was a sweet-nothing, when every little look conveyed deep emotions, when every spare moment was spent thinking about the new special one in your life.

More and more of Jeremy's things ended up in my room, bathroom, and the spare bedroom. Some of his mail started arriving in my mailbox. And soon, his boys were seeing my house as Jeremy's, and they were hanging out in the family room or the back house like it was hangout central. This time, maybe because they knew Jeremy and I were official, they were a lot more respectful and clean than they were back when we first met. And when they left, after homework, or watching videos, or playing the new Xbox 360 I bought Jeremy, we'd turn each other out, make love in new and exciting positions, try out new role plays, and bring each other tears of exhaustion and pleasure. Felt good falling asleep and waking up with Jeremy every day.

Jeremy surprised me with his skills everywhere. That morning, a month or so after Jeremy's pseudo move-in to my place, Jeremy woke up early and made breakfast while I was out on a morning jog around the neighborhood. Came back and the house smelled like a Mexican diner, with the aromas of onions, chilés, frijoles, and sautéd carne asada in the air. I smelled like I'd been without a shower for days after my run. Didn't matter to Jeremy, as he greeted me at the kitchen door with a smile, hug, and a kiss. Felt real *Leave It to Beaver.* Until we ended up making out, all sweaty and greasy, against the kitchen island. Concentrated so much on each other that we chose to ignore the ringing phone. But couldn't miss the message. Especially once we heard Jeremy's name and Omar's voice.

". . . Jeremy's background check that you ordered, so I wanted to see when you and I could meet and go over what I've found. Sorry it's been so long, but been busy with other cases. We should try and meet today if it's possible. You've got my number."

"You had your cop friend check me out?" Jeremy asked and backed away. "Still don't trust me, I see."

Jeremy turned away and walked toward the stove. Emptied the food he'd made for breakfast into the garbage disposal and walked out. I followed him through the family room and hallway toward our bedroom.

"I do trust you, Jeremy," I said, trying to keep up with him. "I did that over a month ago, before you started staying here on a regular basis. I hadn't heard from Omar, so I assumed it was a done deal. Nothing to report."

"Still, you called a cop on me," he said. "After I told you everything I did about my brother. I'm sure it's just a matter of time before the cops come knocking on our door."

Jeremy grabbed a duffel bag out the closet and started

snatching his clothes from hangers, opening and closing drawers to retrieve his belongings.

"Why are you packing?" I said. "Don't go."

"Why should I stay with someone who doesn't trust me?"

"I do trust you."

"Sorry, Kenny," he said. "Play me once, and that's one time too many."

I grabbed at Jeremy's shoulder to try and stop him, calm him, but the only thing it managed to do was anger him even more. Felt the shove, felt myself rolling over the bed, felt my face hit the corner bedpost. Found out just how strong Jeremy's arms could be with the one push.

"I'm sorry," Jeremy dropped his bag and came over to me on the bed. "I totally didn't mean to push that hard. Serious."

He kissed the side of my face, rubbed where my cheek had made contact.

Felt no pain. Thought about my mom. How she would say once a man hits you, it's over. Move. Put him out. Get away. Don't take him back. No need for giving benefit of the doubt. No need for talk or excuses. Please don't say forgive me.

"I hope you didn't mean it, because if you did, that's trouble."

He continued rubbing my face. "Kenny, is this abuse?"

"What?"

"The way I pushed you. Is it abuse?"

"No. Maybe. It just . . ."

"Are we one of those fucked-up couples? Or is this an isolated thing? Every other day or every other week one of us does something to hurt the other."

Jeremy and I held each other. Silence. Both thinking, probably, about what and why we were doing to each other what we were. I knew abusive and dysfunctional relationships. Academically, and through my work with students, I could see the symptoms a mile away. In my own life, personally, it wasn't something I'd experienced or even thought about as a reality or a possibility. I trusted and wanted to believe that Jeremy's shove was not a clue to a larger flaw in his personality, though Jabari had mentioned something to the effect when we found out we had Jeremy in common. Blew it off then, and now, didn't see Jeremy as a real threat to me physically.

Emotionally, Jeremy and I were a different story. And I wondered if our emotional roller coaster was a product of a relationship between two different cultures, two different generations, or if it was just us. That personally, Kenny and Jeremy had no more business together than oil and water. That we just weren't meant to be together at all. Not like Jeremy had gone out and made babies all over L.A. County like DaVon had, and given me something specific to say, "Paper or plastic?"

"Jeremy," I said and rubbed his shoulder. "What are you thinking?"

"I love you. You're the best thing to happen to me."

"I love you, too."

"I need time to think."

"Yeah, I think I do, too."

"Why'd you order a background check on me?"

"I don't know. It was spontaneous, just came up in conversation."

"If you wanted to know anything about me, you could have asked."

"I did, Jeremy. Over and over. And you never said anything."

"This is fucked up, Kenny," Jeremy said. "I can't be with someone who doesn't trust me."

"What are you saying?"

"Dude, don't get me wrong. I don't want to break up, but I . . ."

"Think we need some space?"

We looked at each other and smiled. Not happy smiles. Jeremy said, "Maybe."

I looked at the digital clock on the bedside table. Almost time for both of us to be out the door for work and school.

"I have meetings. You have classes. Don't leave now. Come back and let's figure things out tonight."

"Good idea. Maybe we're just too dramatic, huh?"

We smiled. Chuckled. Rubbed our cheeks together.

"Jeremy, what am I going to do with you?"

"What am I going to do with you?"

There was another long pause, while we held each other and enjoyed the moment and silence. The reality of the day soon kicked in. I showered. Jeremy grabbed a frozen breakfast sandwich to microwave, his hard work in the kitchen down the drain. He left his duffel bag, but took his book bag and laptop case, and I dropped him off at ELAJ. Before parting, we kissed. Physically, it was like always. Emotionally, something felt different. There was a divide, a void, and I wondered, as I drove up the street to my job at CUELA, if this was worth fighting to keep or if my choice in partners needed tuning up. Or if this back-and-forth, up-and-down action meant I was handling things in a mature way by sticking it out.

Chapter 29

As I pulled into the staff and faculty lot, I saw Omar sitting, well, more like lounging, in his LAPD cruiser. Close to where I normally parked. He was right. Officers could figure out anything they wanted. He got out and stood by the car. His departmental polyester blues stretched to accommodate his muscles, curves, and bulges. Thought to myself: Damn, wrong place, wrong time, wrong orientation.

Turned off the truck. Saw that chivalry wasn't dead as Omar opened my door. I gathered my things from the backseat and floor.

"Quickest way to get yourself jacked," Omar said and smiled. "Sitting here, not prepared to exit your car while you organize yourself."

"What? You're going to rob me?"

"'Course not. Just making a point. How are you, Mr. Kane?"

"Could be better, Off-i-cer Etheridge," I said and pointed a finger into his chest. "I thought you had a little more discretion than to leave messages on people's answering machines."

"What? The kid heard me?"

"Yeah. We had a fight."

"I can tell by that shiner on your cheek." Omar touched where my face had hit the bedpost earlier in the day. I hadn't realized it left a mark. "You all right? Need me to arrest him?"

"No. I fell. It was me. My mistake. More an argument than a fight."

"That's what they always say to protect their man," he said. "But if that's how you wish to proceed."

"Jeremy's not like that. I'm just clumsy."

"Really?" Omar revealed a manila envelope kept hidden in his other hand behind his back. "You wanna bet?"

"Jeremy's background check?" I said and reached for it. Omar pulled it away. Tease. "What's up with that?"

"Are you sure you want it? Is it gonna cause more problems for you and the kid?"

"Everything's cool. Really, Omar."

"Fine," he said and handed it over. "Here. Just doing my part to keep you safe."

"What does that mean?"

"Read it," he said. "When you have time. Then call me if you have questions . . . or want to do dinner again."

Omar smiled. Damn. Flirt. Hated and loved the new confidence he'd developed since being at and leaving CUELA. But not cool that he was straight, knew my deal, and still kept on like he wanted more than friendship. Knew it wasn't gonna happen.

"I have a partner," I said. "He wouldn't appreciate me going out on dates with other men."

"Especially after he knows I know everything about him and his family."

I couldn't stand the ambiguity Omar presented. And I had to ask, "Omar. What's up? Are you? Or not?"

"Am I what?" He smiled. Looked me in the eye. Nodded his head. "Say it."

"Are you gay or what?" I finally asked. "You act weird and say weird things."

"Oh, yeah?" Omar took out his pad and pen. "Acts weird. Says weird things. Uh, gay."

"Nothing, forget I asked," I said. "And don't bother exaggerating more stories to DaVon about you and me."

"Oh. That."

"Yeah. That."

"You enjoy shacking up with DaVon again? Jeremy know about that?"

"How do you . . . Right, you were probably casing my house."

"Your secret is safe with me."

"You're kinda sleazy."

"You're kinda intrigued."

Omar lifted his radio from his belt and responded to some call or question from the dispatcher. I didn't like the idea of keeping secrets from Jeremy, but I didn't like Omar, whose motives and intentions I didn't understand, knowing my secrets. Or even Jeremy's secrets.

Waited for Omar to finish his police communication, put the report envelope in my bag, and grabbed the rest of my things out the backseat. Locked my baby, and just my luck, Mrs. Allison Perez pulled up two spots away from me and Omar. Great.

"Morning, Kenny." Allison's face looked "refreshed" yet again. Swore her skin was just gonna fall off one day if she got one more procedure. She gave Omar a long, slow, up-and-down look. "Is this your friend DaVon?"

"Nope," I said, and wanted to add, "Just because he's black?" but didn't. White lady law. Not responsible for being able to distinguish perfectly distinguishable black faces.

"What happened to your face?"

I didn't think it was that obvious.

"I ran into the bathroom door." She waited for additional information, but I gave none. I wondered if it sounded like those denial phrases that mental health brochures say are red flags for physically abusive relationships. Not that Jeremy's and my misunderstanding put me in that category. "See you in the office, Allison."

"Just trying to be nice, Kenny. You still have a job because of me. Remember?"

Allison walked off, her light perfume lingering behind her. She was right. I still did work at CUELA. Big whoop! But I did have a little thanks in my heart for receiving probation and not a pink slip from her, and felt a little compassion for this woman whose husband had a little hobby called gay barhopping. I'd have to be nicer to my boss.

"Sorry about that," Omar interrupted my thought. "Gotta run back to the station."

"Thanks for the report," I said. "And for keeping quiet about DaVon."

"You guys and your secrets. I swear."

"I don't need your commentary, Omar. Thanks."

He patted my shoulder and headed back to the cop car. "Kenny, you're a smart man. I hate to see someone like you make bad choices."

"Bye."

"Call me when you read the report," he said as he opened the door. "If you can."

Watched Omar speed off, the red and blue lights of the police car flashing. Wondered what kind of man he thought I was. And for a second, had me wondering the same thing.

As I walked through campus to my office, felt my phone buzz and saw the red light turn on. Message. A text from Jeremy, saying he wasn't mad, but he'd be staying at his parents' house that night and would call me later.

Signed it, "With Love. Your Man."

If Omar wondered what kind of man I was, it was this: a man in love. Dangerously in love.

Chapter 30

Jeremy's family night turned into nights. He checked in a few times by phone and e-mail, but of course, I wondered if once again, Jeremy was running away from the challenges that came up in a relationship. Said he wasn't avoiding me, but needed to help with some family issues. I still hadn't opened the background check information after three days, and though I'd thought about the contents, I wanted to wait until Jeremy came back to my house and we could go through it together. To give him the benefit of explaining whatever Omar had discovered. Said he loved me, and that keeping my trust was his mission, and that he'd do that once the family issues were settled.

As for my family, I obviously wasn't my mother's son. Said she was this close to ordering a 51-50, involuntary commitment to a mental institution, if I didn't get my act together. Said the symptoms of loneliness and heartache were staring me in the face. Named a list of neighbors and family members whose relationships and marriages never should have happened, and ended in bad breakups, when everyone around saw the red-flag warnings before the relationships started. Even went so far as to call me Whitney (as in Whitney and Bobby).

"I don't blame your mom," Carlos said. He had one elbow

on the dinner table, his chin resting in his palm as he listened. "She's right."

"Whitney?" I asked. "Whitney?"

Jeremy's family time and Ricky's overnight shift at the station meant one thing. Boys' night out for Carlos and me, and on one of the better nights of the week. Saturday. We sat at a cramped table in the middle of Cheebo, this trendy, organic foods restaurant in Hollywood. We had table neighbors just inches away on either side, but the noise and busy atmosphere of the place drowned out conversations deemed private or embarrassing. This conversation fell somewhere in between.

"If the shoe, wig, pipe fits."

"Not cool, Carlos," I said. "Don't make fun of her alleged problems. And don't put me in the same category. Besides, Whitney's clean now and enjoying the comeback of a lifetime."

"Well, you're running around with a gangsta hood-rat masquerading as a college student who says he loves you. And there're no similarities, you say?"

I had thought we were through with this line of discussion and critiques of Jeremy. Thought we were working on getting our friendship back on track. Obviously, Carlos was waiting for just the right moment to warn me of his suspicions of Jeremy again. Jackpot. Boys' night out.

"Are you ready to order?" I asked. "Or are we blowing off the whole night's agenda to discuss Jeremy again? Because we could have had this same, tired conversation over the phone, on the ride over, or on Instant Message."

"Can't you see what being involved with Jeremy has done to you?" Carlos said. "We hardly see you, and when we do it's always some new crisis or problem Jeremy's gotten you into."

"I don't talk about Jeremy . . . that much," I said and tried to recall if I, or Carlos, did the most of the talking about Jeremy.

I thought I'd done a pretty good job of trying to hide things, keeping them quiet, leaving Jeremy and Kenny problems between Jeremy and Kenny. Like a relationship should be. Felt like I let too many people into my business when DaVon and I first started having the paternity test problems. Felt like they talked me, indirectly, into issuing the "paper or plastic" ultimatum. Jeremy and I had not nearly the level of commitment, years of togetherness, or depth of problems DaVon and I had. Maybe if Carlos had showed the same level of concern for me and my relationship choices seven years earlier, I never would have ended up with the courtroom dramas and baby momma issues of the past couple years. Our supposed-to-be fun, boys' night out, was not as fun as planned. And all I wanted to do was get up and walk. All I could do since Carlos drove. Maybe walk farther west on Sunset to the strip of hip, Hollywood jet-setter type clubs. Maybe immerse myself in a new environment where no one knew me, Jeremy, DaVon, and where I could just escape and not think about Carlos, Ricky, DaVon, Vanessa, Kenyatta, Ke'Von, my mom, Allison Perez, Omar, Jabari, fraternities, hazing issues, sitting on this task force or that campus committee, paternity issues, family dramas, or mentoring young people.

"Enjoy your wine, guys," the wine server said as he set a bottle and two glasses on our table. Hadn't even heard Carlos place a drink order. The waiter quickly came over, after our wine was poured, and took our orders. Salad for me. Portobello mushroom sandwich for Carlos.

"Cheers," Carlos said and lifted his glass to mine. Clinked. "I promise not to go on much more about Jeremy. I know you *think* you love him, and if that's how you feel, I have to respect that. I'm your best friend, and I thought we were allowed to share our opinions if we didn't want to see the other get hurt. You and Jeremy are a formula for disaster."

Not again. I gulped the glass of wine in two swallows. Poured another and said, "Let me arm myself for the latest round of attacks first." I smiled. Carlos smiled, a fake smile, and got serious again.

"I'll make it quick," Carlos said.

"Thanks. Because we're supposed to be getting our drink, eat, and dance on tonight. Haven't been to The Catch in a minute. Your minute starts now, Carlos."

I lifted the wrist that wasn't holding the wineglass. I was feeling tipsy.

"And you say you're no Whitney," Carlos said. Catty dig. But whatever. "I'll tell you who you're *really* not. You're no Janie and Jeremy's no Tea Cake. You're no more a boyfriend to that kid, than I am to that singer Obie Bermúdez."

"Countdown continues."

"And I don't want to see anything bad happen to you," Carlos continued. "You stay all isolated and away from us like you're on lockdown, keeping secrets, showing up to work with bruises with the lie that you're clumsy. Please, Kenny, heard that on a billion TV movies of the week. You and I run several miles at a time, and you've never fallen. You're not clumsy. I'm surprised he's not ringing you every other minute to see where you are, who you're with. Oh, duh, he doesn't give a fuck."

"Hmmmm . . . hmmmm . . . hmmmm."

"And I just don't understand why you're so desperate to be with someone who's not on your level," Carlos said. "You are educated, have your shit together, speak English, in your thirties now, own your own house and car . . . You're buying him gifts, giving him money, letting him lay up inside you *and* his ex, and what are you getting in return? Are you that insecure about whatever that you have to be with the first person to come along since you and DaVon? What are you looking for? To create your own *E True Hollywood Story*? You shooting for martyrdom? Trying to come to the rescue for yet another lost soul? Because when it comes down to it, you're going to be disappointed, you're going to have your heart broken, and you're going to run back to us—me, Ricky, your mom, whoever—and wish you never had even met Jeremy.

I love you like a brother, man. Don't want to see you be a fool for some kid."

I couldn't believe how freely people, especially Carlos, felt in telling you exactly everything they didn't like about the person you were dating. Just amazing. Not once had I ever told Carlos anything negative about Ricky, and there were aspects of him that I found challenging to put up with. But, I left those things to myself because it was Carlos and Ricky. Not Carlos and Ricky and Kenny.

I looked at my watch, took another swallow of wine, and said, "So what after that, Mrs. Lincoln?"

"Did you hear a word I said?" Carlos asked.

"Yep."

"And?"

"I heard you out, buddy. Best friend."

"And . . . you have any response?"

"No. I heard you out. Thank you."

"So what now?"

"I don't know about you," I said and touched up my glass with a little more wine, "but I came to have a party."

Wasn't going to let Carlos in on a secret. I had heard everything he'd said, and respected his opinion, and knew part of what he said was . . . well, true. But wasn't going to let on that I thought any part of him was right, that I'd had my doubts from time to time, and that on more than one occasion since DaVon and I slept together, I'd wondered what getting back together with DaVon would be like—familiar, safe, equally yoked. But pride is a bitch. Keeps you in places and states of mind you know are . . . well, you just know.

But Carlos and I continued eating, drinking, trying to get back to a somewhat normal evening of friendship. Knew that black club etiquette stated one should not arrive at one's night festivities until well after midnight. So Carlos drove us up the street to the shopping plaza where Virgin Megastore, Crunch, and Laemmle's Sunset 5 enticed the pretty-crowd shoppers. A little too much wine led the plastic to come out freely and spend money on some goodies for me and for Jeremy. Cruised up Sunset to watch all the hetero types doing their thing underneath the backdrop of the Hollywood Hills. Talked, joked, laughed, and got somewhat back to normal for the evening before driving south and east to Pico Boulevard and to Jewel's Catch One.

Because we hadn't followed black club etiquette and arrived well before midnight, we breezed easily through valet, security, and up the long flight of stairs to pay admission with no waiting. Bass bumped. Early birds lined the walls of the lounge and upstairs dance room. Risk takers shared their goodies and best old school moves on the empty dance floor. Carlos and I looked at each other and laughed. Knew we were wondering if we looked too old, and out of place, like the courageous souls underneath the disco balls who braved dancing alone at eleven o'clock in a black hip-hop club. Dancing too early was a black club etiquette no-no. No worries. We shouted our drink orders to Caprice, our favorite new bartender-friend and former CUELA student, and got hooked up with two shots of X-Rated, and then a full glass of the same stuff on the rocks.

"Damn, I feel like I'm back in undergrad tonight." I raised my voice over Rihanna's "Umbrella," and held up my glass with the hot pink drink sloshing around. "You're definitely gonna have to drive and not let me get lost."

"I got you, Kenny," Carlos said and raised his glass. "Get as wasted as you want. It's our night out."

"And I'm not going to think about Jeremy or DaVon tonight," I said. "And I'm not going to worry about what you think about Jeremy either."

A few minutes passed. Clock struck midnight, and like magic, the upstairs dance floor filled almost to capacity, out of nowhere. Got looks and head nods. Tons of looks from boys, men, and the kind I had found myself attracted to lately. Urban prep. Young. Hot. Running in their multicultural packs, though at The Catch, they were mostly black packs. Checked myself in the side mirror, just to make sure I didn't look ridiculously young and out of place. Triple Five Soul T-shirt over a longer-sleeved tee, low-rise jeans, and a black knit cap tilted. Looked like thirty-three going on twenty-three, but pulled it off effectively. Smooth, tight skin. Used my empty hand to do a quick feel for softness around the waist. None. Thank God I ran, which kept the slowing metabolism at bay.

Bought another X-Rated shot for Carlos and me from the drink server passing by, finished them off, and Carlos and I joined the sweaty, head-bobbing crowd for the next thirty minutes. At some point, I swung around and bumped into Jeremy and his cell-phone-photographer friend from Ricky's birthday party. He held his hands up, shrugged his shoulders, and shouted, "Kenny, Nacho. Nacho, Kenny."

"I remember Nacho." Duh.

Jeremy grabbed my waist and turned me around. Danced up and down my back, kissed my ears, grinded against my leg, held me from behind, slapped my ass, while I reached back and held on to his neck. Danced together, while Nacho and Carlos took a breather, until we felt sweat running off our faces, arms, and backs. Kept whispering in my ears, on my neck, "I love you. I love you. I love you," when other boys leered like they wanted to join in and make a three-some. Felt magnum rising in his jeans, pressed against it, and said, well, slurred, "I'm taking care of that tonight."

"Let's go get drinks and cigs," Jeremy said and grabbed my hand. Elbowed our way through the crowded floor and walked down the back stairs to the downstairs lounge, dance floor, and smoking patio. Grabbed a couple cocktails on our way outside into the chilly night air. Jeremy lit up a cigarette and offered me a drag, which I took, despite the fact I wasn't a smoker. Hated cigarettes and the smoke since growing up in a house of smokers. But whatever. I was unexpectedly with Jeremy.

"How's your family business?" I asked. Not quite angrily, but not friendly either, and handed back his cigarette.

"No biz to take care of at midnight on a Saturday night," Jeremy said and smiled. Flicked ash and took a puff. "I didn't think you'd be here."

"You got caught," I said. "Bad boy."

"It's always cool to see my boo. Hope you don't mind I'm a little lifted tonight."

"Whatever, Jeremy."

He puffed on his cigarette. Chuckled. "Hey, what did that report say that your piggy dug up on me?"

"Haven't opened it yet."

"Where's Carlos and his boyfriend Lurch?"

"Carlos is inside still with Nacho, remember?" I said. "I'll call his cell and find him in a minute. Ricky's at the fire station tonight. Not that you care."

"I don't. Not about Ricky."

"I know."

"You look good tonight," he said and looked over my shoulder. Nodded his head and smiled. "The Catch's most wanted tonight."

I reached for his cigarette and did a slight turnaround to see who Jeremy was eyeing. Knew he was checking someone out. Not born yesterday. Just something to put on the checklist when dating someone ten-plus years younger—the wandering eye. Target: Togo Boy, from the sandwich shop. Made a mental note, but made no scene. Turned back to Jeremy, handed the cig back, and took a swallow of my drink. Told him, "You look good, too. As usual." And he did. Black blazer, wife-beater, baggy jeans, with his usual bling around his neck and in his ears, and black-and-white NY baseball cap tilted back and to the side.

"So I want you to come to a party at my house tomorrow afternoon," Jeremy said. Glanced again past me in the direction of Togo Boy. "My niece's birthday party. The *familia* wants to meet you and see who I been spending all my time with. Wanna come?"

"You want me to?"

He leaned in next to my ear. Whispered with hot breath, "I want you to come all over my face. I want to fucking be inside you and have you inside me. I want to taste that hot cock and hear you fucking screaming out my name, nigga. I want you to treat me like a fucking dirty field worker and order me around and threaten to deport me unless I fucking do everything you want. And then I'm going to spread your ass against the wall, search you for fucking-while-black, and club your ass like it's never been clubbed before. Hell, yeah, Kenny. I want you to come. It's going to be so fucking hot. All you gotta do is say yes."

I blushed, rose to attention at Jeremy's dirty race-play talk, wondered if he'd downloaded the Pat O'Brien, host of *The Insider*, alleged voice mail messages that were all over the Internet a year or so earlier. Jeremy moved back to his original standing position. Closed-mouth smile. Eyes squinted. Looking cocky as usual. At me? At Togo Boy?

"Yes," I said and closed-mouth smiled back. Nodded my head.

"I'll ring you after the club, then." Took one last drag of his cigarette. Pulled out another. "Make plans for you to come."

"You're bad, Jeremy."

"You make me that way," he said.

Suddenly felt the urge to pee and knew I needed to look for Carlos. He could hold his own in a majority-black crowd for just so long.

"I'll be back in a few," I said and finished my drink. Set it on an empty table. "Want anything from the bar?"

"You know what I want," he whispered and leered as I started to walk away. "Text me to let me know where you are."

Togo Boy gave me that look, part envy, part I'm-up-to-something, as I breezed past him and inside the club. Had given that same look to other boys, back in the day, when all the scene was about for me was drama.

Walked past the kitchen, wondered why and how people could eat so much fried chicken and shrimp so late in the night, found the first available stall in the bathroom, washed hands, rang Carlos to meet me at the downstairs bar, and ordered two more drinks. The downstairs lounge and bar were beginning to fill with fans of 80s and 90s house, R&B, and dance music. In other words, music of my generation: Ten City, Crystal Waters, Inner City, Cajual and Cashmere, Martha Wash. Waited for Carlos. Got Togo Boy instead. Smiled. Mouth full of metal. Looking much like a Jeremy clone. Knew the crowd at Catch would peg me a nonblack dater with all the Latinos I'd been hanging with that night.

"I'm Juan," he held his hand out and smiled. Firm grip. "'Sup?"

"I'm Kenny, Juan," I said/shouted over a remix of Jody Watley's "Don't You Want Me." Now that I knew Juan's name, couldn't go back to calling him Togo Boy in my mind. "Not much is up. Just waiting for a friend."

He sipped through the straw in his drink. "JJ?"

"Nah. Another one." Hadn't heard the name JJ used for Jeremy since the whole Jabari name-game months earlier. Felt a tap on my shoulder. "Oh, here he is now. Carlos, Juan. Juan, Carlos."

Shook hands, smiled, exchanged typical club greeting, "Good to meet you."

"I'm going to the bathroom," Carlos said. Turned to Juan. "Nice meeting you, Juan. Sorry to be so rude. Too much to drink, bladder the size of a goldfish."

"No biggie, man," Juan said and smiled more. Could have been nicknamed "Giggles" or "Chuckles" or "Braces" because all he had was a perpetual smile and happy look. Far from the indifferent look at the sandwich shop. Couldn't believe I was standing and having conversation with Togo Boy, er, Juan, who'd seemed caught up in Jeremy back at the sandwich shop weeks earlier, and who, tonight, was the object of Jeremy's wandering eye. Juan leaned in more for conversation. "Kenny, it's so cool that you and JJ can be friends. There's no way I could stay friends with any of my exes."

"Is that what he told you?"

"Well, not exactly."

"What exactly did he tell you?" I was careful not to raise my voice. Kept it friendly and light. Smiled a lot, too, to match Juan's body language. Needed to tread lightly in solving this mystery. "Where's Jer . . . JJ now?"

"Went to the car with some buddies to blaze up," Juan said. "Not my thing."

"Oh, okay. Just wondering. So what does JJ say about me?"

"Well, that you guys are good friends. That you used to mess around like more than friends, but now, that you're like his mentor. Which is so cool, because I sometimes wish I had an older gay guy to kinda show me the ropes and . . ."

Went into blah blah blah mode. Good *friends*? *Used* to mess around? *Mentor? Older* gay guy? Looked at Juan as he continued talking. Couldn't have been any more than twenty-one, like Jeremy, but definitely naïve and not streetwise like Jeremy. I downed my drink very quickly. Grabbed the other one waiting for Carlos. Too bad, Carlos.

"So what do you think of my friend?" I asked. Still in detective mode.

"He's a good catch, totally," Juan said and smiled. Knew that young, just-out-the-closet, first-crush look once, too. "Know what I'm saying."

"Yeah, totally."

"We went to the movies yesterday night after I got off from work," he said, not realizing he was tightening a noose around Jeremy. "And then he asked me to meet him and his crew out tonight. This is my first time at Catch One."

"Nice."

"Is this weird, Kenny? Talking about your ex like this?"

"Not at all," I said. Smiled. Lied. "No need for drama, you know."

"Older guys are so patient. No drama. So cool. Maybe if things don't work out with me and JJ, you and I could—"

"Let's not go there, Juan," I said. "So you guys made any plans for a relationship? Just kicking it? Hanging out?"

"JJ wants to take things slow," Juan said and smiled. "That's cool with me. I have school, work, I lead a Boy Scout troop, and my band."

Now I knew what the term "Punch Drunk Love" was all about.

Too much wine and X-Rated, combined with the confirmation that Jeremy, er, JJ wasn't all I thought he was transported me into a weird, depressed, yet happy mood. Knew where I stood with Jeremy. It wasn't going to work. That he was out making plans and making happy with someone else. Funny, when reality finally hits and you finally accept it, how calming and nirvana-ish it can feel. No matter how much I hoped or did to make it work, it just wasn't going to work. But I could have fun with the downfall in the meantime.

Jody Watley transitioned into Whitney Houston's "I Wanna Dance With Somebody," and I finished the drink I'd been saving for Carlos. Looked at Juan and said, "Wanna dance?"

"Yeah. Sure. Doesn't look like JJ's coming back for a while."

"JJ's through."

"So 2006."

Juan and I elbowed through the standing-room-only crowd on the dance floor. Smiled, laughed, and danced our asses off to Whitney, then Salt-n-Pepa, then Paula Abdul, then Karyn White, then LL Cool J, Slick Rick, Run DMC, and then JJ Fad's "Supersonic."

Them big, everlasting ears.

I should have seen Jeremy barge through the crowd.

Should have heard him shouting and cussing and flashing his hands in the air. But definitely felt the pull on my shoulder. Heard him shouting about me staying away from Juan, or Juan staying away from me. Saw the shove on Juan's chest. Listened to the emotionally violent words coming from Jeremy's mouth. Rage. Jealousy. Betrayal. Everything slow motioned. Felt like I was watching a scene in one of the *Matrix* movies. Watched as the security guards broke us up, put Jeremy in a headlock, and my elbows behind my back. Turned Jeremy over to Nacho and escorted them down the alley to their car. Turned me over to Carlos and escorted us out to valet.

Carlos stared at me while we waited for his car. No words needed, but looked back at Carlos and said, "I know . . . you're right."

Chapter 31

The room spun. My head rang. So did the phones—my house and cell. All night and all morning. Like a billion times, it seemed. I was hung over. Well, not quite hung over, but not quite sober. Hadn't had a Sunday morning hangover in years. Definitely since before life with DaVon.

Used the bathroom. Brushed my teeth. Washed my face. Grabbed a couple aspirin and downed them with tap water. Looked at myself in the mirror.

This was the face of a man like everyone else. Solid exterior. Healthy looking. Able to put on a happy face for the sake of appearances. As Countee Cullen wrote, "We Wear the Mask."

Behind the face was a man not like everyone else. Or so I thought. Unhappy. Desperately, dangerously in love with someone who flirted with danger and trouble, despite his clean-cut and happy exterior. Confused and bitter that someone could be so obviously open with his cheating, lies, and being on the edge of the law, and yet expect you to stand by his side. Angry and embarrassed at myself for wanting to stand by his side, yet knowing, for sure after the incident at The Catch, that being with him wasn't the best thing for my mental or physical health.

Had to admit a lot to myself. Had to admit that my mom, Carlos, Ricky, DaVon, and Jabari were right. That sucked.

Didn't know if they would allow me to save face and move on, as if this time with Jeremy never existed, or if I would hear "I told you so" about Jeremy and face scrutiny on any future dates and partners. At this point, I just needed to end things with Jeremy once and for all. Dating someone else, including DaVon, was not in my near or distant future.

House phone rang again. Went to the family room. Checked caller ID. Jeremy. Twenty-fourth time calling. Couldn't avoid the inevitable. Didn't want to delay any further.

"What, Jeremy?"

"Good afternoon to you, too, sweetie," Jeremy said. Could hear the singsong happiness tone of his voice. I looked at the wall clock. Almost three. "How you doing?"

"That's a joke, right?"

"Oh, last night, huh?"

"Duh, Jeremy."

"I'm sorry about that," Jeremy said. "I think they put some shit in the herb. Made me kinda crazy, huh? I'm sorry."

"I can't take your apology," I said. "I can't take this anymore. I want you to get your things and the car I'm hiding in the garage. The keys and a garbage bag will be waiting on the front porch for you."

"You can't break up with me, bro. I love you. You love me."

"I thought I did."

"Dude, don't play me like this," he said. "I said I'm sorry. You're the best thing to happen to me, Kenny. I tell you that all the time, because I mean it."

"If you cared like you say you do . . ."

"I love you. You're the one I want." While he talked, I picked up the remote and flipped to VH1 Soul. Retro Sunday. Saw the stupid Xbox 360 I'd bought Jeremy. Started making a mental note of everything I'd have to gather and put in garbage bags. Clothes. DVDs. Cologne. Toothbrush. Danielle Steel novels. Video games. The dog tag chain with our picture etched on it. "Hello? You still there, Kenny?"

"Yeah."

"You know you don't want to break up with me. The way I put it on you in bed, how I make you laugh and make you feel like you're twenty-one again. No one else can give you the excitement I give you, Kenny. Don't break up. I promise I'll do better."

"Sorry," I said. "It's over. Paper or plastic?"

"You're funny. That's what I like about you. You keep up with me. I need a boy that'll ride or die 'til the end."

"Whatever, Jeremy. Your things will be on the porch in a bag. You can pick them up—"

"When I pick you up. My goddaughter's birthday party, remember," Jeremy said. "My family is expecting you to show. You can't leave me hanging in front of them."

"Your family doesn't know me as anything but the man you used to sleep with," I said. "They won't care. And I thought it was your niece."

"Well, whatever, it's a little girl party," he said. "Please, just do this for me. This one last favor, and I promise, I'm out. I won't holla at you no more. Won't try to convince you to be with me—shouldn't have to, but I'll chill. Pweese?"

I could imagine Jeremy's puppy-dog face. Remembered how much I loved and laughed at the face. And then would end up doing what Jeremy wanted. I had no plans for the day. Didn't feel like running or working out or anything else.

"Just this one last thing, Jeremy."

Knew it was probably silly, but what the hell? One last outing, so Jeremy could show off his black, smart, hip-to-be-older catch. I could play the PR game for a couple hours with the Lopez family in East L.A.

"Thanks. I do appreciate this, man."

"What time?"

"A couple hours. I'll pick you up."

"I'll be ready. So will your things."

"Don't eat anything, boo. We got a grip of food and drink over here. My uncle bought a keg."

"No drinking for me," I said. "But I'll be on time and waiting. Bye."

Hung up. Walked to the kitchen and poured a glass of water from the fridge door. Ate a piece of bread. Decided to give Carlos a call, let him know I was okay and of my plans.

"So what's happening with the young, hung, and restless?" Carlos greeted me. "You ready to call a restraining order against the De La Hoya wannabe?"

I grabbed a garbage bag from under the kitchen sink and said, "I'm breaking up with him. We just talked."

"Good for you. Amen. Everything okay?"

"Well, I love the boy," I said. "But I just can't be with him. He's coming over to get his things. I'm loading everything up in bags now."

"Breakups are hard, I know."

"Yeah, you who've been with Ricky for going on eight years now," I said. Found a stash of Jeremy's weed peeking out from between sofa cushions. "But he actually took my ending things pretty good. Just asked me one favor."

"Uh oh. What's that?"

"He wants me to go over to his folks' house this evening. It's his niece's or goddaughter's birthday party, and he says the family wants to meet me. Whatever."

"You're going? You believe him?"

Threw more Game Boy Advance cartridges in the bag, along with dozens of bootleg DVDs and CDs Jeremy had copied at my place. "It's just a party. I'll make an appearance and he'll bring me back here."

"Want my gun? It's NRA-registered," Carlos said and laughed. "Not that it's funny, but Jeremy's got violent tendencies if you haven't figured it out already. How do you know he's not going to try and harm you?"

"He won't. Jeremy's a good kid, just a little rough and growing into who he's supposed to be."

"You sure? Kenny, I don't want anything to happen to you."

"Trust me, I'll be fine. I'll say 'hi' to the folks. You remember where he lives, don't you? Remember the Executive Suite night?"

I gave Carlos the exact address again, what time I expected Jeremy to pick me up, and by when I expected to be dropped off after the party.

"Be careful," Carlos said. "I'll 9-1-1 you at some point if you want. For old times' sake."

"Sure," I said. "Why not? Try me around six-thirty."

Hung up and continued going through drawers in the bathroom and bedroom, rummaged through the closet we shared, picked up a sock here or there, and reveled that in a matter of hours, Jeremy's things would be out my house, and he would be out my life.

Chapter 32

"Whassup, pa. I'm outside your place, but I don't see my shit."

After showering, trying to choose a casual, yet impressionable outfit, and cleaning my house of Jeremy's things, I hadn't had time to put the bag of stuff out on the front porch. Besides, I didn't want my neighbors, like Mrs. Li and company, to see there was domestic drama on our block. Leave that for *Desperate Housewives* or *Knots Landing* reruns.

"I'll be right out, Jeremy." I did a double take in the mirror. White Lacoste Polo, jeans, white sneakers. Perfect for a Sunday evening party and family meet-and-greet. Perfect for leaving a lasting impression on Jeremy and his family, their first and last time spending time with me.

Arrived at the front door, trudging a heavy garbage bag behind me. Jeremy got out the car, walked to the door, and reached to grab the bag. Grabbed my wrist instead and rubbed.

"You sure about this, man? I promise I won't fuck up anymore," Jeremy said and gave me the puppy-dog face he always gave when he knew he was in the wrong. But never again, again. I wasn't changing my mind. "I swear on the grave of Froylan, and on my brother Eric in Iraq's honor, that I will completely devote my time to making things better. I only need one more chance."

"It's too late, Jeremy," I said. "If I find anything else, I'll mail it. Now, are we going to your niece's birthday party, or are we spending the evening on my front porch with you begging for another chance?"

"I would stay here with you, but she's counting on me. And my family is counting on you coming over. For reals." I handed the bag over to Jeremy, who pushed a couple buttons to release the trunk of the car he arrived in. "Shit, I can't figure out this ride."

"Whose car is this?"

"I don't know. José Luis let me use it."

"Great," I said and rolled my eyes. "Rolling in your twin's car, the firestarter. What about the one I'm hiding out back? Why don't I follow you in it, and then you'll have everything."

"Man, you really tryna get rid of me, huh?" Jeremy smiled. "We'll take care of the car, I promise, tomorrow. Just get on in and enjoy the ride with me."

Stuffed the bag in the backseat, hopped in the front, and rolled south on Atlantic for a couple miles until we were in East L.A. Jeremy and I talked and laughed on the ride. He grabbed for my hand a few times, but I didn't let him hold it. Needed to hold to my resolve and be done with him, in the romantic sense, after the party. Friendship. Maybe. Jeremy had brought a lot of excitement and energy into my life, a little more than I wanted at this point, but still, it was a few months that I knew I'd never forget. For the good times and the bad.

We pulled into the driveway, crowded with family members' trucks and SUVs. One of those inflatable jumpers that kids love to get in and romp around was in the front yard. Huge balloon arrangements adorned the white metal fence surrounding the house. I could hear the sounds of popular Mexican *narcocorridos* and *cumbias* pulsing from the backyard and neighborhood stereos. Sunday afternoons, particularly sunny and warm ones, were perfect for family parties and get-togethers.

All eyes were on me when Jeremy and I entered the backyard. I recognized the smoky, hoarse-sounding voice of Jeremy's mother from the phone, when she greeted me. His dad, who looked just like Jeremy but thirty years older, as dark brown as me, and dressed in a yellow guayabera, held out his hand. "Kenny, whatever you want, whatever you need, just let us know. We got a keg over there."

"Tacos with all kinds of meat—cabeza, pollo, carne asada. Fill up," Jeremy's mom said in Spanish and patted my back. Then in English, "You're a growing boy like *mijo* here."

"Mi casa es su casa," Jeremy's dad chimed in again, with hints of his New York Dominican roots coming through his voice. "Have a seat and Jeremy or his mom will fix you a plate."

I sat at a table with a few of Jeremy's uncles and cousins, brothers and sisters-in-law, and nephews and nieces, including the birthday girl. Noticed the too-close resemblance between José Luis and Jeremy, and figured this was where Ricky and Carlos might have made the arson flier assumptions. First, Jeremy's family stared like I was a foreigner invading their territory. Then, I thought, duh, I'm black. At a Mexican family party, well, with mostly Jeremy's mother's Mexican relatives in attendance, and the Dominican dad. I'm dating, er, was dating their nephew, son, cousin, uncle, brother. Probably weird for everyone. One of the girl cousins broke the ice. "Finally, Jeremy brings home a decent one." Everyone laughed, held up a beer to toast, and chided Jeremy as he brought over two plates of food—one for me, one for him.

"You're the best one Jeremy's brought home," his sister, Yadira, joked and chuckled. "And there's been a lot of them, huh?" She had the same intonation as Jeremy.

Again, laughter, beers toasting in the air.

"What do you do again, Kenny?" asked another relative. "Jeremy talks about you all the time, but he exaggerates sometimes."

I explained the story of me. How I grew up in Toledo, went to Northwestern University and Indiana University, how I ended up in L.A. working at CUELA. When that information came across as dry, not *chisme* enough, someone asked how Jeremy and I met. I was impressed. They were truly interested and seemingly not homophobic at all. Apparently I'd made the grade, met with their approval, and received the stamp of acceptance with *la familia* Lopez of East L.A. Jeremy and I looked at each other. He grabbed my hand, tapped his foot and leg against mine under the table, and smiled. We had an invisible pact, not to tell the family about our problems or breakup. Just like any other couple who might have been having problems, but kept it quiet and between themselves in public.

Jeremy's dad brought over a plastic cup of foamed-up keg beer and handed it to me.

"Sorry, it got kind of warm," Jeremy's dad said. "We need some ice for the keg tub. Who wants to go get some fucking ice?" Obviously, the apple hadn't fallen too far from the tree in terms of word choice at times.

Uncles, aunts, and cousins shrugged their shoulders, looked away, some complaining they were already too buzzed or drunk to drive up the street to the closest store. Others saying they didn't know the neighborhood well enough or where to go.

"I'll go," I said. Hadn't drunk. Hadn't touched the food majorly, but would definitely eat when I returned.

"Jeremy, go with Kenny," José Luis said. Jeremy's mom and dad nodded. "Can't have a brotha getting lost in this part of town," José Luis continued.

"Just don't get lost in a parking lot or alley or back at your house," Yadira chimed in. "We need brotha Kenny back so we can fill him in on Jeremy."

"Yes, we love you, brotha Kenny," Jeremy's mother said. "You're keeping my boy out of trouble. At least one of my boys is going on the up-and-up."

"Thanks, Mrs. Lopez," I said and smiled. Felt good hearing them say how much they liked me and how much they think I'd influenced Jeremy's life over the past months. And wondered if they knew how much Jeremy had put me, well, us, through.

Jeremy rubbed the palm of my hand with his middle finger, released, and stood up. So did I. His mother ran over with a twenty-dollar bill for us to take to the store for ice, paper plates, and plastic forks.

José Luis yelled out, "Foo, don't use up all my gas. Fill up the tank, *ese.*"

"Fuck you, foo," Jeremy yelled back. "Hit me with some cash."

I interceded, before a family fight started between the look-alikes. "I got the gas. We'll be back."

"Thanks, Kenny," Yadira said. "Save the drama, José Luis."

"I like this nigga," José Luis said and gave me a long leer as Jeremy and I started walking down the driveway and back to the car José Luis had loaned him.

A little girl ran behind us in the driveway. "Take me with you, *Papi.*"

"Not right now, *mija.*"

"Your daughter?"

"It's complicated. Gabriella, this is Mr. Kenny. Kenny, Gabriella."

Jeremy picked up the little girl and handed her to me. She hugged me.

"Bring me back something, *Papi.*"

"I will, *mija,*" Jeremy said. "Go back to *Tía* Yadira. I'll be back in a few minutes."

We watched her run away back to the festivities and the hot-air balloon jumper in the yard.

"Sorry for my ghetto family," Jeremy said and winked. As if nothing. "But they like you."

"I like them. They're cool peeps. I'm sure our families would get along." As if nothing.

"You think?" Jeremy asked.

"You have a daughter?" I said, asking the obvious. "Since when?"

"Well, she's my brother José Luis's daughter, but I guess I'm kinda raising her since he's never around. Firestarter. She thinks I'm her father."

"Truth?"

"For real. No lie. You can ask my moms when we get back. She'll tell you exactly what I told you."

"It's always something with you," I said. "That's cool that you're taking that little girl under your wing in a way."

"We could raise her together one day."

"I don't think so," I said. "I think you've got it handled on your own."

"I like you, Kenny. So much. I can't imagine being without you. It's crazy, I know. I can't explain it. But no matter what, I can't help myself. I like and respect you so much, Kenny. You just don't know."

"Oh, do you?"

"You know I do," he said and beeped to deactivate the car alarm. "I love you, Kenny Kane. You can't disappoint my family now by leaving me."

"Jeremy. Stop." I got in the passenger side. "We'll talk later. Once the party is over."

"You mean I got a chance?" Started up the car, backed up, and started driving toward our errands—the store and gas station.

"I can't promise anything, Jeremy," I said. "But I can't turn off my feelings either. Not like that."

"I love you, man. You're the best thing to happen to me. When I tell you that, I really mean it. You don't know how much my life is different because of you."

"Hmmm . . . really?" I said and looked at Jeremy. He winked at me, smiled. "Okay, I'll stop being sarcastic, Jeremy. I believe you."

"Thanks. I know I got some problems and issues. I'll get help. Just don't leave me."

"I'll think about it and we'll talk. After the party, okay? That's all I can promise. We'll talk."

"Thank you."

"But you and I both know we're probably better off as friends, or just—"

"Don't say it," he said. "Let's just pretend like we're going to be together. Like we're going to grow old and take care of each other. Imagine. Wouldn't that be crazy?"

"So idealistic," I said. "But who knows?"

A few minutes later, we pulled into the lot of the grocery store. Drove around in silence, until we found a parking spot. "You real cool," Jeremy said. "If you take me back, I swear, no more drama. Done with other boys. The secrets. Whatever you want. And if I get tempted, I'll talk about it with you. Communicate."

"All right, geez," I said and laughed. "You don't have to bring me the Rock of Gibraltar to make me take you back. We'll talk."

"Thanks for giving me a chance, Kenny," he said and smiled. "I won't let you down."

Jeremy played with my hands, tapped me on the head, acted like a young kid, a boy in love, as we headed toward the store.

"Whassup, *ese,* where you from?" The voice of a preteen called out from an aisle away in the parking lot. *"¿De donde eres, maricón?"*

"Ignore him, Kenny," Jeremy said. "Speed up."

"Why?"

"We're getting hit up, probably thinking I'm José Luis or something," Jeremy whispered. "Stay calm and he'll leave us alone."

I thought about the news stories—Highland Park and South L.A., African-Americans being targeted by some.

Another boy emerged from another direction. "Whassup, *ese,* where you from?" Hand in his pocket. Head nod. "Where you from?"

"Kenny, go back to the car."

"Don't run, foo." The boys walked closer. A third emerged from yet another direction, pulled down the waist of his pants to show off the butt of a gun. "Where you from?"

I pulled out my wallet. Probably a stupid move, but this wasn't my normal, everyday interaction. What does one do when getting hit up? "You want money? Here . . . my watch."

"Where you from, foo?" the first boy asked again. "Not you, nigga, the wetback spic here."

One Latino kid using a slur against another Latino, but not really important at that point, but a little disturbing. Like black people calling each other the "n" word.

"Jeremy?"

"You two fags? This your nigga?"

I looked around. No one to even yell out to in the parking lot. People drove by, stuck to their routines, not paying one iota of attention to Jeremy and me, in the parking lot, being hit up by punk kids probably being initiated into a gang. I didn't know what to do, or say, but knew at that moment that I loved Jeremy enough to do anything to protect him. Maybe even give my life to defend him. Crazy, the thoughts that flash in slow motion before you when your life seems in jeopardy. Thinking about my mom, dad and stepdad, sisters, and what it would be like if I never saw them again . . . all for defending Jeremy against a couple street boys.

"Fuck these foos, they just a bunch of punks," one of the boys said and put his arms around Jeremy. Gave him a hug and a pat on the back. "Let's jet, foos."

I said a silent prayer and thanked God that nothing had happened, and that the kids ran off without doing anything to us. Jeremy and I walked, stunned and in silence, to the store entrance. Put a quarter into the gum machine at the store entrance, got some Mexican candies for Gabriella. Found the ice freezer at the front of the store and I grabbed a bag.

"Kenny, why does it feel so warm?"

I looked back at Jeremy. Blood dripping slowly from his lips. Blood on the floor, tracing the steps we made inside the store to the ice freezer. Didn't want to panic. "Stay still, Jeremy."

"Whassup, babe? I'm hot. My back feels hot."

"I love you, Jeremy. Stay calm," I said and looked around. Shouted, "Help! Help! Can somebody please help us?"

"Kenny, my back," Jeremy said, more blood flowing from his mouth, tears welling at the corners of his eyes. "Can't . . . breathe . . . What's happening? Want . . . Mom."

"Don't worry," I said. "I'm here. I'll take care of you." I dropped the bag of ice, put my arms around Jeremy, my hand filling with Jeremy's blood. Melted into my arms, his weight pushing us against the ice freezer, his eyes rolling back. That boy had apparently stabbed Jeremy, easily and quietly slipping the blade in and out, in the back during that hug.

"Love . . . you."

"I love you, Jeremy," I said and looked around at shoppers milling about. "Help us! Someone help! Jeremy stay awake . . . Keep your eyes open for me . . . I love you. Stay awake for me."

"Love . . . you."

"I love you, too. Stay calm. Help is coming."

"Can't wait . . . tired."

Chapter 33

There are some beds that are just right and for the right occasion.

For newborns, it might be an incubator or a new bassinet purchased by happy parents looking forward to providing a prosperous and privileged life to their child. For preadolescents, it might be the brand-new canopy or bunk bed for their first stand-alone bedroom, where the prospect of hosting numerous sleepovers and slumber parties awaits. In college, it's the allure of the single twin bed, or, if adventurous with design, the loft bed built in a dorm room, where virginity can be lost, and new, temporary "loves" can be explored after a frat party or dorm dance. For college graduates, it's the futon that serves as both sofa and bed in an efficiency, studio, or two-bedroom apartment shared with one or more roommates. With newlyweds, or for those who don't have the legal right to marry, the bed is the place where dreams are shared, love is made, children might be created (or not), and where rest for a weary soul, mind, and body can be found. It's where the shoulder and ear of the one you love can be easily accessed and reached out to in times of need. It's where you can find solace in a lover/partner/spouse and where you can count on a hug, kiss, and an "I love you" on a daily basis. And if you're alone, without a special person or partner to share it with, the bed can be a source and symbol of independence or loneliness, pleasure or pain, longing or lust fulfilled or unfulfilled. It's often taken for granted that we'll have a bed to come home to and sleep in each night. For others, it's part of the daily question of survival: Where will I rest tonight? Who will let me in?

For a twenty-one-year-old, there are some beds that are just not appropriate. Especially when there's so much life, love, and happiness to look forward to. Especially when there's so much potential, fulfilled and unfulfilled, yet to be discovered. A twenty-one-year-old should not be in an intensive care unit hospital bed, unable to function, move, open his eyes, respond to your words, tears, kisses and hugs. A twenty-one-year-old should not be moved to life support or fed from a feeding tube. A twenty-one-year-old should not be without a doctor's most optimistic medical prognosis: a speedy recovery and return to life as usual. A twenty-one-year-old should not be sobbed over in his hospital bed, said goodbye to by streams of family and friends, given last rites. A twenty-one-year-old should not be in a coffin, a permanent bed, a final resting place. Anything other than old age . . . just doesn't seem right, natural, or fair.

I still think about Jeremy. All the time. Mainly at night, when I'm at home, alone in my bed. Some of the old gospel singers and preachers talk about how deep in the midnight hour, when one's soul seems lost and weary, when you think you're alone, that's when your door is open for a conversation with the one who guides your universe. I talk a lot with the one who guides my universe. I talk and wonder out loud. Wonder if I spent too much time questioning Jeremy's existence and purpose for being in my life, rather than seeing our time together and his life as a gift. Wonder if I spent too much time listening to what other people said, rather than just listening to my own heart. Wonder if what others see as flaws in someone else's relationship, they see in their own.

Wonder if Jeremy and I had been brought together for some higher purpose that I shouldn't have questioned. There is always a reason for the people who are drawn into our lives, and our mission is to learn, live, and let those lessons make us better people.

I learned a lot from Jeremy. Living life spontaneously. Protecting and loving your family, even with numerous faults and dysfunctions. Working hard and playing hard. Loving hard, too. There's a lot about him that I never learned, and still, to this day don't have the answers. But Jeremy still teaches me something every day. When I listen to the one who guides my universe, I get a window of insight, a thought, even a phrase, about my life, and I feel Jeremy is near.

When I visited Jeremy's family, to finally drop off the Jeremy/José Luis getaway car, the unopened background check, and the last of Jeremy's things he'd kept at my house, his mom hugged me, thanked me for being there for her son in his last conscious moments, and for guiding him to be a better person. Said I'd given him a chance that most people wouldn't, especially with the obvious family issues and gang-banger brother. And that I'd given Jeremy reason to live for himself, and not just for protecting his brothers from trouble. She gave me something she said Jeremy would want me to have, and that she wanted me to keep. A journal he'd started right after we met. Filled with poetry, scribbled entries, spontaneous thoughts about his life, school, work, dreams. But mostly about me. Things I never knew. I look at his journal from time to time, and find myself surprised and saddened seeing our life through Jeremy's eyes. Find myself wanting to live up to a wish Jeremy expressed in one of his latter entries: *For Kenny to love and trust again.*

My bed is empty now. Just me. No DaVon yet, though he's separating from his wife and wants to explore options with me again. But, for now, I'm cool being alone. It's the way I want it now. At least for a little while. Choosing to share it with someone in the future is something I don't want to take lightly. The right side of the wrong bed might work for some, especially those adventurous types. But I've learned that like the old folks used to say, if you make your bed, you have to lie in it. And I want mine to be comfortable, a place of refuge where, once you slip in, you won't want to slip out.